VOLUME #3

MOSUTHA'S MAGIC

ORON

by David C. Smith

ZEBRA BOOKS
KENSINGTON PUBLISHING CORP.

This one, again, for
Dave Clement
friend and ally,
who wanted it to happen a lot sooner.

ZEBRA BOOKS

are published by

KENSINGTON PUBLISHING CORP.
475 Park Avenue South
New York, N.Y. 10016

Printed in the United States of America

Foreword

I wrote *Oron* when I was twenty-one years old. It began simply as an experiment during the summer between my third and fourth years of college. I'd already been writing short stories for two years—mainly horror and heroic fantasy—and was selling them to fanzines like Gordon Linzner's *Space and Time*. I took the summer off and challenged myself to write something in a long format. After some frustrating months spent with an aborted pirate novel and a historical Rome-vs-the-Germanic-barbarians-saga, I decided to write a fantasy. I've always been fond of the ancient Homeric epics and the *chansons des gestes*, and was familiar with Robert E. Howard's heroic adventure stories. I went through my notebook with the intention of tying together short story ideas to build something of greater scope. The first note I made concerning my planned book ran something like, "Have a king go mad under the influence of a sorcerer. Kossuth." Later, trying to decide on a suitable name for my mad king, I discarded several unsatisfactory ones (the common complaint is true: there are far too many "Thundors" and "Gorks" in the genre) and finally found the sense of ambiance I wanted by dropping the "i" from the Greek hero

Orion's name. I named my tragic hero, and titled his epic, *Oron*.

I thought I'd be able to write the story quickly, during the remainder of the summer, by not having to spend time on hard research (which had crippled the two previous projects). Adventure-fantasy, of course, is never just "made up," but rather relies on a very keen appreciation of what is plausible, honest, or potential in an imaginary culture. I didn't have to do much research, that's true, because I was able to rely mainly on what I'd absorbed from texts on ancient history. But as the book progressed, my "deadline" receded far into the future as *Oron* grew from an experiment into a very large story of epic proportions. Details wanted to be pinned down, characters wanted to have their say, and the Alexander-like Oron began to take on some real dimensions. This can be a good thing; when a story takes on a life of its own—but because I didn't know then about useful shortcuts or self-helps like outlines or story cards, I wrestled through three partial and three complete drafts of *Oron*. In a crude parallel to natural gestation, I spent nine months completing my "summer project"—an epic way over one hundred thousand words long in final draft. I cut and revised it, much to the story's good, but it remained pretty hefty.

I was able to work into *Oron* a number of things that (at the time) I thought might be revolutionary. Specifically, I wanted to make Oron himself a more complex character than was usually found in adventure-fantasy. I wanted him to have archetypal depth, natural intelligence, but to retain his essential element of natural energy and strength. He was a barbarian, but he was not a savage, and he was not a simple-sly ogre. (I might have gone too far in develop-

6

ing these "humanizing" qualities, though, because I was eventually asked to excise humorous scenes, terms of endearment, and other bits of business that didn't seem to fit the mold of a rough-and-ready warrior.) But even more than this, I wanted Oron to be a truly tragic character, a man with something manifestly fateful in his makeup, a man with a destiny he did not comprehend. He was the "Na-Kha," a world hero, descendant of a line of mighty heroes who had been born to help maintain the very tenuous balance between man's civilization on earth and the very strong, demonic, antihuman elements of the rest of existence.

Flawed though it is (and as, I suppose, it must be, written by a neophyte twenty-one-year-old with more ambition than experience), I felt that Oron was a good solid story, and I was fully confident that it would be accepted immediately for publication by some farseeing, revolutionary-minded editor. Wrong. The manuscript began to collect its disappointingly routine share of rejection slips as it was returned, time after time—often with comments to the effect that the market for "barbarian fantasy" had played itself out. I turned to other things (including a second adventure-fantasy set in the same milieu of Attluma, four hundred years after the events of Oron), wrote some more short stories, and poetry, and film articles, changed my address a few times, and turned the Oron manuscript over to an agent. When Zebra decided to publish the book (after they'd first printed two Howardian adventures I'd written for them; The Witch of the Indies and For the Witch of Mists, the latter with Dick Tierney), it appeared during the summer of 1978—fully five years after I'd first started work on it. In a stroke of luck, Clyde Caldwell was commissioned to paint a strong cover for Oron and do

7

a dozen faithful, beautifully rendered interior illustrations. (I later learned that Clyde had made his public debut as an artist in the same issue of *Space and Time* where my very first published story appeared!) Zebra did a good job with the book, [and despite some typographical errors the only really upsetting flaw was the failure to typeset] where Part III, "The Na-Kha," begins in the novel. (This occurs with Chapter 17, thus breaking the book evenly into three stages of Oron's growth, awareness, and destiny. Those of you who have copies of *Oron* may want to mark this in your edition.)

The book [sold] [fairly] well, going into a second printing two years after it was first released, and talk began concerning the possibility of my writing additional novels featuring Oron. At first, quite frankly, I was reluctant to do this. At the time I wasn't interested in developing a series character and, too, I thought I'd said all I had to say about my hero in *Oron*. If I were to write additional stories, would I be compromising my character and my original intention? At the same time, though, it would be foolish for me to turn down an opportunity to keep my name in print; besides, since *Oron* was selling well enough to interest readers, it was common sense that those readers might be on the lookout for more books about him.

I considered the idea. A few helpful friends mentioned the possibility of "resurrecting" the slain Oron by some artificial or sorcerous device, thus to have him battle Kossuth again—and again—for three more books. Well, not only would this become interminable and boring, and not only would it insult my readers' intelligence, it would also invalidate the intrinsic verisimilitude of the fantasy milieu I'd created. If I were to write more adventures about Oron, the only reasonable possibility was to go back to his youth—back to the early days among his barbarian tribespeople, his wandering days, his legendary period as the Wolf and leader of renegades in the forests and mountains of the Nevga River Valley.

I'm a storyteller, and I trust my instincts; if an idea excites me, it has the potential to excite readers. If I were to return to Oron's youth, to incidents only hinted at in the original epic, I could put him through some interesting paces (and have fun doing it) and at the same time *anticipate* much of his later career. Ironies suggested themselves to me, poetic nuances, parallels, scenes of intrigue and rough-and-tumble action. Scene after scene appeared to make this "alternate" Oron—this young Oron—a character that demanded to be uncaged.

The result is this book, *Reign, Sorcery!*, the first of three novels telling of Oron's adventures as a young barbarian. These will be fun books. There'll be some grimness to them, certainly adventure, but some sensitivity, too. Inevitably, the character Oron will have more depth and "reality" to him than I achieved in that first—my very first—novel. (The only drawback—and this depends on how you look at it—is that Oron battles sorcery and the supernatural in these stories, things he seemed ignorant of in the original epic. But that's what makes him an "alternate" Oron.) Still, in all, when you reach the conclusion of the third book, you should be able to open your copy of the original *Oron*, start at page one, paragraph one, and have a clearer feeling of the Nevgan's background, his fate, his character. I'd always intended for Oron to be the kind of hero who would take on a life of his own, and with these three additional books, maybe he's starting to do that.

Besides, there's a lot of truth in these books, just as there has to be in all myths, legends, and illusions. Truth—and fun. (Fun, after all, is only painless learning.) And if telling stories isn't fun, and if reading stories isn't fun, then having anything to do with them doesn't make much sense at all.

David C. Smith
Youngstown, Ohio
December, 1981

Prologue

The Man Without A Name

He had traveled far, he had nearly died, he was wounded by the bitterness in his heart. He was nameless. Young, he desired vengeance; a vengeance so great that in its making he might no more be a man. Forsaken, he sought to forsake all, and renew himself in a baptism of new life.

He had come by forests, over rivers, down mountains. He had traversed swamps. He had survived long days and cold nights without food, he had glutted himself on the corpses of dead warriors he found wasting in the aftermath of battle. He had fashioned his own weapons and used them, awkwardly, to bring down game and to fish.

And always, always, he continued on his journey. It took him three years, through forests and over mountains, across deserts, into deep swamplands as old as the earth, to reach his destination.

And when he arrived at his destination, he feared that he would be killed before he had his chance to be reborn in hell's name.

"He is but a boy," hissed the elder serpent. "Let us eat him."

"He comes to us for knowledge. Shall we not give

11

him knowledge? His heart is full of hate. Shall we not feed that hate?"

"What does he promise us?" inquired the elder serpent of his son.

"He comes to the swamps seeking old magicks. He wishes to harm the world, for it has harmed him."

"I hate men as much as he, but—see you!—men drove me away, long and long ago, and now I should give my weapons to a boy with a heart full of hate?"

"What shall we do with him, then? Feed him to the lamiae?"

The half demon-half serpent elder choked something like a laugh. "Bring him in. Feed him the Fire Spirit. Make him die, and pull out his heart—blacken it at the furnace and let his spirit look upon it—and if he agrees, then place it again in his breast and let it blacken him forever. Let him trade his soul to Hell, and become an unman. Then we will teach him magicks. Let him brand himself with the Star, and then we will fill him up with knowledge, and he may harm the earth. . . ."

"It shall be done."

"Bring him in."

And he was brought in, and the shadows were bright with flames, a ring of serpent-things hissed dryly at him, their master sat upon its throne, and around them the walls of the cavern dripped with the seeping moisture of the swamp.

"You have entered Hell, mortal youth. An you be strong enough, yes, we will teach you things. But you will damn yourself. . . ."

"Give me power," he said, "to kill my people. For they have wounded me, cast me out and banished me. I am no more of them. I have no soul any longer, but let its shadow belong to Hell, for my heart is there already, and my mind and will."

"Let it be done, then. Place the human on the altar and feed him the flames."

He screamed. And screamed. And screamed.

Looked upon his charred heart.

Felt his broken ribs bent back from his severed chest, felt his heart pulled out, and, hot, flaming, replaced to torment his forever. . . .

He screamed, and screamed, and screamed. . . .

And was reborn, in a swamp-womb of serpents and ashes.

Arising, he took for himself the name Mo'sou-tha' ah: "Hell-returned," in the language of the serpent-folk, his demonic masters. And, learning from them, he spent many long winters and dismal summers in the swamplands before returning to the world of men. . . .

PART I

THE WOLF

When summer's end is nighing
  And skies at evening cloud,
I muse on change and fortune
  And all the feats I vowed
  When I was young and proud.

The year might age, and cloudy
  The lessening day might close,
But air of other summers
  Breathed from beyond the snows,
  And I had hope of those.

—*A.E. Housman,*
"Epitaph on an Army of Mercenaries"

1

He was tall, well built for his age (sixteen winters) and at home in the forest. A young barbarian with dark brown hair tied in a tail behind his head, and a beard and moustache to proclaim his manhood. He was dressed in the raiment of his tribe, the raiment of any barbarian tribe of the wide Nevga River Valley: vest of deerskin, antelope-hide trousers, thick well-worn boots of ox hide. His belt was woven of gut and was stronger than strong rope. His sword he had forged himself on his uncle's anvil, and it was a strong sword: longer than most used by men of his tribe, but light-weight and sturdy, due to his endless patience with hammer and fire. He had carved an inscription into the blade of the sword: Pictures (since his tribe had no written language) of the animals he had killed, and at the hilt of it he had fashioned a wolf's head. He wasn't old enough yet to have passed his manhood rite and been given a totem name or a war name. His father was Aksakin the Skull-Splitter, a name well earned from ferocity displayed in battles with bandits and the killers of other tribes. His chief was Ilgar the Moon-Hunter, renowned for sure sight and killing stroke in moonlight as well as sunlight. But the young bar-barian had a simpler title in mind for himself when he passed his manhood ritual this autumn. He thought of himself and referred to himself simply as a wolf. He had even killed a wolf two summers ago. Alone in the forest, a lad of fourteen with a spear and a short sword had slain a mad wolf. He deserved his title.

Oron the Wolf.

Today was his third day in the forest. He came often into the forest, preferring to spend time by himself on the hunt, or relaxing in the trees, or climbing the mountain outcroppings to see if he could catch glimpses of the strange many-hutted cities that were said to sprawl like huge nests far to the east, beyond the mountains. He could survive easily in the verdant wild, and he found it more to his liking to do it than to sit around with the other young men, listening to the war tales of older fighters, or stealing wine skins and drinking from them with young comrades not yet tattooed with the warrior's sigil.

He was fishing—something he liked to do because it was relaxing and gave him time to think. Of himself. Of his father. The tribe. Esa. His manhood rites. He was already a strong fighter and a good hunter, and he had already let it be known that he would ask for Esa as his mate this fall. (Not from her father, since Esa was an orphan, but from her strong-willed aunt.) Esa was pretty and strong. So far as Oron knew, no one else had yet asked for her, and he suspected this was because of old Aunt Lunda, with whom Esa lived in a hut far to the edge of the village. Lunda was always upset, crabby, and complaining about everything. She scared away prospective suitors. But Oron, in pursuit of Esa, had spent some afternoons talking with Lunda, and he'd discovered that once he'd won the old woman to him (by bringing her fresh fruit and fish, and by complimenting her on her cooking, claywork and weavework) she came to appreciate his visits and encourage his attraction to Esa. At least some of the time.

So life was good. The tribe was strong; their village was the largest in the southeastern forest of the valley. The men hunted well; other warriors respected them. In council with other Fathers of other tribes, Ilgar was given great deference because of his years and his ferocity. His battle plans for stealing forest land and other prizes from tribes farther to the south always succeeded. As part of the tribe of Ilgar, Oron could justifiably feel proud of himself. But he felt proud of himself anyway. He, too, was respected as one of the finest young sons of the village. He had intelligence, skill, strength, and craftiness. He could plan ahead for things, he was independent enough to be his own man, yet open enough to understand that what was best for the tribe was also best for him. He had learned well from Ilgar, and he knew that Ilgar liked him. There was a loyalty shared by Ilgar and Oron that was lacking between Oron and his father, Aksakin. Aksakin was brutal, selfish, always eager to prove himself — a childish young warrior in an older man's body. And he had always been cruel to his son, perhaps blaming Oron for his wife Usuma's death, suffered during Oron's birth. So Oron had been raised in a troubled hut, and part of his life's dream was to better his father in war skills and heroics. Den-Usutus, the old shaman with the white tail of hair, had once told Oron that the young warrior had the blood of ancient heroes in his veins. Oron took pride in that, too, just as he did in his slaying the wolf and his love for Esa.

The sun was high above the crowded trees as Oron's gut fishing line jerked and pulled. Quickly he yanked it in, lifting onto the bank a large trout, one of those more often found in the wider part of the river, leagues to the north. A good catch. He added it to the three other fish he'd caught this morning, then wound up his line and pushed it into a pocket of his boot. Wrapping the fish in his leather vest, he headed farther up the embankment to the small camp he'd made beneath an oak. The ashes of his fire would yet be warm; Oron would have a blazing fire within a short while and a good meal to keep his belly full for the rest of the day.

It was on his way back to his fire, however, that he realized he wasn't alone in the forest. Oron heard the noises and recognized instantly that they weren't the sounds of passing wild elk or boar, a bear or a pack of wolves. He paused and listened and understood the passing of men through the forest. But not the men of his own tribe, and probably not warriors of other tribes. These unseen trespassers were making far too much noise to have any real understanding of what they were doing.

Oron reached his camp and hid his fish. In a small hole in the ground which he'd filled with water and wet leaves, he deposited his fish and covered them with a rock. Then he went to investigate the sounds, not drawing his sword but keeping one hand on his side-knife as he went.

In a few moments he'd climbed a small hill and pushed his way through trees, brush, and foliage to settle behind a mossy boulder and observe. On a path below (one that eventually led to the hut of Slum the Carver, later to Tree Lake and, three days down, to the village of Kilum the Oak) he saw soldiers.

Soldiers. Not barbarian warriors, not tribesmen from his or any other place of huts, but soldiers. Oron knew about soldiers; he'd talked with mercenaries once, men who'd fought in the east. And these soldiers were dressed in regulation regalia, all the same, wearing bronze and steel armor, carrying arms much too foreign in their design to be the product of any village forge Oron knew of. Long swords, shields, axes, bows, and well-crafted arrows in leather pouches, spears and knives. These men, in fact, were so overburdened with weapons that Oron, spying on them as silently as the breeze, wondered if they had the freedom of movement necessary to use them to their advantage at all.

But he'd already decided who they must be. Not because he'd seen them before but because he and the entire warriory of Ilgar had heard rumors of these soldiers over the past several weeks. They were sorcerer's soldiers. A deployment of men from— What name had Ilgar spoken? Mosutha?

Mosutha.

A sorcerer.

A sorcerer with skills far beyond the skills of any tribal shaman or old magician. Which is why, Oron decided, he must be a sorcerer. It was difficult for him to comprehend just what sorcery might be (just as it had been difficult for him to understand the difference between soldiers and tribal warriors, before seeing soldiers: for didn't both kinds of men do the same work?), but he'd been given some indication of how strong sorcery must be by Den-Usutus's reaction to Ilgar's remark that a sorcerer was in the area.

Old Den-Usutus had gone white and had removed himself to his hut for a whole day and night. When he came out he said that he'd fasted and prayed to the earth spirits and had reviewed many old animal-skin pictographs that he, as tribal magician, had inherited from his father and his father's father and an entire descendancy of tribal magicians.

So Oron looked upon these soldiers, these emissaries from a sorcerer, with a twinge of apprehension and uncertainty—the discontent that a mystery, one perhaps with a harmful solution, always brings to the belly. He counted eleven of the soldiers, all dressed in the same armor, passing through the forest below him with what he supposed they considered exaggerated caution. He saw that a number of them had bloodstains on their boots and their armored vests. Human or animal blood? A ferocity began to thrum in his brain. Foreign killers or foreign hunters in the territory of Ilgar's tribe.

The troop proceeded at a quick pace; too quickly to pay any real attention to what was going on in the forest around them. If this sorcerer Mosutha had recruited them for their keen senses and advanced tactics, then he had certainly misspent his meat and salt. And his gold. Probably, as Oron understood it, the sorcerer paid them in gold. Oron had seen gold coins and he knew that these men, most likely mercenaries, must be paid in gold. Gold coins; which were flat discs with impressions and inscriptions carved on them. It was the same gold which Uth and Sith used to decorate the metal pins and bracelets and other things they made, and it was the form of barter used in the cities.

Oron allowed the soldiers to pass without taking any action against them. He might have easily fallen upon them and slain at least half their number, and before being killed himself perhaps kill all of them. But it wouldn't have served any purpose. Sorcerers could probably make new soldiers appear at random, or was it possible that these men, as agents of a sorcerer, weren't men at all, but spirits in the form of men? Oron's imagination went wild, contemplating the intruders. But as the troop passed on, out of sight but not beyond his hearing, Oron quietly withdrew and scurried back into the forest to his campsite. He had no intention of acting against Ilgar's instructions, which were: "Take no action, but report to me what you see."

In his camp he buried his fire, threw upon the place leaves and dirt, covered everything over and fanned the area with a tree branch to ensure that it might look as undisturbed as any other portion of the forest. Then he took his fish up from the hole, dropped the rock back in place, and began trotting at a steady, noiseless pace toward the tribal huts, half a day to the east.

Ilgar was not pleased with the news. He sat in his hut, squatted on his small dais of wood and animal skins. Crouched at his right hand was Den-Usutus. Otherwise, none besides Oron disturbed the somber quiet of the chief's brooding.

"West?" Ilgar asked Oron again, cocking his right eye at him. The chief was a huge man, built like a bear. He had many tattoos on his body proclaiming his conquests, his totems, and his symbols. He was dressed in rough buckskin breeches; a plain iron and bronze amulet hung around his bull neck identified him as leader of his people. There was no other ornament or affectation to him. Long knives and a naked blade, thrust openly through his belt, gave him an almost mercenary look.

"West," Oron repeated. "I had made a camp to hunt and fish, and at noon-high today I heard them. I counted eleven of them and they didn't see me. They did not look like any of the soldiers I've seen before, and they trailed from the north and headed south along the way to Slum the Carver's. Some of them were blood stained, but not because they were wounded."

Ilgar nodded, saying nothing more for a moment. He looked over at Den-Usutus. The old magician caught the look and passed it on to Oron, then leaned forward and in the dust of the floor of Ilgar's hut traced with his finger a sign.

"Did any of the men on them possess this mark. Either on their persons or on their armor?"

Oron studied the drawing—a star of seven points. Mutely, he nodded.

"On their flesh?" Den-Usutus asked him.

Oron shook his head. "Each man wore on the breast of his armored vest such a sign as that. I assumed it part of their protection. They were done in bronze or copper and attached to their chests."

"Keh!" Den-Usutus shivered his old white head. "A part of their protection, maybe. It is the star of sorcery."

Oron's eyes went wide. "Then these men are from Mosutha?" he asked eagerly.

Both elders stared at him sharply. "Do not speak the name!" Ilgar told him quickly.

"But it has been spoken, my chief—"

"Aye, but only in rumor. We will prepare our defenses, but some men of our huts would become as wayward as children if they knew we fought sorcery. Do you understand?"

Oron had to answer truthfully. "I do not understand, my chief. I do not understand what sorcery is."

Den-Usutus explained. "It is an old weapon. It was used by the gods on the young earth until the demons stole it from them and passed it on to the first evil men and women. It is stronger than my magic or the incantations of any shaman. It is stronger than your sword, Oron, and perhaps it is stronger than the sword of Ilgar."

"How can something be stronger than a strong sword and a warrior?" Oron was perplexed.

Ilgar found himself somewhat bemused by the

young man's naiveté. "Sometimes dreams are stronger than life, Oron. Sorcery is stronger because it is the power of the gods brought down to earth. It is not solid like a sword or heavy like a hammer, or even real like flesh. You know how sometimes the lightning and the storms, or a fire, or a flood can be more powerful than a sword? How in floods we lose people from the tribe? How we tell stories of the gods doing things without actually making them happen? How the earth was formed and the first deer and boar and elk and bear, and the first men and women, and the demons from dung and rotten clay and old vegetables?"

"Yes, my chief, I know these stories. But they are only stories."

"Is a story less real because it is a story? Do you not believe in the spirits or in the gods, young Oron?"

"Yes, I believe in them. But I have never called upon them. I have gone my own way and they have gone theirs, and we've never interfered with one another."

Ilgar unleashed a loud laugh at the logic of the young man's words. "You're a great hunter and you do not need the gods, eh, Oron? And they do not need you?"

Oron considered that. "My chief—my shaman—I have never prayed against them and I have never scorned them. But I am myself. Two summers ago I slew a wolf and I did it myself and I did not call upon the gods. But I slew the wolf."

Ilgar nodded and decided to cut short the talk. "All to the well, then, Oron. Listen to me. I will announce to the tribe tonight that enemies are in our territory and so we must prepare for battle. But if anyone asks you what you have seen, tell them only that you have seen warriors afoot to the west. Do you understand that?"

"Yes, my chief."

Ilgar's tone became less stern. "You have sixteen winters?"

"Yes, my chief."

"Have you not taken your manhood rite yet and named yourself a name?"

"This fall, my chief, I will take my ritual and call myself the wolf."

Ilgar nodded. "A good name for a strong young warrior."

Oron smiled. "I'm strong and I killed the wolf, Father Ilgar. I'm the only son of Aksakin the Skull-Splitter." He said it with pride in his father's renown, but not with any love.

Ilgar frowned. "Well, then, Oron. Go now and eat your meal that you caught. I will talk with you later."

"Yes, my chief." Oron stood up and slapped his chest in a gesture of respect and exited the large, shadowy hut.

Ilgar brooded a moment more, then said aloud to Den-Usutus: "The son of Aksakin?"

"Aye." Both men shared a wariness for the tribe's skull-splitter. Den-Usutus spoke: "Oron has the blood of old heroes in his body, from the first days."

"Is this true?"

"As we are descended from the People of the Sword, so Oron is descended from the Heroes of the Sword. I told him this once; he smiled. The secrets passed on to me from my father from his father, and so on into the past, tell me that Oron has the blood of great heroes in him."

Ilgar grinned curiously. "No doubt," he spoke, "that is why he feels he has no need for the gods."

Oron took his fish to the hut of Lunda, Esa's old aunt. When Lunda pulled back her drapes and saw who it was, she scowled. She would have scowled if one of the young gods of the trees had come to her, to take her on a magical flight of love to the mountaintops.

But Oron disregarded her scowl and held out to her the skin full of fish.

Old Lunda's expression changed. "They are fresh?"

Oron nodded. "I caught them today in the forest."

Lunda bobbed her head, motioning him inside. "Bring them in. You may sit with Esa while I prepare them."

Oron entered and saw Esa sitting by the firepit in the middle of the hut. She looked at him shyly and set down the weaving she was at. Oron walked to her and sat down beside her, crossing his legs, while Lunda, on the other side of the fire, began expertly scaling the fish with a small bone knife.

Oron touched Esa's hand; she did not draw hers away, so they held hands. He asked her what she was weaving. She told him, "It is a belt for you. I am weaving it for you with the sign of the Wolf, so that when you become a man in a few moons you will wear this and everyone will know it is from me, and that you are the Wolf."

Oron smiled broadly at that. "Let me see it."

But she'd hidden it, tucked it beneath her as she sat so that he wouldn't see it until it was finished. "Not yet," Esa told him. "Let it be a surprise for you."

Lunda, protectively eyeing them, asked Oron what he had done in the forest for three days. He was burning to tell her of the sorcerer's soldiers he'd seen, but checked himself and instead calmly reported, "I slew three bears and one wild gazelle. No? You don't believe that? One bear, then. You still don't believe me?"

"You tell stories!" Lunda laughed at him. "You tell stories like Sub the Speaker tells stories! Tell him you want to be a storyteller instead of a hunter. You're a good storyteller!"

"But I'm a good hunter, too. I killed a deer in the forest and ate for two days, then set a trap for a bear with what remained and went to fish. I caught the fish but before I could see about the bear, I saw something else in the forest."

"And what was that?" Lunda asked him, pressing the fish onto spits and setting them over the fire, expecting more stories. "Two gods as big as mountains?"

"I saw warriors."

Lunda paused at her meal-making and eyed him critically. "Strange warriors?"

"Yes. I reported them to Ilgar and tonight he will talk to our warriors." Oron wasn't afraid to tell this much to the old woman. She wasn't a gossip and, besides, Ilgar had told him he could speak of it. It made him something of a hero in Esa's eyes. Oron held her hand the tighter and told her, "I considered attacking them and killing them all, but thought it might be better to come back and warn Ilgar."

"I'm glad you didn't attack them," Esa said in a low voice, watching the fire."

"Where did you see the warriors?" Lunda asked him.

"Half a day to the west, on the third trail."

She nodded thoughtfully. She was an old woman and she had seen many raids and attacks in her day, and as she cooked the fish she tried to remember how many attacks had come from tribes in the west, and when. But all the tribes to the west were more or less on terms with Ilgar's people, and if something had happened to change that agreement, it would be known by now. So Oron had told her more than he realized, although Lunda could not decide how the knowledge of warriors to the west might affect her and her niece and her tribe. A mystery.

But she said nothing of it to Oron or Esa as she handed them the first of the fish. They ate, and scooped brown bread and chopped fruit and vegetables and roots onto plates to supplement the fish. Lunda poured grain beer into small bowls and passed them around.

Neither Oron nor Esa said much to one another as they ate; it seemed more private if they simply sat beside one another, aware of one another, listening to each other eat and wordlessly sharing the feelings they had.

Halfway through the meal, however, Lunda said something which froze Oron's heart. "Aksakin," she told him, "has been visiting while you were gone."

Oron stared at her. "For what reason?"

He felt Esa look away, shamed, as Lunda replied, "He has been to see Esa."

Oron set down his plate and stared into the fire. "He knows that I want Esa for my wife when I pass my manhood test."

Lunda shrugged. "He is your father and he is a warrior; he has the right to request Esa if he wishes her. You have to wait until you are a man."

Oron told her, "You can refuse to give him Esa."

"Yes. But if I refuse, he can complain to Ilgar. Ilgar might agree with Aksakin. Esa and I are only women, alone in the tribe, with no men. Is there any good reason why Aksakin should not have Esa if he wants her?"

"Only that Esa does not want him; she wants me. Ilgar knows that. Ilgar does not like my father."

"Few in the tribe are friends with your father, but that is not the issue. Everyone knows you and Esa want each other, but you do not have the right to ask, and even if I refuse to give Esa to Aksakin, Ilgar may say yes to it."

Oron thought for a long while. "I will talk with my father. He can have any woman in the village. He only wants Esa because I want her."

Lunda agreed with him. "This is true."

Esa said nothing. She was pained. Shy, in love with Oron, she was terrified of his cruel father but, because she was bound to certain realities of the tribe's life, it was impossible for her to speak up for herself. Although when she was with Oron she was as wild and free as a young deer and Oron loved that in her, when they were within the eyes of the tribe they naturally fell into the roles ascribed for them by tribal code. Oron hated it, too; but he felt that if he made his position clear to Aksakin and to Ilgar, then nothing bad could come of this.

Oron stood up and told Lunda that he wished to walk to clear his mind. Esa rose to her feet and announced that she wanted to walk with him. Lunda sadly nodded her head in agreement. As she watched them leave her hut, there was a grave light in her eyes.

They did not walk far, however. Lunda's hut, on the edge of the village, sat beneath the shadows of the first trees on the great forest. Oron wished to walk behind the hut and, with Esa, pace the forest. In the cool night air, scented with pine and oak and maple, they could share hands and speak freely to one another as they liked to do. But as Oron and Esa went alongside the hut, a loud voice stopped them.

Oron turned slowly, knowing the voice, knowing the man.

Aksakin, now in his middle years, was as tall as his son, and as broad as an ox. His movements were slow but forceful. Because he'd had an eye punched out during one of his many battles and fights, he wore a rag around the top of his head to hide the cavity. And now, to add to his intimidating posture of savage manhood on the decline, he was very drunk of wine, which probably gave him the courage tonight to confront his son and his son's lover, as it had given him the courage every night to visit Lunda's hut and threaten and frighten Esa with his kisses.

Oron stood squarely and defiantly before his father. "Go away. We're alone."

"I wish to speak with Esa. You aren't a warrior."

"I'll talk with you later; we will talk to Ilgar in his hut."

"You aren't a warrior. Your words mean nothing."

Oron sucked in a breath of cool air. "Esa doesn't want you. She and I are alone. Go away, father."

Aksakin stumbled forward, belched, threw out an arm and leaned against the side of Lunda's hut. Lunda heard the commotion and came out. Aksakin, not turning around, staring at Oron, growled to the old woman, "Lunda, I have come to speak with Esa. Tell the little puppy to go pee in the woods."

Lunda did not speak. No one said anything. There was only the sound of Aksakin breathing heavily as he stared at Oron and the sight, as the moon came up, of Oron, bold before his father, hatred in his eyes, with Esa hugging close behind him.

"Go away," Oron told Aksakin again, "or I'll bring this to Ilgar."

"Ilgar is not your father. I am your father."

Oron growled, "No. You are not my father. My father was a wolf, not a half-blind, drunken old man."

Aksakin nearly fell backward in shock. Both Lunda and Esa let out small gasps of astonishment. Hatred or not, jealousy or not, there was blood here, and Oron was not yet a warrior; he could not dare to talk to his own father, a warrior, in this manner.

"Oron," Esa ventured, "let me talk to him. Perhaps—"

"No more talk!" Aksakin bellowed. Snarling, he threw a hand to his sword pommel and pulled free his blade. It glistened like a tongue of silver in the flat moonlight. "Oron, draw your sword!"

"I am not yet a warrior. You can't challenge me. It's a crime. Go away." There was no fear or terror in his steady voice. "And I am your blood-son, so I cannot fight you."

"You're not my son!" Aksakin yelled at him. "You are a son of a wolf, huh? You are a traitor to your father and to your tribe, huh? Draw your steel!"

And furiously, drunkenly, he jumped forward, swinging his weapon in a wide arc.

Oron instantly jumped back, throwing out an arm to push Esa away. Aksakin's blade barely made its mark, but it sliced Oron's free arm and drew a line of blood.

"Now draw your sword!" Aksakin bellowed hoarsely, "or I'll kill you as you stand, son or no son!"

Lunda threw herself on Aksakin's back, pleading with him. He pushed her off and ambled forward, spitting and snarling, whipping his blade in the air.

Oron began, "I will not—"

But his father swiped again, cutting the air, proving that he meant what he said.

Reluctantly, Oron pushed Esa far behind him and, as Aksakin lunged at him again, he drew his own sword and skipped out into the open, prepared to slay, prepared to kill, prepared to murder, as he had murdered the wolf two summers earlier.

2

With his second swipe, Oron drew blood. His father howled angrily and fell back a pace examining the red on his hand. A neat slice over the knuckle bones. His hand still worked, but the blood there would make his hold unsure.

"Whelp!"

"Father, let it end here!"

"Come ahead, pup! Come ahead, *wolf!* Wolf pup!" Aksakin lunged forward.

Oron drew back. "I don't want to kill you!"

"One of us must die!"

"Father, don't—!"

But Aksakin lunged again, and this time he kept swinging furiously. Thrusting, pulling back, swerving, hacking up, slicing back, hammering down. Oron guarded himself well, his blade always a heartbeat faster then his father's. Sparks shot in the night from their blades, the crude steel clicking and clacking, scraping as the swords slammed together, whisked apart.

Lunda grabbed Esa and pushed her back. "Get inside!"

Dumbfounded, Esa stood staring in shock at the swordplay.

"Get inside, girl!" Lunda pushed her, pushed her

again. The roughness awakened the girl from her trance. Shaking her head in disbelief, she ran quickly to the shadows of the hut, then stopped and looked back. Lunda came up to her and blocked her view.

"He will kill him. . . ." Esa whispered softly, her wide eyes darting to her aunt's.

"They are warriors. They are men—"

"Oron will kill him."

"Get inside!" Lunda grabbed the girl by an arm, pulled her around the corner, and took her inside the hut.

"Damn you, pup!" For the second time, Oron had drawn blood. "Think you'll carve me into pieces?" Drunken with wine and ferocity, Aksakin moved away from his son. He breathed, leaning forward and panting. Spittle drooled from his gasping mouth, and hung in silver threads down his long beard.

"It is ended, father."

"I'll cut your heart out, pup! You're no son of mine! Son of a wolf!" With an astonishing leap that took Oron by surprise, the Skull-Splitter jumped at him, swinging his blade in a short, pointed thrust aimed at the heart.

Aksakin was swift, a swift warrior. But Oron had slain a wolf. With a motion that matched speed to agility he slid to the side, and when his father's lunge carried him past, Oron brought his blade down with a hammering shock. Aksakin howled.

Nervous pain shot up the Skull-Splitter's arm as his sword cracked in half beneath his son's shattering blow. The tip of the blade tumbled in the air and disappeared with a rustling loudness in the forest bushes. Aksakin stared down at the halved sword; the hilt in his hand, the sundered end clean and frosty in the moonlight. It was as though Oron had demanned him in some shocking, novel way.

"No more, father," Oron told him in a low, commanding tone. He stood in the clearing, sword up, tall and almost regal in his pride. "Let it end."

Aksakin shook his mane of hair and pulled himself erect. A growl curdled softly in his throat and his eyes flashed black brilliance. Hatred. "Pup. . . ."

"Lay down the sword, father. We will go to Ilgar; speak to the chief."

Slowly, slowly Aksakin shook his head. "No more words, son of a wolf. . . ." As quickly as he had before, the solid bear of a man abruptly moved; became a shadow of motion lit with the blurring dazzle of his halved sword.

Oron leaned forward, lifted himself onto his toes, and raised his blade, measuring for the stroke, watching the rush of his father.

Aksakin was at him. Frenziedly, the old warrior struck up with his blunt blade and pulled back in a deft slice. Oron felt a cold burn whisper across his chest; felt cold air breathe through hot raw flesh.

"Skull-Splitter!" he screamed. The intensity of his sudden shriek stunned his father. "*Now* we are done with words!"

Aksakin dropped back a pace, twisted his sword deftly in his grip and held it like a knife. He jumped.

Oron's blade moved as his father's bulk moved. His sword was a streaking curtain of ghostly silver, a fanning blur. As his blade swept up, as his father lunged forward, Oron slid to the side. It was done in a moment.

Aksakin tumbled ahead, stumbling awkwardly. Ahead of him, impossibly, he saw his hand, still clutching his blunted sword, speeding on a trail of black blood. Dancing stupidly in his dazed surprise, he glared down at the spouting stump of his right arm. Quickly he covered the pouring stump with his left hand, trying to stop the blood flow.

Lunda shrieked.

"Dog. . . !"

"Now give it up!" Oron yelled at him.

"Dog!" Aksakin howled, and stared fiercely at his son. In a moment he had drawn his side-knife, the silver tongue of metal he carried at his waist. Gripping it in his left hand, he lunged, wholly madened, lusting for death.

Oron met him. He did not fall back to measure the stroke or his enemy's movement. His mind was gone; there was only blackness, and if the enemy was indeed his father, Oron at this moment did not realize it. He saw only fierce eyes, screaming mouth, a hand with a knife.

The knife swept past him, brushing his long hair.

Aksakin growled.

Never stopping in his own rush, Oron punched upward with all his strength. The tough crunch of metal breaking into bone twisted his sword arm slightly. He pulled back with his blade, jumped free, and raised the dripping metal high for another stroke.

Before him, his father went limp. Wide, surprised eyes. Hanging mouth. Spouting stump of an arm. Wide patch of slick, shining red on the front of his chest.

Suddenly lifeless, Aksakin dropped back in a few weak steps, turned awkwardly, and fell backward. He crashed to the ground with the noise of a felled oak.

Oron stared at him. He shivered tremendously. His arms ached, his lungs burned, his head pulsed. He breathed rapidly, with no pictures in his mind, no thoughts, no words. He had slain. Slain as he had slain the wolf.

Slain his father.

He swallowed thickly. Shook his head. Dropped his sword.

It struck the ground softly.

His hands were jumping as though with lives of their own; frantic, nervous, with coiled tension unleashed suddenly.

Lunda shrieked.

Slowly, dumbly, Oron looked over at her. He saw Esa's aunt in the shadow of her hut, falling to her knees, hands covering her face, sobbing and shrieking.

And he saw the others.

All of them. Three hundred, four hundred warriors, gathered at the edge of the clearing, some with torches in their hands, all with hardness in their eyes. At the head of them was Ilgar. All witness to his crime.

"The boy has slain his father," whispered one voice, quietly. But in the abysmal silence of the death-plain, it rumbled as loudly as a thunderclap.

Oron looked into Ilgar's eyes.

I'm strong and I killed the wolf, Father Ilgar. I'm the only son of Aksakin the Skull-Splitter.

Stared deeply into his chief's eyes. . . .

"The boy has slain the father," whispered the voice again.

The silence of the death screamed in Oron's brain, and he was afraid.

He sat awake in his father's hut ~~all~~ night long while warriors stood watch outside and I——— his hut to decide on justice. Oron knew th———— fair as he could be in the matter———— But he also knew that his only———— Hukrum, his father's brother, ————— in the name of vengeance. Or———— and if Ilgar passed down a ————— Oron would face it manfully

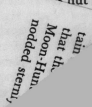

tain
that th———
Moon-Hun———
nodded sternly

him that he must die before attaining his warriorhood. Yet he did not want the vote for his death cast by Hukrum, because he knew Hukrum to be a crafty, temperamental man, as selfish and brutal as Aksakin. Oron did not wish to die in the cause of blood vengeance; he wanted his story told, his peace made, and his death done with honor.

When the first of the sun shined through the smoke-hole at the top of the hut ceiling, the drapes were drawn aside and four warriors entered to escort Oron to Ilgar's hut. He felt ashamed as he was led down the dirt paths to his judgement; he had hoped that most of the people would be sleeping, yet all were awake and watching from their doors, or standing by the paths, silently looking at him as he was taken.

In Ilgar's hut the chief sat on his small dais. To his right sat Den-Usutus, on the ground; to the Moon-Hunter's left sat Hukrum. If there had been more relatives, all would have sat in a line to the chief's left. But there was only Hukrum, and in the dimness of the hut, lit in the gray dawn by many torches, the uncle's eyes were black and malicious, and in his posture he leaned forward as if wishing to deal a deathstroke with his fists.

Oron bowed slightly to his chief and slapped his chest. The warriors that had escorted him stood behind him, watching him carefully. The young man's weapons had been taken from him, but these warriors knew Oron to be a strong and swift youth, and if he became angered, he might attack his chief as he had his father.

Ilgar stared at the boy, and despite his role as chief and law-giver of the village, there was no doubt there was sympathy and sadness in his gaze. The Moon-Hunter wiped his tired eyes with a big hand, and said to Oron, "Is there anything you have to say?"

"My father provoked me, O Ilgar. I had no wish to fight him. He drew his sword. I did not wish to harm him. But he—he caused it himself."

"We have heard the story."

"Have you spoken with Lunda? She knows how it—"

"She is a woman. what right has she to speak in tribal matters?"

"She knows why this happened."

"I know why this happened, Oron. You wished Esa; but you are not a warrior. Aksakin, a warrior, wished her. It was his privilege."

Oron trembled with subdued rage. "But he would not have if I did not desire Esa. I was his own son. He only wished to—"

"I know your father's temperament. I know the man he was. All men have passions, and that is why we have laws. Laws are to control passions. And where they cannot control passions, they punish them. The law says that a warrior may choose a woman if he has no woman; it does not say that a man who is not a warrior may choose a woman. That is the law."

"I know the law. But it does not—"

"It is the law of this tribe, Oron. There is another law stating judgement when a warrior kills another warrior, and when a son kills his father. These are not harsh laws; they are necessary for the tribe."

Oron's belly became ice. He was not afraid to die, he was not afraid of Ilgar's judgement, but when he looked into his uncle Hukrum's eyes. . . .

"I have made my decision," Ilgar said.

Oron watched him.

"You are a strong man. You would make a strong warrior. But you are not a warrior. The earth needs good warriors. You slew your father. It is not good for a son to slay his father, his parent and his blood. But I think you are a reasonable man. Your father was not reasonable. And I do not wish to make the earth suffer for lack of good warriors or for lack of reasonable men."

Oron was trembling in his anxiousness. Hukrum watched him, sneering.

"It is my decision that you will live, but you will be banished from this tribe. You will not become a warrior of this tribe. You will no longer carry the name of this tribe or of your father. You will leave this tribe now, and you will not return. If you return, you will be killed. We no longer know your name, you no longer know our names."

He heard. Understood. Looked deeply into his chief's eyes.

We no longer know your name. . . .

Banished?

He could not speak the word. He could not believe it.

Banished? Away from his tribe? Forever?

He stared into Ilgar's eyes. "Banished . . . my chief. . . ?"

Sternly, but with a tremulous voice, the Moon-Hunter told him, "You will go now. You will be given your weapons, and you will go. Forget the path that leads you to the village of Ilgar the Moon-Hunter."

"Banished. . . ?" Oron took in a deep breath. He was trembling terribly. Banished! Away . . . forever? He would rather that he had been killed. What was a man without a tribe, without his name, without his people? That man was no man; he was a wild animal; he was no better than—

Oron swallowed thickly. Tears swelled at his eyes and he fought to hold them back. "I—my chief—"

"Do you accept this judgement? You must accept

this judgement, Oron."

"I—I wish to speak with Esa. Before I go. Let me speak with—"

"No."

"—Esa . . . please. . . ."

"You are no longer of this tribe. You have no business with Esa of Lunda's hut, you have no business with any man or woman of this village."

Choked, Oron turned his head away. Self-pity gripped him, and then anger, wrath. Was this fair? He loved Esa, and Ilgar knew it, and he was of the tribe.

"I will kill you!" Hukrum shouted.

Oron turned, snarling, to face his uncle.

Hukrum hunched forward on his knees, slamming his fists on the floor of the hut. "Dog! Dog! Blood-slayer! I will kill you, you have—!"

Instantly Ilgar was on his feet. The chief jumped from the dais and with a mighty swing back-handed Hukrum, cuffing the man so fiercely that he dropped to the side. When he pulled himself up, Hukrum's nose was bloody and one eye was red. He stared evilly at his chief.

Ilgar's shadow hovered over him dangerously. "*I* am the chief!" he yelled to the man. "*I* am the law! You curse your nephew for spilling blood, and now you would draw *his* blood? You are a warrior! You are bound by oath to me! Act like a warrior! *I* am the law!"

Humiliated, Hukrum repositioned himself in his crouch and carefully fingered his tender eye and bloody nose. He did not look at Ilgar; he stared at the floor of the hut. But as the chief sat again on his dais, Hukrum shot a vengeful look of utter hatred at his nephew.

Oron, regaining his composure, realized that there

was nothing he could do or say to argue Ilgar's decision. His chief had been as fair as he could be. As fair as he could be in banishing—banishing—casting out a man of the tribe. . . .

The Moon-Hunter told Oron broodingly, "Go now, Wolf."

The respectfulness of that order was not lost on the young man. Harmed in his heart but unbroken in spirit, he turned silently and exited the hut. Outside, mist was rising and sunlight warmed every home, lighted every pebble and leaf and stone, as bright, morning sun does. A warrior handed Oron his sword, his knives, his small hand hatchet. He was dressed in his boots, breeches, and a vest. Without a word, he looked upon the villagers assembled to stare at him. Lunda was there. There was utter sadness and desolation in her face, and Oron had never seen such strong emotion reflected in her before.

But Esa was not there.

Heartbroken, angry, but alive—banished—Oron turned from his people and walked down the path of the village, aware that with every step he passed by huts he would see no more, glimpsed people he would see no more, suffered agonies that would burn and writhe in him—agonies, eventually, that would cauterize into scars.

With every step, he left the sunlight of his village and entered into the sunlight of the remainder of the world.

He was alone, banished, without hope in anything save himself. He was afraid. Not afraid of the world, but afraid of what he had left behind. . . .

In the hut, when Hukrum had left, Den-Usutus said to his chief, "It is good that you did not order him slain."

Sadly, tensely, he answered, "How could I order

him slain? He will become a great warrior. He is the man his father never was."

"He has the blood of the gods in him, Ilgar."

"Then the gods must guide him, for this tribe no longer will."

Den-Usutus stood up, stepped beside his chief, looked Ilgar in the eyes. "You looked upon him as a son."

Ilgar drew in a deep breath. "I have no son, bone-reader. No son. . . ."

He wandered for his first day in the forest, not going far from his village, but staying outside its bounds, and staying away from the paths he knew its warriors used. Becoming hungry, he silently debated about starving for a while, as a self-inflicted punishment, but he did not. He fished in the river to fill his belly, and by the Nevga in a great oak tree, as if marking out his own territory outside the tribe, Oron carved a crude picture of a wolf and a sword. His tree; his totem; his river.

As the sun came down he climbed high into a tall oak and from its great height watched the lit fires of Ilgar's village. He made himself a nest of boughs and vines and studied the silent, distant village, listened to the night birds and the insects. As he became tired, he cried. He was a young man, almost a warrior. He was the Wolf. He was banished and alone, without a hut, and because the village was no longer his home the forest no longer seemed his home. He cried, angry, and fell asleep.

He awoke with the first of the dawn and abandoned his nest, walked through the forest and ate fruit for his breakfast. He decided that he must do something. He must make a plan, come to a decision. He at first considered wandering west to join other tribes, but even if he were to do so, word would soon spread of his crime, and no tribe wanted an outcast.

He knew that bands of other criminals and rogues and free swords lived in the forests and in the mountains of the wide Nevga River Valley, but he did not wish to join them. He was not a thief, or a pillager, or a cannibal. He was Oron, the Wolf.

He decided to move east, circle around his village and, in a day or two, enter the eastern lands with their cities of big nests and tall huts, and join with armies of warriors who had the many different kinds of weapons and even (he had heard it said) moving huts of war. That seemed to Oron a good decision. It appealed to his sense of adventure to do what no one else in his village had ever done. So following his breakfast of fruit, he began walking east.

He circumvented his village, came upon a small stream that flowed east, and followed it. As the afternoon came down he felt that he must not be very far from the cities of the east, but just to make sure he climbed a tree and looked.

No cities.

He climbed even higher. The tree was very tall and its branches sturdy, so Oron kept climbing until he felt that the smaller branches high up might no longer support his weight. All around him spread the dense green roof of trees with their clustered boughs and spiring heights. He could not even look back to the west to see Ilgar's village; it was entirely hidden by the thick forest. Beyond him, to the east, Oron saw the blanket of tree tops spread wide in all directions and vanish in a misty haze against the flat blue of distant mountains. Were the cities beyond those mountains? If that were so, then it might take him another whole day to reach them. Those cities were far away, indeed, farther away than Rall the Serpent Bow's village was from Father Ilgar's.

A strong breeze blew and Oron suddenly became aware of how high up in the tree he was. Cautiously, he descended, and when he eventually found himself back on the ground, he began mulling over what he must do.

He missed Esa.

Wandering through the woods, walking vaguely east but sometimes backtracking toward the west, he began working on a bow for himself and plotting a strategy about Esa.

He loved her, that was certain. And she loved him. Maybe he was not a warrior of Ilgar's tribe but he was a man, and he would become a warrior in his own right. Therefore, he had a right to a mate. He had already chosen Esa, and she had chosen him. No one, and no law, had the right to keep them separated. Oron told himself that, and he was a man, and he believed it.

As night came down he finished his bow. He'd carved it well, notching into it a picture of a wolf. He stopped at a stream and watched carefully as a buck came down the opposite bank to sip water. Silently Oron stepped down his side of the bank and aimed with his bow. He had but one arrow, and that one unfeathered. The buck lifted its head and sniffed the air, then dipped its head to the water again.

Oron released his arrow.

Due more to the strength behind it than the precision of its design, the arrow shot true. It pierced the buck cleanly through one eye, burying itself in the brain. The proud animal jumped up, kicked its legs, fell back on its haunches and dropped to one side. Oron leapt from the bushes and splashed across the shallow stream. He knelt by the still-twitching buck, cut its throat with his sword, and proceeded to carve a meal for himself from its fresh meat.

That evening, by his campfire, he oiled his boots and vest with grease and fat, and sewed deerskin into a meat-carrying pouch. When night fell, Oron extinguished his fire, climbed into a tree and made a nest for himself.

On the morrow (he decided) he would return west, take Esa from her Aunt Lunda's hut, and with her escape to the cities of the east. There, they could become married to each other; they could live in the big-hut cities, and Oron could become a warrior with the army-warriors of the east. Their life would be good; they would forget about the village, have children, and make their home.

As he slept, high in the tree, far from the village, Oron did not notice a great fire lighting the sky to the east, and he did not smell the black smoke that rose high to the clouds and was blown by the winds to the south.

3

As he approached the village late the next afternoon, Oron smelled the dirty, heavy stench of smoke. His heart raced. He had intended to come close to the village and wait in hiding until nightfall, but now he sensed something gravely wrong, and he hastened westward, running at a rapid, steady pace, looking for signs of rooftops.

He saw none.

A short distance from the village he thought it best to climb a tree to get a view of things. He was still banished, whether or not harm had come to his people, and he would be treated as an intruder. As an intruder, or worse—for if harm had come to the village, his people might consider him somehow responsible.

From the height of the tree he saw a scene of devastation that seared his brain and chilled his heart. There was no village. There were only smoking huts, burned trees, piles of corpses. . . .

Oron scrambled down the branches, jumped to the ground, and ran as fast as he could.

None questioned him or tried to stop him as he walked into the ruins of the village. Numbed, dazzled, he took it all in at once, and slowly began to pick up the details: The corpses of dogs and children—

smashed against trees, heads separated from bodies, or burnt into black ashes; a strange blue glow that hung like a wispy cloud upon flung weapons and some of the mutilated bodies.

And a few survivors. Ghosts, they seemed to be. Oron did not speak to them, nor did they say aught to him. No warriors. For everywhere, he saw the shattered corpses of warriors, as well as women, children, and animals. An old woman here was stumbling, roaming from body to body. As she heard Oron approach she looked up at him, screamed, laughed, pulled at her hair, then shivered and went back to wandering from corpse to corpse.

Over here a dog was sniffing at bodies. It saw Oron, crouched low, tilted its head to one side, and barked at him viciously. Oron noticed that one full side of its head and body was burned raw, the flesh black and red, the hair gone.

Fear began to chew inside him as he trod the blue-glowing paths of the desolated village. Hukrum? Ilgar? Esa? High gods, what of Esa!?

Hurrying as well as he could, numbed by the destruction, Oron made his way to Lunda's hut.

He saw no sign of Esa—no corpse, no shred of clothing or jewelry. But Lunda was lying outside her hut, which was intact but burned in patches. Lunda was babbling. Oron saw that she, too, had been severely burned.

Kneeling above her was Den-Usutus.

Oron approached them.

Den-Usutus looked up.

In a dull voice, Oron asked of the burned, frail shaman, "What has happened?"

Den-Usutus tried to speak; he shook his head. With a black, clawed hand he motioned for Oron to come nearer.

Oron bent down beside him, looked at Lunda, who lay with closed eyes and barely moving breast, and stared into Den-Usutus's dull eyes.

"Shaman," he said in a low, careful voice. "Tell me what has happened."

Tears rolled down Den-Usutus's pink-burnt cheeks. "Soldiers," he whispered gutturally, coughing and rasping. "Mosutha. . . ."

"What?"

"Mmmm—Mosutha. The sor—cerer. . . ."

"He did this?"

"His—soldiers. Warriors. Mosutha. They—burned—"

Oron moved suddenly. He grabbed Den-Usutus by the shoulders, and the old man winced with pain at the strong hold. Fresh tears rolled down his face.

Oron removed his hands, astonished that Den-Usutus's flesh felt hot as fire coals. "Esa?" he asked.

Lunda, half-dead, heard him. Her body quaked, like a corpse reanimating to life, as she tried to sit up and shrieked in a crazy howl, *"Esa-ah-aha!"*

Oron stared at her, chilled.

Den-Usutus bent over her, held Lunda's hands, and shook them until she calmed.

"What of Esa?" Oron demanded again of Den-Usutus, becoming angry and afraid.

"They—they took some people."

"Esa?"

"Yes. Yes. . . . They took Esa."

"Are you sure, Den-Usutus? Look at me."

"I am dying." He faced Oron, a wounded old man, his face pink and blotched, his mouth black with dried blood. "I am sure," he wheezed. "They took—Esa. Took—women—young men. Ilgar—dead. All of them. Burned. . . . Blue fire. . . ." His face creased in perplexed astonishment.

"Where, shaman? Where did they take her? *Tell me!*"

Den-Usutus began to sob. He drew away from Oron. "Don't hit me! Don't—! I want to die!"

"Shaman . . . shaman, please. Where did they take Esa?"

Den-Usutus began to laugh. "North. Yes . . . to the north. Sorcerer lives in the north—across the river. We never told you. Ilgar—fool! 'No, don't tell them, they are warriors!' Fool! Now he's burned." The shaman began to rant in a singsong voice, rocking back and forth, and Lunda began to shriek, accompanying him as a chorus of the damned. "Now he's burned . . . now he's burned . . . sorcery in the north. . . . Now he's burned . . . the dead are burned. . . ."

Oron rose to his feet, wary of the maniac. Yet, he had to make certain. "He took Esa?" he asked Den-Usutus again. "To the north? Listen to me! Mosutha did this?"

Den-Usutus ceased his singsong, and rocked still. He regarded Oron carefully, held out his black-charred, clawlike hands. He tensed. "Mosutha!" the shaman screamed suddenly. *"Mosutha!"*

Birds squawked and fluttered from nearby trees at the sound of the howl.

"Yes! *Yes! Mo-sutha!*"

Oron cautiously lowered his hand to his sword hilt. "And where is Mosutha?" he asked gravely. "In the north? He took Esa to the north?"

Den-Usutus's eyes went wide as if with some inner brilliance. "Mosutha is in Hell, Oron! I am in Hell! You are in Hell! Hell, Hell, Hell!"

Lunda, thrashing on the ground beside him, shrieked: "Hell! *Hell-lllll!*"

"Hell! Hell! *Mosutha is in Hell!*"

"Hell! *Hell-lllll!*"

Oron backed away from them, turned, and hurried through the village.

"Hell! Hell-lllll. . . !"

Dazed, frightened, he wandered down one path, and turned onto another. Everywhere lay the smoking desolation, the black ruins, the blue-glowing corpses. He saw Ilgar's hut, or what remained of it. And outside it—

Outside it, sprawled in a pile, were a dozen corpses, Ilgar's on top. Ilgar, the last to fall. All charred, burned black, fused together—bone and flesh and metal weapons—as though with the heat of a Fire Demon.

Oron stared at the corpses.

Stared at Ilgar and the men of the tribe, the retainers of his chief.

The black corpses . . . the blue glow.

And a madness exploded within him. A clarity. An uncaged agony, an unsuspected sight through new eyes.

"*No-oho-ahhh. . . !*"

Howling, he drew his sword from its sheath. Turned this way and that. Hair flying, muscles tensed—needing an enemy to kill.

No enemy.

He jumped up and down on the ground, hammering his sword into the black earth.

"No! No! *No-oho!*"

Clods of earth and bits of stone rained up and down, spattered him in the face, as he hammered madly at the earth.

"Damn you! *Damn you! Damn you!*"

Furious, unable to kill anything, Oron reared back, lifted his sword and, angry at the world, hurled it with all his strength.

"*Mo . . . soo . . . tha . . . aahhh. . . !*"

The sword flashed through the air, flew half the length of the village and hit the ground, slid crazily, and bumped into the half-burned dog that was sniffing at a corpse far down the path. The dog growled at Oron and scampered away as the sword slid still.

"Mo . . . soo . . . tha . . . ahh!"

Roaring, Oron ran after his sword, the wind in his face, the sweat pouring down him. The stink and rot of the village filled his lungs. Not slowing down, he picked up the sword as he ran and continued running until, exhausted, he reached the end of the path. He fell to his knees at the forest edge.

"Mosutha!"

Holding his sword high in his hands, he challenged the unseen, unknown evil thing that had slain his village, desecrated him, shattered his soul.

"North! Mosutha!"

Furious, he drove the sword with both hands into the earth, hilt deep.

"I am Oron, Mosutha! I am the Wolf! I will come north and slay you, sorcerer! *I . . . will . . . slay . . . Mosutha!"*

Trembling, Oron rose to his feet, pulled free his sword and held it to the smoky sky defiantly, as if to brand the clouds with it.

"I will slay Mosutha! I am Oron! I am *Oron!* I am the Wolf! Esa!" he screamed. *"Esa!* I am *Oron!* I will slay *Mosutha!"* he shrieked. "Slay . . . himmm. . . !"

Thunder boomed high above, growling over the forest, answering his challenge.

"Mo . . . soo . . . tha . . . ahh. . . !"

Night descended with the rain of the thunderstorm as he came upon a village—another village devastated by an attack of sorcery. There were still men alive in this village, but they were not strong men. Many of them were wounded and burned. They invited Oron into their huts and, as they roasted meat over their fire pits, they spoke with him. From all around came the dull groans and the screams of the wounded and the dying.

"Mosutha," they said, agitated, "—the soldiers of Mosutha—they came with fire and magic. Our shaman died, our chief was killed, our warriors were slaughtered. They took our women and our young men, slew our children. The rest of us hid. They came and destroyed us . . . took our people. . . ."

"Where did they take them?"

"North."

"Come with me. You have weapons. I am heading north to free the prisoners and slay Mosutha."

Harsh laughter and derisive comments answered him. "Who are you, a boy, to slay Mosutha and defeat his warriors? Free his prisoners!"

"I am Oron, the Wolf."

"You are a boy."

Oron saw that he could not press them into fighting for themselves. "Mosutha is in the north."

Nods.

He told them, "I will sleep a night in your hut. In the morning, I will walk north, and I will find Mosutha and kill him. You are free to come with me."

But they shook their heads, and in the morning, as they fed him breakfast, they told him, "We are feeding a corpse."

"I will slay Mosutha," he assured them.

"You are a hunter?"

"Yes."

"Do you think Mosutha is a bear or a deer? Did you not see what he has done to our village, or what he has done to your village?"

"What he has done to us, we can do to him." Oron

stood up, severely disappointed. He asked them, "Are you not men?"

"We are farmers and builders. Our warriors fought and were slain."

"Are warriors the only men who can hold weapons?"

"We are afraid," one of them responded, shamed.

"I am afraid, too," Oron admitted to them. "Yet I am angry. Are you not angry?"

They looked at him and did not speak.

"They took your women, butchered your children, killed your men. Are you not angry?"

But he couldn't dislodge the overriding fear in their bellies, so he went on.

Into the forest.

North.

Convinced that those men were cowards afraid to turn their fear into anger, afraid to make of their fear a weapon.

The rain let up, and late in the afternoon Oron spied loud tracks in the forest. Bootprints. He examined them and decided that there were six soldiers ahead of him. Soldiers, not warriors.

Mosutha's soldiers.

He went on, invisible and soundless, moving through the trees and the vines, the bushes. He ate fruit. From time to time he double-checked the tracks. Six of them, progressing north.

As the sun began to go down, Oron came upon the soldiers.

They were at a meal. They had built a small fire and were roasting pieces of cut meat over the flames. Soldiers, dressed in armor like the first Oron had seen, and wearing the sign of the seven-pointed Star on their breasts. They were heavily weaponed. That amused the Wolf.

He watched them from high in a tree, looking directly down upon them. The smoke of their fire almost reached his nose. Carefully, Oron fashioned a long rope out of vine, all the while staring at the men below him. He knew that he had ample time; these men were bloated and tired, and they would rest awhile longer before moving on.

When he finished his rope, he made a lasso at one end of it—the kind his father had always made when setting a trap for animals—and slung the rope over a strong limb. Coiling it, Oron placed the bunched rope securely in a crotch of the tree. Then he took down the three spears he had fashioned on the trail this afternoon—he had bundled them together and placed them in some branches above him. Now he yanked them free, tearing with his teeth the gut that held them. Crouching on his tree limb, getting comfortable so that his legs wouldn't go numb, he waited.

Six of them.

It was becoming darker in the forest, which was to his advantage.

He watched. In a short while, one of the men stood up and said something to his companions. A second stood up, and together they went off a little ways into the bushes to urinate.

Oron waited until those two were standing still in the bushes, and then he struck.

Holding his three spears in his left hand, he fed them one by one into his right, precisely, and with no wasted motion. Crouching, measuring well, he hurled the first downward.

It struck the chest of a soldier who was lying by the fire, dozing off. The man grunted as he was hit, and his three companions immediately leaped to their feet. One of them bent over to examine the stricken man.

Oron threw his second spear through this one's

back. The soldier screamed as the sharpened pole crunched through him, the point of it breaking through his belly and burying itself in the body of the first, pinning the squirming soldier to his companion.

The other two had seen the second spear fall from the tree above. Drawing their swords, they stared up and yelled to their comrades in the bushes. They tried to see into the thick foliage above, but Oron was invisible to them.

His third spear smashed one of these soldiers clean through the belly. The force of it knocked him back to the ground, where he writhed and howled, stretching and kicking his legs like a beetle pinned with a bone fishing hook.

The fourth man reacted by moving away from the base of the tree. Oron glanced over into the bushes. The two who had been relieving themselves were awkwardly making their way back to the camp.

Oron dropped his noosed vine.

It fell around the fourth soldier, trapping his arms to his sides. He squawked wildly.

Oron drew his sword. Holding tightly onto the other end of the rope with his left hand, he dropped from the tree.

The roped soldier, acting as a counterweight, was yanked upward, screaming and kicking his legs, as Oron dropped down beside him. As the dog flashed by him in midair, Oron stabbed him quickly with his sword.

The first of the other two ran into the camp as he swung down. The Wolf caught him full in the head with his boots, knocking him senseless to the ground. The sprawled body cushioned the shock of Oron's fall; bones snapped loudly as Oron landed on top of him. Grunting, he jumped aside and let go of his rope. As the last of the six soldiers jumped through the bushes, the roped man plummeted earthward, shrieking pitifully. He crashed into the small fire of the camp with a loud crunching sound.

The sixth dog was totally stunned. In the space of a few heartbeats his companions had been exterminated. And by what? This boy—this barbarian—this—?

That was all he had time to think.

Shocked, he fumbled with his sword, trying to free it from its scabbard.

In that moment, Oron leaped forward, his own blade a mist before him. With a bristling, choking noise the soldier's head snapped from his neck and dropped free to the earth, as his spouting shoulders dappled the surrounding bushes with a scarlet downpour.

Grunting, half-poised, Oron pivoted on his heels and surveyed the camp.

All was death.

Bodies prone with spears protruding from them. The man in the fire, his face and hands crisped, bent in an awkward position, arms still pinned to his waist. A crumpled, armored heap a little farther away, the neck snapped and the head twisted around, the flesh bulging and swollen. One decapitated corpse, the leather and bronze of the armor washed with dark red blood.

Methodically, with no expression in his eyes and only the deep, ravenous fire of wrath in his heart, Oron moved from corpse to corpse and freed the swords of the men from their sheaths or from their frozen fists. He dropped them in a pile. Then, just as methodically, he severed the heads from the five corpses in the camp, chopping once each time with his heavy, wolf-sigiled sword.

He collected the six heads into a pile.

He drove a sword through each of the six heads.

Then he nailed the heads to the logs set around the campfire, shoving with his strong arms so that the points of the swords, protruding from the backs of the skulls, adequately secured the severed heads to the timber.

He looked at what he had done.

It was good.

The mark of his vengeance.

He yanked his three spears from the bodies of the dead soldiers, for he would have use of these spears again. In the darkness, then, he moved on toward the north, running at a measured, loping pace, so that all that could be heard of him was the occasional breeze like rustle of bushes, or the low dim wolf-pad of his boots on the earth.

Late in the night, he found more of them.

It was a camp. Once more Oron hauled himself up into a tree to survey his enemies, and grunted with subdued rage at what he saw.

Wagons, with cages mounted on them. Tens of wagons, thirty or forty of them, arranged in a wide circle in a clearing of the forest. In the center of the circle sprawled hundreds of soldiers, all in greased leather and dull bronze, all with that seven-pointed Star on their chests. They roasted meat or sipped wine or drank bowls of soup or slept in the light of tall campfires. Off to one side, within the circle but huddled within the shadow of a small black tent, Oron saw five or six men who were not soldiers. They were all of them tall, slim men with white faces and deep-set eyes. They wore robes of some kind, but no armor: robes similar to the hide robes that Den-Usutus, the shaman, had worn when he tranced or sang loudly in his fever to reach the gods. And outside the circle of wagons, where crowds of horses were tethered, Oron saw a patrol of soldiers moving tiredly, walking around in the forest as lookouts.

He tried hard to see if Esa was within one of the cages, but the distance and darkness were too great.

Blood thrummed in his brain, his nerves jangled, his belly thrilled with the promise of death and vengeance. The night was yet young—long to go before sun-dawn. If he moved swiftly and stealthily, hid himself well, used his weapons certainly, he could slay every soldier in this camp. He would be the lone wolf of the trail, maddened and fierce, ripping down, one after another, every enemy of this pack.

He did not keep to the trees, for that offered him no mobility. He moved on the ground, silent as a shadow, through the trees and leaves and bushes. He did, however, make good use of another weapon he had fashioned on his way northward from the last village. With deer gut from the buck he had killed, Oron made a strong sling, forming the pocket of it with a circle of hide. As a boy he, like other boys of his tribe, had used such slings to kill birds and rabbits. Occasionally, too, the warriors of Ilgar's tribe had used them when routing enemies during battle. With practice, the sling was a deadly weapon.

In Oron's hand this night, it was a very deadly weapon, indeed.

Chary of using his bow in the dark, clogged forest, he had safely left it high in the tree. But he had hidden his spears on the ground, where he knew he could return for them. And as his first weapon of attack he used his sling—sharp-edged stones found on the floor of the woods were perfect for him. He kept three or four at all times in his left hand, and fed them as he used them into the pouch of his sling. Moving as a breeze does, he circumvented the perimeter of the camp and struck, at first, only isolated soldiers. Those who, on their rounds, had paused to rest or sleep. Oron would come close to them, hide behind a tree, drop a stone in his sling and whip the weapon until it whirred with the noise of a loosed bow.

The first soldier died in the middle of a sweet dream, when Oron's sharp stone buried itself in the center of his forehead. A second died when the stone ripped into his eye socket and lodged itself in his brain. Oron caught a third at the back of the neck, in he weak spot where the skull joins the spine. A fourth went down with a stone embedded in his temple, and a fifth died as a stone ripped through the throat. All died quietly, leaving only grunts or wheezes on the wind.

But other patrol soldiers became suspicious when, calling out for their companions, they received no responses. Oron withdrew a little farther into the forest. When a seventh soldier came looking for his comrades, he went down with a stone in his skull. An eighth appeared, calling out. Oron, while not particularly fond of the gods, nevertheless whispered quietly to the mountain deities to keep his aim true and the deaths of his enemies silent.

Perhaps the mountain deities, that night, decided that Oron had slain enough in one day. Perhaps his sureness and his quickness offended them. Or, perhaps, the Wolf was simply becoming fatigued.

The eighth soldier caught a stone in his belly. It ripped deeply but did not kill him. Wounded, he howled in pain and stared into the forest, in the direction from which it had come.

Immediately there was a commotion in the camp, and Oron heard the mad pandemonium of boots, leather, and drawn swords.

"Damn you to your gods!" he hissed at the loud soldier, loading another stone.

As the gasping wounded guard drew his sword and peered into the forest, Oron struck him with a second stone full in the face. He went down with a groan, eyes shooting blood, and fell into the dark bushes.

Instantly five others appeared from all directions to examine his corpse.

Oron moved. He slid into the forest, returning to the tree where he'd deposited his spears. Retrieving them, he hastened back toward the camp. Two soldiers were running in the direction of the commotion, where the last soldier had been killed. Stones would take too much time and precision. Oron hefted a spear, aimed, and felled one of the latecomers. When his companion stopped, shocked, he caught a shaft in his belly.

A third came running and Oron hurled his final spear at him. It did not kill. Thrown too quickly, the spear struck the side of a small tree and skewed off to land harmlessly in the bushes.

"Erith and Corech!" Oron swore, blaming the gods.

"They're over here!" screamed the guard. "Over here!"

Oron had no choice.

He drew his sword and ran.

The guard looked up, wholly surprised to see a body suddenly fly toward him from the recessed darkness of the forest. Oron, hurled himself in a strong leap, his body balled up, one arm out, with his sword a dazzling length of pure silver.

"They're o— —!"

The head, chopped free, slapped loosely back between the shoulders, blood spurting out in a tall river.

And Oron was gone that quickly, smashing through the bushes, heading into the camp.

The soldiers, he knew, were all collecting at the southern end, where he'd killed the one guard with two stones. Quickly, making noise, the Wolf hastened around to the east, behind the soldiers' attention. He did not run directly into the camp but hurried toward the wagons on that side.

If he could break them open, free the captives and arm them, get them the swords piled by the fires.

"Oron!"

His blood froze.

"*Oron!*"

Esa!

He stared across the encampment, saw her head and hair sticking through the wooden bars of her cage, her white-knuckled hands straining for freedom.

"Oron, *Oron!*"

Fury welled within him. Madness possessed him. Esa saw him and, now, so did the soldiers running up behind her cage. They tore into the camp, racing toward him.

Fiercely, Oron raised his sword and smashed at the wooden bars of the cage nearest him.

The men and women trapped inside screamed wildly at him. "Free us!" "Let us out, let us get our weapons!" "Harder, young warrior! They come!"

Sweat drooled down his face. His arm ached. Out the corner of one eye he saw the army of soldiers thundering across the camp. He swiped again and again, smashing at the cage.

"Free us!"

"Hurry, we'll—!"

"*Barbarian!*"

He looked up. A man staring at him, behind the cage. A man in a robe.

"*Dog!*" Oron screamed at him, frightened now, feeling that he had lost control. Swiftly, with the grace of long practice, he knelt and pulled a knife from his boot, jerked upward and hurled it at the robed man.

The robed man snarled and threw out a hand.

The knife glowed blue.

Oron gasped as he saw his knife slow down tremendously in its arc and land—position itself—softly within the robed man's outstretched fingers.

"Erith and Corech. . . !" he whispered, numbed.

Quickly the robed man jumped at him. Growling, Oron took a moment to make one last swipe at the wooden cage bars. A quick army of guards surrounded him, and the white eyes of the clay-face man in the robe blazed.

Oron moved his sword.

His strike stopped in midair as the robed man's arm lashed out swiftly. His fingers barely touched Oron's bare bicep, but instantly the Wolf burned with a tingling of fire, and he felt himself falling forward into a pit of darkness.

4

When he awoke it still was night. He came alert instantly but did not move. Opening his eyes slowly, Oron looked about him in the darkness. He felt a burnlike sore on his arm, but other than that no real discomfort. He realized that he was lying in one of the wagon-cages.

As he sat up, his hand instinctively went for his sword. It was gone. Of course—they would have taken all his weapons. Understanding this, he nonetheless felt in his boot and all around his waist for any knives they might have missed. He was weaponless.

He stretched, and looked at the people around him. He did not recognize them as members of his tribe, although a few faces looked somewhat familiar. They were from other tribes in the Valley. All were men, and strong men; brawny warriors. Oron shook his head to clear the last of his dizziness and studied the men as well as he could in the darkness. They watched him.

He nodded to one of those crowded nearest to him. "I am Oron, of Ilgar's tribe. Who are you?"

"Kosun the Ax-Maker, of the tribe of Nor the Bold."

"All of these are your men?"

Kosun grunted. He told Oron, "You fought well.

We heard them say you killed nine of them. But you were foolish to come into the camp."

He shrugged. "I have no intention of staying here."

Kosun smiled grimly. "You're a boy. You speak brashly. They have our weapons and the men in the robes have powerful lights in their hands."

Oron regarded Kosun for a long moment, then he looked away, and studied the camp. There was no use arguing with a man already defeated. He saw that the camp was no better fortified than it had been prior to his arrival. Obviously these people considered his interruption a fluke. Perhaps it had been. . . .

He looked back to Kosun. "How long was I asleep?"

"Half the night. You took a powerful touch. He could have killed you."

"Uh. Where are we going, do you know?"

"The camp travels north, to Mosutha's fortress."

"And they are attacking villages as they go?"

"There are none left to the north," Kosun replied. "Ours was the last; unless the tribe of Himgum is still at home farther up the river. But I heard his people went west after he died of a fever."

Oron glanced around the camp some more, and said to no one in particular, "We should plan our escape."

"When an opportunity presents itself," Kosun cautioned him.

"Will the soldiers talk to you? If they come over here, we can grab one of them and stab him; take his steel."

"Then the men in the robes will burn you."

Oron considered that. "Listen to me. If we all crowd to one side of the wagon and rock it back and forth, we can tip it over and smash it. We can free our—"

"The wagon it too heavy," Kosun reminded him.

"And they will see us doing it."

Oron glared at him, becoming upset with Kosun's irritating pessimism. "Then what of this? I still have flint and steel in the bottom of my boot. I can set fire to the wagon. That will weaken it and we can get free."

Kosun shook his head patiently. "You seem to forget, young Oron, that we are surrounded by armed men, as well as men in robes with the powers of demons."

A few behind Kosun chortled gruffly, and Oron reddened. He disliked being treated like an unthinking pup.

"I attacked this camp and killed nine of their men. How many have you killed?"

"I have no wish to discredit your kills," Kosun reminded Oron. "But you are now a prisoner with us. Think like a prisoner, not like a free man."

"No," Oron told him. "No. I cannot—"

Their conversation was broken suddenly by a commotion across the camp. Oron listened and crawled to the bars.

"Oron! Oron, can you here me?"

Esa!

"Your woman?" Kosun asked him.

Oron gripped the bars of his cage and fought with them. "Esa!" he cried out, seeing her now, far across the camp. "Esa! I am here! I am alive!"

Soldiers came at her and beat the bars of her cage with the flat sides of their swords. Driven back, Esa stumbled and fell into the crowded women behind her. She screamed.

Oron thought she had been hurt. *"Esa!"* With renewed fury he attacked his bars, twisting them, pulling at them strongly.

Kosun moved up, crouched behind him. "Calm

yourself!" he warned the youth. "This will do no—!"

"Esa! *Esa!*"

Incredibly, the thick poles that made the cage bars began to turn in Oron's grip. Feeling it happen, he threw himself against them even more powerfully. But to free himself he would have to snap the heavy bars in two, for they were sunk deeply through the very sides of the wagon.

Soldiers angrily drew their blades and trotted toward him.

"Barbarian dog, you—!"

"Esa!"

Once more, however before the soldiers could reach him, one of the robed men moved from the tent near Oron's cage and swiftly crossed the campground.

Kosun saw him. "Oron, get back! He'll kill you!"

"Let him try!" He was straining with all his young might at the wooden bars.

The robed man hurried to the cage. Lifting an arm, he threw back the sleeve to bare his hand and a slim wrist. The flesh shone.

"Oron!" Kosun yelled.

But Oron refused to let go of the bars.

Kosun leaped. Grabbing Oron by the shoulders, the warrior shoved the youth back. Oron slammed into the wall of bars on the other side of the cage.

But the robed man did not slow his pace. Furious, white eyes glowing like bits of molten metal, he reached through the bars, trying to grab Oron's foot.

In the darkness, he caught hold of Kosun.

The warrior howled in agony as he tumbled back, thrown as though hit by a lightning bolt. His leg smoked as he writhed painfully on the straw of the cart, and still the robed devil held onto him.

Oron, crouched on his feet and knees, stared in shock.

The robed man saw him. The brilliance of his eyes burned into the barbarian's brain.

"Erith and—*Corech!*" Oron screamed, doubling his fists and tensing to pounce.

But in the next instant the robed man grunted and jerked awkwardly. His head bent abruptly to one side as a stream of blood erupted from his open mouth. Despite the darkness, Oron saw a length of pointed wood jutting from his chest, tenting the robe and staining it with a shimmering red blotch.

"Gods!"

The robed man tumbled back, twisting, turning, letting go of Kosun to grab hold of the arrow that had pierced him. He could not pull it free. As he tripped backward, dying, a second arrow caught him in the side and pushed him around. He gawked, blood poured down his chest and he fell sloppily to the ground.

Astonished, Oron watched as the camp soldiers all hurried to their feet and drew their weapons. They began running, uncontrolled, in all directions as a sudden rain of arrows dropped upon them. Screams rent the cool night air as many of them stumbled, shrieked, and went down with stained shafts in their chests, throats, bellies, skulls.

"Who—?" Shocked, Oron glanced at his fellow prisoners.

"Get back!" yelled a voice from behind, and half a dozen large men crashed through the forest, running to the wagon. "Get back, we'll get you free!"

Oron and the others scrambled away as steel blades chopped at the bars. Splinters bit into flesh. From surrounding cages came similar sounds: the crunch of steel biting wood, the mad gleeful howls of the prisoners, the loud yells of the intruding attackers.

Oron was first through the broken bars. Quickly, he

68

hurled himself out of the cage and ran for the weapons piled by the campfires. He hoped to find his own sword—his wolf sword—but, rummaging, he was thoroughly satisfied to make do with the first heavy, scabbarded blade he got into his hands, as well as two knives and a small hatchet, which he thrust into his belt. As more and more men pushed their way around him, grabbing for weapons, Oron broke clear and, pivoting, surveyed the battle in the camp.

The attackers had surrounded the site. They were barbarians, that was obvious—most likely a squad of uprooted Nevgan Valley dwellers fighting back, in force, against Mosutha's army. They were out-numbered, that was certain, but their surprise maneuver had already downed at least twenty-five of the sorcerer's soldiers.

And one robed man.

Oron saw others of them caught in the melee—hurrying black robes with bright-burning white eyes. He hated them. And as they variously tried to escape or defend themselves, Oron took a moment to pull one of his knives from his belt and hurl it.

It struck one of the robed ones true in the back and sent him, gasping and hunching, sprawled to the ground.

"Esa!"

Her cage had not been smashed open. There were swords fighting in front of it, strokes being traded between barbarian steel and soldier blades. Oron tried to move around the fray. His paramount concern was to free Esa. But as he ran for her cage, one of Mosutha's soldiers jumped in front of him.

The Wolf made short work of him, A stroke, a parry, a dazzling sidewise movement that threw his opponent wholly off guard, an upward thrust, and the man crumpled to his knees, blood jetting from the crater Oron had ripped under his rib cage.

"Esa!"

She called to him, hanging on to the bars of her cage. "Oron! Hurry, please!"

He ran and threw himself and his sword against her prison with a maddening flurry of strokes. The wooden bars shattered, ripped, splintered apart.

"Oron! Oh, gods—!"

"Hurry, Esa!"

He grabbed her hand, she threw herself from the wagon. He paused only a moment to gaze into her eyes, look upon her hair, feel the real weight of her hand in his.

"Run!" he told her.

"Come *with* m——!"

"Into the forest!"

He dragged her. Far stronger than she, and eager to see her free, free and with him in the forest, Oron dragged her, and Esa, in her panic, nearly fell to her knees. Away from the whooshing, flashing blades, the bodies erupting and spattering blood, around past other cages, around pockets of swordplay, blood, screams, shining faces, red-painted fists, kicking legs, oozing ripped bellies. . . .

"Oron, Oron, we can't—!"

Panting, furious, sword out, he pulled her here and there, tugged her and shoved her, staying clear of the blades, and running men.

"Oron!"

"Gods!" He turned, threw Esa behind him.

It was Hukrum, freed with the rest of them during the raid. "Now you die, *murderer!"*

Madness! But it was Hukrum, charging at him from a circle of moving blades, a sword in his fist. He loped quickly toward his nephew to embattle him in the very moment of their freedom.

"Fool!" Oron howled at him. He half turned to push Esa toward the forest, but there was no time. Hukrum was upon him, swinging his steel. Oron cursed and brought up his blade; sparks shot, the fever gripped him as, howling, he jumped upon his uncle.

"Are you moon-mad? We are *free!*"

"Die, blood-murderer!"

Hukrum thrust. Oron cut down; pushed his uncle's blade aside. Hukrum moved to the side; sliced. Oron caught the stroke with his blade and jumped forward. Quickly—to kill his uncle quickly, and escape with Esa. . . .

But Hukrum would not let him. His mind was gone, he was without his senses. Chaos raged around them, sword battled sword, men in robes fell screaming in the night-dark, fires flared, arms and heads and bits of flesh and bone jumped into the air, shrieks erupted high and pitched in agonized dying wails as Hukrum the madman sought to slay his nephew.

"Fight me, *fight me, pup!* I'll cut your—!"

"Madman!"

Esa shrieked.

Oron could not chance a look. Furious, he moved ahead and struck once, twice, three times against his uncle: numbing blows that sent sparks of pain up Hukrum's arm. He howled in anguish. He drew back, deterred.

And Oron looked behind him.

They had Esa.

"Dogs!"

Hukrum screamed.

Two of them. Mosutha's soldiers. Not cutting her, but with naked weapons, holding Esa between them.

Oron lunged at them.

Two more ran at him.

He turned to them as Esa, screaming, was pulled

71

back to the center of camp.

"Oron . . . *Oron-nnnn—!*"

"*Gods, no!*"

The two were at him. He met the first, shoved his blade aside, screamed to the stars and lopped off the dog's head. The blood nearly blinded him. He swerved to one side, swung his steel around him like a scythe. The second soldier, moving too quickly to pause, fell directly into the stroke. A wide rip tore across his belly and his entrails splashed out like a red gray swamp, tripping him and bringing him down.

"*Esa-ahh. . . !*"

But they were dragging her off. He saw two large men in armor, Esa's flying hair, and Hukrum, battling two more. While others ran at him from the center of the camp.

The camp was no longer under siege. The barbarians, whoever they were, had made their maneuver and freed many. Now they, along with those freed who still lived, were retreating into the dark safety of the forest.

Oron saw them moving away. But he could not join them. He turned to face three more of Mosutha's men while, beyond them, Esa was carried off.

Gods of death, was there no end to it?

Would he kill forever without getting Esa?

The three came at him, and for the first time Oron felt the pain in his chest, the leadeness of his arms, the ache of his legs. He was exhausted. Frenzied, maddened, but exhausted. He would move falsely, he would strike too slowly, and they would have him again, or they would spill his brains.

Barbarians. Two of them. Crossing the camp diagonally behind Mosutha's men.

Oron met the soldiers' charge. He dealt swift strokes, cut one along the arm before the two raiders, from behind, fell upon the dogs.

They howled as forest swords smashed them through their backs. Oron stabbed the one he'd wounded, cutting him clear through the chest, and within a moment the three armored corpses lay in a heap.

"Into the forest!"

"No," Oron yelled at them. He was panting hungrily.

"Into the forest, boy! There's no time to—!"

"My woman!" he growled, and threw a glance in the direction where Esa had been dragged off.

"We'll raid again! Into the forest!"

"No!" Oron shouted, and turned, lifted his sword, looked into the camp—

He grunted as his blade was knocked heavily to his side, as two strong pairs of arms grabbed his. He grunted and fought to free himself, but he was tired, and they swiftly pulled him with them in to the dark trees.

"Damn you, free me! I must save Esa!"

He was their size but they had him in bulk, and their twin hot tempers adequately matched his own frustrated fury.

"Damn you, I've got to—!"

"We'll come back for her! Now be a man!"

They were soon under the cover of the forest. Behind them, in the camp, loud voices howled and pandemonium carried in their direction.

The hard hands relaxed slightly, and Oron shirked the two men from him. But he didn't try to run back,

"You going to calm down, now?" one asked him gruffly.

"It won't do you any good to run back there and get killed, boy," the other said to him. "If your woman is still alive, we'll get her in the morning."

Their roughness had quieted Oron. The madness had passed, and he understood the truth of their words. But he had had Esa! Had hold of her! Was running to freedom with her—when his demon of an uncle had interfered. . . .

Deep in his heart, Oron swore that his father would not be the last of his blood to die. He damned his uncle, and vowed to kill Hukrum, to torture him with slow strokes and slow bloodletting, as surely as he would kill Mosutha the sorcerer.

"Quietly, now, lad. Our camp is not far."

He went with them, continued with them. Not begrudgingly, but downcast. He thought that he still felt the warmth of Esa's hand in his, knew that he still heard her voice, clear and painful and real.

He trudged through the forest, utterly desolate. As the shock and tension of the battle eased within him, his massive fatigue bore down on him and his senses began to blur.

One of the two with him slapped his shoulder. "You can rest soon. But keep your step up now, lad, or you'll give us away."

Oron grunted and moved more quietly.

"What's your name?" they asked him.

"Oron. The Wolf."

"I am Akrim, my companion is Host."

"What tribe are you from?"

"We were men of Ghen the Knife. But he was slain by those sons of Hell. Now our leader is Adrum, a warrior."

"You are renegades."

"Yes. From four villages. Five, with you."

"I am the last of my village, except for the prisoners. My chief was Ilgar the Moon-Hunter."

"A brave warrior. I am sad to hear of his death."

Oron nodded solemnly. "He was a good chief. He

was a fair man, and a good chief. . . ."

Their camp, a hastily concocted place of stones and logs and no fire pits, was situated on a small rise deep within the belly of the forest. It was backed by a verdant outcropping, and there was a stream nearby.

As Oron and his companions came close, Akrim, behind him, whistled a birdcall. That allowed them to enter freely into the company of mixed swords that now, silently and busily, tended to their wounded and counted their survivors.

Someone said to Akrim, "Adrum is wounded. He is ill."

"Was he badly hurt?"

The speaker shook his head. "They caught him in his side. Deep. He bleeds."

Akrim walked ahead while Host, obviously a warrior of few words, moved away and joined a group of men seated beneath a tree, munching on fruit and strips of venison. Oron stood for a moment and looked around, taking stock of his new companions. For they were his companions now. His future resided with them, and it was as though he had joined, by chance, a new tribe.

He was very tired, and he was hungry. Someone handed him an apple as he walked around the knots of busy men, and he accepted it, thanking the shadow, and moved on until he found a resting place. It was a vacant log, and Oron sat down on it and munched at his apple.

From close by, just behind a dark copse of trees, he heard Akrim's voice in conversation with others.

"Does he speak?"

"He is sleeping, Akrim. Let him rest. We have applied cold water, and Uira is making a poultice."

Akrim cursed. "Some of these will disband if

Adrum is too ill to hold them."

"They will not disband. We all know why we are here."

Akrim grunted something.

Oron chewed on his apple. His jaw felt so sore and tired that he barely had the energy to swallow. He tried taking another bite, but he was far too fatigued. He lay back on the log, but his position was uncomfortable. He slid to the ground, tilted his head back against the log and closed his eyes.

"Adrum, can you hear me? Speak, warrior!"

"He will live, Akrim. Let him rest."

Noise—someone else approaching.

"What do you say, shaman?"

"Do not call me a shaman. I am more than a shaman."

"Then save him, more-than-a-shaman. If he is ill, save him!"

"Is your temper endless, Akrim? Would you have me—"

"Stop. Uira comes."

Oron vaguely heard the words, vaguely heard the conversation. His mind went blank, and emptily he began to doze.

"The poultice is ready. It is all I could do. Father—can you hear me?"

Oron, falling asleep, was somewhere in him mildly surprised to hear a young woman's voice, before he lost consciousness altogether and slumbered.

5

When he awoke, it was to the feel of soft hands on his forehead and to the bitterly bright light of the first of dawn.

He grunted and rolled onto his side, awkwardly moving for the sword at his belt.

"Calm yourself, calm yourself! You are well and safe!"

He looked up into a pair of pretty dark eyes, stared into the face of an attractive black-haired young woman.

"I am Uira," she told him, "daughter of Adrum."

"And I am Oron, the Wolf." Sitting up, he shook his head, and stretched his arms.

"So Akrim told me. You have no fever. You were not wounded."

He watched her, somewhat unsure how he should react, and Uira regarded him just as frankly. From behind him, Oron heard one of the voices he'd overheard the night before, just before falling asleep.

"He's still feverish. Bring more water." It was a gruff, commanding voice—a strong but strangely odd voice, cadenced deliberately.

"Du-ubas," Uira told Oron, with no trace of friendliness.

"Who is Du-ubas?"

"A powerful shaman. He lives in the forest. My father forced him to come with us and help us. He refuses to help, but he stays with us. He will not fight the slavers."

Oron remembered Akrim's concern of last night. "Your father is ill?"

A pained look of sorrow clouded Uira's face as she answered, "He was badly hurt during the raid. I do not think . . . he will live. . . ."

Even as she said it, Akrim came through the knot of trees and, saying nothing, looked grimly down at her. Startled, Uira quickly got to her feet.

"Go to him," were Akrim's words.

"What—?" And Uira hurried away.

Oron got to his feet, a question in his eyes.

Akrim shook his head. "He is dead. Now many of these dogs will desert."

Oron scratched his belly, hunched his shoulders. "Will they not try to free the rest of their people?"

"Against the robed men? Against—?"

Uira's sudden cry of anguish stopped his words; both men glanced in the direction of the trees and listened to her loud sobbing.

Akrim told Oron, "Go find something to eat," and he turned away to go to Adrum's daughter.

Oron looked around. In the misty light of dawn, the camp looked far more desolate and deserted than it had last night. He saw that there were, indeed, few tribesmen left to continue the fight. They stood in knots of two or three, gesturing and talking among themselves. Some still lay, half-asleep, against logs or stones, while others were eating fruit or strips of meat. Oron started walking toward one group of men; they seemed to have a full satchel of food they were sharing, and his belly was growling.

But before he could reach them Oron paused to

watch a troop of seven men pass through the camp and approach Akrim. The big warrior moved from the protective shade of the outcropping where the dead Adrum lay. He stood solidly, waiting for the seven to say what they would say.

"We believe it is foolish to continue this war," their leader spoke. "At least until we find more men."

Akrim sneered at him. "Will you wait for more villages to die so that we can recruit the survivors?"

"We are few in number, Akrim. Adrum is dead. Will you lead us, and die next?"

"You are afraid of the warriors, and the men in the robes."

"We are afraid of nothing! But we are not *fools!*" The spokesman spat the word contemptuously.

Akrim took it as a personal affront, construing it as slander against Adrum, a great warrior only freshly died. As Oron watched, Akrim drew his sword and dared the speaker to come forward. "I'll kill you now!" he vowed in a yell. "Or you may face the men of Mosutha! But you spit on Adrum's body and you will die by the blade!"

"Fool!" was the retort. But he did not reach for his own weapon. "I have no wish to fight you, Akrim. Too few of us remain. But you are not my leader! We—!"

A howl, from deep in the forest.

Oron jerked at the sound. Akrim, grunting, looked into the trees.

"They come!" screamed a voice. "They have found us! They—!" His cry ceased abruptly as it lifted on a high, dying wail.

"Gods of death!" Akrim shouted. To the leader of the renegades: "Now you *will* fight, cowards!"

Immediately Oron drew his sword. But, unfamiliar as he was with the camp and its defenses, he held still in his anxiousness and threw a quick look to Akrim.

"We have no defenses!" the warrior yelled to him. "We have few men!"

Came a distant cry, "They have surrounded us!"

The camp became a swarming confusion of furious motion, with awakening sleepers trampled by warriors already hurrying to fight with whole groups of swords rushing to the surrounding forest. Quick screams rose from all directions, and the clatter of steel.

"Dogs! *Dogs!*" Akrim yelled.

A shrieking man reeled into the camp, smashing through the underbrush; a river of blood poured down his chest, darkening his belly and legs. Groaning, he fell, and from the thick behind him three of Mosutha's soldiers burst into the clearing.

"This way! We've found them!"

Immediately Adrum's men were upon them, crashing their weapons upon them. But the cry had roused others hidden in the forest.

Akrim jumped. Moving to Uira, he gripped her by an arm and pulled her to her feet.

"Move, woman! They have us!"

"I must stay with my father!"

"Into the trees!"

In her panic and anguish she began to kick and scratch at Akrim. He shook her severely in an attempt to bring her to her senses. Yells lifted from the center of the camp. Akrim looked. Three men had gone down before a small army of Mosutha's butchers. Some of the barbarians attacked them, others sought to escape. One man running for cover behind a stout tree was surprised by a sudden sword; he went down with a slashed throat.

Akrim roared to Oron, "Take her!" He threw Uira toward him.

Uira stumbled and cried out terribly. Oron didn't know what to do. He ran to the young woman, held onto her as Akrim hastened to join the fighting.

"Come on! Into the woods!"

"My father—!"

"Dammit, come with me!"

Screams—shrieks—the clacking of steel—*Gods of death! would it go on forever? Was all the world at war?*

—and Oron turned, went cold to see Akrim, in the middle of a clot of four soldiers, swinging his blade in all directions as flying blood and shimmering steel obscured him.

He swore at Uira. He must fight! Why had Akrim—?

"Erith and Corech!" he blasphemed. "Come with me!"

"My f——!"

With the hilt of his sword he lightly cracked her on the head. Uira moaned and went slack; Oron heaved her up, threw her over a shoulder and ran with her into the forest.

Off to his right he heard soldiers smashing through the trees. He looked ahead of him, saw no one, so kept running. He hurried until the sounds of the battle in the camp were dim in the distance.

He could leave the girl here in safety, then. He was gasping for breath; she weighed more than he realized. As he plodded along, slowed by her dull weight he hoped that he hadn't killed her. He came to a small stream. Pausing, Oron thrust his sword into its scabbard and, crouching, rinsed his free hand in the cold water. He wiped the water onto Uira's face, then stood up, looking for some place to leave her so that he could get back to the camp.

"Wake up, damn you, wake up. . . ."

Now he heard no noise behind him at all. Could he have run that far? It ate at him that he had run away without trading a single stroke with one of the dogs.

Uira moaned, and began to kick her legs and move her head.

Oron loped to a tall oak tree. Squatting carefully, he slipped the young woman from his shoulder and rested her against the bole. He slapped her face lightly a few times, and felt the lump on the top of her head.

"Are you awake?"

"What—? I—?" She opened her eyes and stared into his.

"Shhh!" He held up a hand. "Stay quiet! They're all around us!"

She seemed frightened of him. She began to tremble visably. Oron was upset with her; he wondered if Uira were entirely useless. But he noticed that she had a knife slung on a belt around her waist. A good knife, too, by the looks of it.

Noises, behind them.

But no further sound of battle. . . .

Oron glanced up at the tall tree. "Can you climb, Uira?"

"I'm—dizzy."

"Come." He stood up, lent her a hand to help her to her feet.

"What are you—?"

"You'll be safer up there. And from the tree we can scout the forest."

Still dazed, she nodded to him, agreeing.

"I'll help you up. Come on. . . ."

Uira turned around and looked up. There was a branch above her, just out of her reach. She felt Oron's strong hands cup her waist.

"Jump."

She crouched and pushed herself up. With his help Uira was lifted to the branch; she hung on, swung back and forth a few times, then slackened weakly.

"I — I'm dizzy."

"Climb, woman!" Oron pushed her with his hands; his fingers sank into the soft flesh of her buttocks, urging her up.

Uira grumbled at him, but she started swinging back and forth again until she managed to pull herself up by wrapping her legs around the limb. Carefully she eased her way toward the bole of the oak, then started climbing onto the next limb higher up.

Oron jumped, caught hold of the first limb and agilely moved upward. Uira moved slowly and carefully, but in a short while they had positioned themselves high in the tree. The young woman nestled herself in the crotch of two wide branches and leaned against the bole for safety.

"You can relax," Oron told her. "You won't fall. But don't look down. Close your eyes."

Then he climbed up even higher, as high as the branches would support him, and surveyed the forest.

Through the denseness of the foliage and the crowded trees of the forest, Oron was able to perceive the campsite. What he saw did not inspire him: piles of corpses and no living thing, no sign of movement of any kind. The battle was over. Looking in other directions, he discerned stirrings in the forest farther north, and he supposed those must be signs of Mosutha's soldiers returning to their camp. He saw no suspicious sign of movement near his tree.

He descended to Uira. "We must wait a little while," Oron told her. "Then we can get down, go back. Steal after the wagons."

She told him broodingly, "And we must bury my father."

"Yes. We will — bury your father. . . ." It occurred to him that he had buried none of the dead of his own village; he had been that wrathful and eager to chase after Mosutha — thinking, naively, that the sorcerer must be hidden somewhere nearby. How angry their shades must be with him!

Oron, his temper calming, studied Uira frankly, looking at her face, regarding her body. Another new companion for — what? A day? A night? But she was a very appealing young woman. He wondered that she didn't have a man.

"Will you go with me, after the wagons?" he asked her.

Her voice, to his surprise, betrayed a strength, a courage, which Oron had not sensed in her before. "Yes. I will go with you, and help you kill them. I'll help you kill all of them."

He felt a glimmer of pride toward her.

"Uira, are you hungry?"

She shrugged.

"I'll climb down and find us some food. You stay here."

"Let me —"

But that quickly he was on his way down the tree, moving lithely and silently. Uira leaned forward, careful not to lose her balance, but she saw no sign of Oron. Hidden by the branches and heavy foliage, he might have been invisible, and he had left no sign of his presence.

She sighed, rubbed her sore head and reminded herself that she should be cross with the man for dealing with her so brutally. And yet — what else could he have done? The moment of the battle. . . . The thought of her father, dead, lying ignobly in the ruins of the campground, was a hot arrow in her heart, but Uira fought to hold back an explosion of tears. There would be time enough to mourn. Life was for the living. Her father had taught her that. Adrum had impressed upon her, as he might have impressed a son, that life is a struggle and that it goes as often to the crafty and the swift as it does to the strong and the violent. Had he not been dead, Adrum would have been first to push Uira toward the safety of the forest during the attack.

Oron returned. He had removed his vest and filled it with fruit, and was carrying it in his teeth as he climbed the tree. Uira looked down at him and almost laughed at the sight of him—his wide eyes staring up at her, the satchel in his mouth, as though he were a pet dog returning to the hut with spoils.

"Here. . . ."

She took the vest from him as Oron pulled himself up and sat beside her, balanced carefully but securely on the wide limb.

"Apples," he told her, opening the vest. He threw her one and Uira bit into it hungrily, sucking at the juice that ran down her hand.

As they ate, they did not speak. But occasionally they glanced at one another. Oron wondered again why Uira did not have a man. Certainly she was pretty enough. She had shiny black eyes and dark hair and a full mouth. Her body was well proportioned but muscular. He imagined that young men of her tribe must certainly have looked upon her with smiling eyes, and followed the stretch of her legs and the fullness of her breasts whenever she passed by them. Perhaps her man had been killed.

Uira was conjecturing similar things about Oron. Her eyes did not miss the muscular expanse of his shoulders or the deepness of his chest, the obviously strong and well-shaped muscles of his legs. He had almost a full beard, too. Surely he had a woman. Had she been killed during a raid? Was she one of the captured?

Oron caught Uira looking at him, and she did not

avert her eyes. He felt moved to speak. But as he leaned forward to tell her that—"

A noise.

Below them.

Oron leaned over and grabbed a branch to steady himself. He motioned Uira to silence.

Someone was walking on the forest floor below them. Oron watched carefully, following the sounds with his ears before the figure came fully into view. His body tensed and his belly tightened with the expectation of a kill, for surely it was one of Mosutha's troops ranging this far south, looking for renegades.

Yet it was not a soldier. Keeping silent, Oron saw a tall, slim man dressed in an animal-skin robe move slowly and cautiously through the brush.

Uira, bending over his shoulder, whispered to Oron, "Du-ubas."

"The shaman?"

"Yes."

They watched as Du-ubas passed directly beneath them, unaware that he was being spied upon. As he passed out of their vision, "We should follow him," Uira whispered to Oron.

"Why?"

"Oron, my father forced Du-ubas to join him because he thought the shaman knew something about Mosutha. Du-ubas is more than a shaman; my father said that he worked magic."

"Where is he going now?"

"To his hut, I think. I do not know where his hut is, but I know it is south of here. If we follow him, we can force him to help us."

Oron was torn. Chasing the shaman meant little to him; he had it in mind to stay after the slaver caravan.

"Should we not follow him, Oron?"

He didn't answer.

"He may be able to help us."

Quietly, Oron told her, "My woman is in the cages
f Mosutha. I must free her."

Uira fell silent for a moment. "Your wife?" she
sked.

Oron shook his head. "I wished to marry her. Her
ame is Esa. I was not yet a warrior when—when the
oldiers raided my village."

Again Uira was silent for a heartbeat, and then she
aid to him, "It might be good for us to follow Du-
bas. He can't live far from here. We know that the
lavers are always going to be north of us. And it will
ake them many days to reach Mosutha's fortress."

"You know this?"

"That is what my father said."

"Mosutha lives in a fortress?"

"My father said he lives in a mountain, in a house
hat is as big as a village, carved out of the mountain."

That impressed Oron. Mosutha must certainly be a
owerful sorcerer to live in a hut like that.

"Oron, can we follow Du-ubas?"

Deciding, he grunted, "If he won't help us, we can
lways kill him."

They followed Du-ubas through the afternoon,
Oron never losing sound of him—for even when Du-
bas was lost to his sight, the Wolf's quick ears picked
p the dim rustling of a bush, or the passing of a
eather boot over an exposed root.

Neither he nor Uira said anything as they trailed
he shaman, and Oron made certain that the girl
tayed well behind him, moving quietly but slowly.

As they came to a clearing in the forest, Oron
aused. Uira approached him.

"What is it?" But Oron held up an arm, indicating
ilence.

Before him spread the small field, ringed by thick forest. A small brook gurgled to his left. It wound in front of him and coursed on, softly tinkling, across the field and into the forest to his right.

Oron motioned again to Uira; she leaned close. "He has stopped," he whispered in her ear.

Uira's wide eyes scanned the landscape before them, but she saw no clue as to where Du-ubas was or where he might have gone.

"Stay here," Oron whispered. Despite a low moan of protest from Uira, he moved ahead.

He stepped carefully across the brook, never making a sound as he moved from stone to stone. Coming out of the woods, Oron paused and lifted his nose, studying the clearing for any evidence of the shaman's passage.

It was possible that he had—

"Barbarian."

Oron growled, threw himself to one side, pivoted and brought out his sword. Snarling, eyes fierce, he glared into the face of the shaman, who stood a length away from him in the shadows of the trees.

"Why do you follow me?" Du-ubas asked him. His voice was cold and measured.

Oron stood there, watching the man, a wolf eyeing a poisonous serpent. Uira ran up to him and stayed by him, holding back from the shaman.

"Uira," Du-ubas spoke to her. "Your friend is mute. Tell me why you follow me."

Oron grunted, "I can speak." He trembled with rage, humiliated that the shaman had been able to take him by surprise.

Gripping Oron's shoulders, Uira said slowly, carefully to Du-ubas, "We wish to know of Mosutha."

"What is there to know?"

"Tell us where he lives. Tell us how to get there."

Give us some of your secrets, Du-ubas. My father begged you for your help."

"I am no priest," the shaman answered, irritated. "I do not learn mysteries to share them with everyone and enlighten the earth. What you ask for is very deep. What will you barter me in return?"

"Oron growled to him, "A sword in your belly, if you do not help us."

Du-ubas smiled cruelly at him. "Fool. I knew you followed me, every step of the way. Do you think you can take me unawares?"

"Everything that breathes can be—"

"Oron," Uira gently cautioned him, "please. . . . We need his help."

"*I* do not."

Uira faced Du-ubas frankly. "Shaman, let us sit and talk. We can come to barter. I will trade you what you want, if it is in my power. But you must aid us in killing Mosutha. He will destroy the Valley if we do not."

Du-ubas looked upon the young woman, and there was obvious appreciation in his gaze. Oron did not miss the look. Shaman or no, he was a man, lascivious, but strange, and as trustworthy as a lying demon.

"We—" Du-ubas began, looking from Uira to Oron, and back again "—we can barter, yes. But you must promise me not to hold back on your word."

"What is it you want?" Uira asked him. "My body? You wish to rape me? Save the Valley, give us a weapon that will slay Mosutha. Then you may take me."

Oron stared at her, shocked.

"Can we barter, Du-ubas?"

He smiled grimly. "Yes, we can barter. Come with me to my hut."

He turned and led the way, starting across the field.

Oron was severely disappointed. "Why do you make such a bargain?" he demanded of Uira.

"My family is dead, Oron. My father is dead. I have no man. If I can trade myself for the safety of the Valley, so that you can kill Mosutha, what is the harm?"

He pondered that. "But no woman would—"

"Besides," she reminded him, "you will be there. Two hunters can more easily trap an animal than one."

"Trap him, yes," Oron replied. "And kill him."

She warned him, "He is powerful. He knows things more than a shaman should know. He is a magician. That is why he lives alone, away from the tribes of the Valley."

Du-ubas, ahead of them, looked back, that cruel smile on his lips. He waved them ahead as he entered the forest.

"To trust him, even for a moment. . . ." Oron complained.

"But we must trust what he knows, Oron. We must steal what he knows . . . somehow."

Oron was in reluctant agreement. "If what he knows will help us kill Mosutha, then we do that. But then we kill him."

Uira smiled at him. "Why do you always wish to kill?" she asked him.

"To stay alive," Oron told her. "To stay alive. . . ."

6

Du-ubas's hut was situated against a wooded hill just within the forest. He had cleared a small space in the front of it as a yard, and had penned there some goats and chickens. Despite the presence of the animals, the atmosphere of the place was pervasively silent and chill. Though sunlight fell upon the hut and the yard was pleasantly shaded by fir and maple trees, to Oron Du-ubas's hut had no feel of life to it, no sense of belonging to the land, as had the huts of his tribe.

Apparently the shaman did not keep his door barred, for he approached his hut and opened the door casually. Oron suspected that the hut, like the shaman, had a reputation: Who would dare to venture here and interfere with his things while he was away? Uira passed through, after Du-ubas, but the shaman, standing at the threshold, held up a hand to Oron, barring his entrance.

"Stay outside."

Oron's fingers plucked at his sword. "Do not harm her," he growled threateningly.

"I will tell the girl what she wishes to know. You will wait outside."

Oron looked to Uira for her answer; she blinked her eyes slowly to him and said to him in a whisper, "It's all right. If I need you, I'll call."

Du-ubas seemed pleased.

"I'll be here," Oron reminded her—and the shaman.

Du-ubas closed the door in Oron's face, and he stood there for a long while, waiting, listening. He could not hear their voices. Worried, he looked around the yard. He walked to the short fence that penned the goats and chickens and talked to the goats. When one came near, Oron scratched its head.

It was late in the afternoon; dusk was beginning to darken the forest, and the sunlight that dappled the yard was orange and red. Oron returned to the door of Du-ubas's hut, to listen. Still, he heard nothing that sounded suspicious, and so he prowled around to the other side.

He was tired. He had gone long on little sleep and not much food. Sitting down on the ground, he leaned against the wall of the hut. He meant to press his ear to the logs, to listen for any sound from the hut's interior, but as he sat there, eyes on the softly blowing sunlight and the leaves of the trees and bushes —already beginning to turn colors—a heaviness descended upon him. To relax, Oron sprawled his legs out before him and stretched his arms. He tilted his head back and closed his eyes.

No sounds from the hut.

His eyes were heavy, and a looseness weighted down his body. He was exhausted, utterly exhausted. As he heard the tinkling sounds of the rustling leaves and branches, his body seemed to react to the darkening quiescence of the forest. He tried to open his eyes but decided not to; it would do him good to—

Did he hear something from the hut?

No . . . all was silence. . . .

As he rested, pictures and voices began to hurry through Oron's imagination. All that he had been through: His fight with his father, Ilgar, the village, Esa trapped, himself caged, killing, killing—always killing for freedom, for anger—his father, his heavy blade, spewing blood, Esa, Esa, Uira, Esa. . . .

"Oron. . . ."

Esa. . . .

"Oron."

He grunted. That voice.

"Oron. . . ."

He opened his eyes—and his heart jumped.

"Oh, Oron, I have found you. . . ."

Esa!

Du-ubas's hand was a taloned claw; it scraped painfully at Uira's scalp as he brushed his fingers through her long, dark hair. She shuddered at his touch, and her belly squirmed coldly as she stared into his dark, malevolent eyes.

"You are very beautiful." Du-ubas moved his hand down to her breasts as he continued to stare into her eyes. As if he were testing the quality of meat or fruit, his hand pushed and kneaded Uira's breasts, then scraped down her side. "Remove your clothes," Du-ubas ordered her.

Uira answered anxiously, "There is time enough for that. Tell me where to find Mosutha. Tell me how to destroy him."

"If I tell you now, I cannot trust you." He grinned foully at her.

Uira thought. Stepping back from the shaman, she lifted her hands and began undoing the laces of her vest. "Mosutha lives in a fortress?" She paused.

Du-ubas, smiling hugely, understood what she was doing. "Yes, yes," he told her. "He lives in a fortress, north of the Valley."

"How far distant?" She undid more of the laces.

"Three days from here. Follow the river. It lies across the widest part of the river." His tongue slid through his lips as he watched Uira slowly undress.

She undid more of her vest. "Why does he want the captives, Du-ubas? Why did he order the raids on the villages?"

"I do not know."

Uira let her hands fall to her waist. "You lie. You are lying to me."

A cloud passed through the shaman's eyes. "I am no sorcerer; I am a forest magician," he told her. "What do I know of Mosutha's raids?"

"You are no fool. You know something."

"Perhaps. . . . Take off your vest, woman."

Uira clenched her teeth; her hands shivered as she raised them and pulled loose more of the ties.

"Esa!"

"Oh, Oron! I got away! They stopped the wagons and I broke free!"

He was astounded; still, he sat where he was. A chill possessed him, and when he tried to rouse himself a numbness gripped him.

"Esa, is it—?"

"Oh, Oron, I have traveled for so long, all night long—!"

He knew it was not Esa. Esa did not speak that way; she did not move that way. This creature's eyes were too dark, too hate-filled to be Esa's. And yet. . . .

She came toward him, dressed in her skirt and vest—just as Oron had remembered her, or imagined her. She moved just as Oron imagined Esa would move. Sobbing, this Esa of the forest approached him lithely and bent down beside him.

Oron shuddered. Moving his hand toward his sword, he found that his muscles responded to his will very slowly. The chill or numbness that possessed him had shrunk his reflexes to an incredibly useless degree.

"Oron, aren't you happy to see me?"

"You are not . . . are not Esa."

"Oh, Oron, aren't you happy to see me?"

She crouched at his side and stared into his eyes. What was she? Some hauntsome she-demon of Du-ubas's invention? Slowly, coldly, Oron's fingers reached for his steel.

"Oh, Oron, aren't you happy to see me?"

"You . . . are not . . ."

She moved her hands upon his chest; they were icy tongues. Her breath was rank, as though she had feasted upon days-old forest carrion. And her eyes. Her eyes. . . .

". . . are not—"

Her eyes glimmered with a scarlet fire, burned like misty blood.

Erith and Corech! What was this thing? Sent by Du-ubas to—?

"Oh, Oron, I am here! I need you!"

Slowly. Slowly . . . like ice. . . .

"You . . . are not—"

She smiled at him, baring sharp teeth, and leaned to kiss him.

"He is a barbarian," Du-ubas told Uira. "Mosutha was driven from the Valley many years ago. All thought he had died. Perhaps he is slaughtering the villages for vengeance' sake."

Her fingers trembled nervously as she undid the last of the lacing. "He is a . . . a barbarian?"

"Remove your vest, woman. Your flesh glows, you are beautiful."

Keeping her eyes on him, Uira took another step back and pulled open her vest. Her heavy breasts, large and pointed, dropped free, the nipples shining like dark berries. Du-ubas stared lasciviously. Uira let her vest fall to the floor.

"You have magic that can harm him, shaman."

"Perhaps."

"Tell me now," she warned him, moving her hands to the belt of her breeches.

"It takes a powerful magic to battle a sorcerer," Du-ubas told her. "Perhaps a certain amulet I possess. . . ."

"Let me see it.'

The shaman smiled and moved toward her.

She had promised herself to Du-ubas, but now Uira regretted her rash words. At this moment, seeing his eyes, reading his thoughts, she decided on impulse not to turn herself to the dog if she could prevent it.

Du-ubas reached again for her breasts, cupped them, squeezed them. He flicked her nipples with his nails, making Uira wince. For years he had harbored hatred against the people of the Valley, and here was a naked woman of the Valley, his willing victim. . . .

"Get me the amulet, shaman."

He showed his teeth. "Do you think," he hissed to her, "that you will ever leave this hut?"

Uira's hands were at her belt. Her knife, sheathed, rested on one hip. If she moved quickly enough, while his hands played with her breasts. . . .

His fingers touched his sword, and instantly a warm thrill shot through him. In that moment, Oron felt as though he were awakening from a slumbering half-death.

The rank breath was on his throat. The eyes burned into his, and he saw in them dances of old shadows, red misty phantoms of delirium, promises of forest rot. . . .

"What . . . are you?"

"Kiss me, my Oron. . . ."

He moved, jerking his head away.

The phantom Esa hissed, and like a striking serpent her head jumped forward, her mouth open.

Oron rolled. He pushed himself aside and kicked out with his legs. Lurching, he pulled free his sword. He heard it scrape on the ground.

Iciness gripped him. The shadow of Death come to life and fallen upon him, sinking into his pores, swarming through the caverns of his brain.

"Kiss me, my—"

It was clinging to him, holding him down.

"You—!"

Holding him down. . . .

"You—!"

The eyes.

As it hissed. . . .

"Get . . . me . . . the amulet."

His hands moved from her breasts to her hair.

"Perhaps," Du-ubas cooed. "Perhaps. . . ."

"Get it now."

"Woman, you seem to—"

Pounding against the outer wall of the hut.

Du-ubas, startled, turned.

In a fluid motion Uira brought up her knife, aiming for the shaman's belly.

It was only a woman, a phantom, unreal. But the weight of it, and the pain of its cold, the fever of its shadowed eyes. . . .

It moved again, aiming for his throat.

Oron lashed his head to one side, screamed out loud, and with all his power yanked on his sword, though his arm was pinned awkwardly beneath the thing.

It hissed. Gurgled. Fluidly moved away.

Oron threw himself forward and swung again with his sword, this time in a wide stroke.

The blade passed through the phantom-woman as if she had been smoke, and she shrieked hellishly at the touch of his steel.

Gasping, Du-ubas stumbled back, throwing his hands to his stomach.

"Woman, what—?"

"Tell me where the amulet is!" Uira screamed at him. "Tell me! I'll stab you! I'll stab you again!"

Du-ubas gained his balance, studied his fingers, and carefully poked at the slice in his robe and flesh. He was bleeding, but the wound was not very deep. Snarling, he glared at Uira. "I tell you nothing!"

"Damn you, shaman, I'll—!"

"Stupid woman!" Du-ubas jumped as Uira moved forward, threatening him with her knife. Quickly he shoved his hands in the front pocket of his robe and pulled out a shining stone.

Cackling, Du-ubas held up his hands. Pressed together, they guarded the glowing stone. "With this I can—"

The door crashed open. Du-ubas looked up, eyes burning with wrath. Uira, surprised, stared in shock.

In a moment, Oron took it all in. Uira, half-naked, holding out a bloody knife. Du-ubas, hands clasped in a threatening posture. Only for a moment, he stood at the threshold, his weight and bulk filling the frame.

Then he moved.

"Stand back, barbarian!"

He was a human storm. In three steps he crossed the floor, sword up. Du-ubas growled. Oron leaped, Du-ubas raised his hands. . . .

The steel was a blur. Du-ubas's lifting scream broke

awkwardly on the sound of splitting bone and spurting blood. Oron's sword caught the left half of his head, cleaved down through the shaman's shoulder and chest, and ripped out the side. Du-ubas's shattered head and chest and one arm ripped free and flew back loosely on stretched muscles and tendons. The body, tilted awkwardly, danced nervously and fell sideways, crumpled to the floor. The stone fell from the twitching fingers, glowing no more.

Only a stone.

Only a man.

Within a heartbeat the only sounds that disturbed the stillness of the hut were Oron's panting gasps and the gurgling patter of Du-ubas's blood as it poured from his butchered corpse and became a runnel on the floor.

Uira made a noise.

Oron's head snapped in her direction, and she caught the murderous stare that veiled his eyes. Then the shadow passed, and Oron pulled himself erect, the wolf in him restrained once more.

"He had some damned—vampire out there," he grunted to the girl. "What happened to you?"

In answer, a ridiculous laughter broke from the young woman's lips, and her arms fell weakly to her sides. "We were bartering," she told Oron. "Gods! but we were bartering, and I was a fool!"

He didn't contradict her. He walked to the halved corpse of the shaman and studied the blasted head. It was possible that some evil life still lurked there. But Oron sensed or saw no indication that Du-ubas's magic in any way prevailed over his death, so once more he regarded Uira, smiled at her and said, "You could put your vest back on."

She smiled and bent her head, wiped her knife blade on her breeches and sheathed it.

Oron began poking around the shaman's hut. Nervous, calming down from the tension that had pulled him taut as a bowstring, he needed something with which to occupy himself. "Does he have any food around here that isn't cursed or poisoned?"

"I don't know. We'll have to look." She drew on her vest but didn't bother to lace it.

Oron glanced at her. The shimmering of perspiration in the deep valley between her breasts brought a tingle to his groin, so he turned back to his search for food. On a shelf by the fireplace he found a loaf of bread, half a brick of cheese, and a gourd of wine. He wiped his sword clean with a curtain that hung against a wall, then took down the food and wine and deposited them on the wooden table that sat in the middle of the floor.

"Hungry?" he asked Uira

"I—I don't know. . . ."

Oron sat down in an unsteady chair and tore free a piece of bread, ate it, and washed it down with wine. "It's edible," he reported. "Have some. You must be as starved as I am."

But Uira had begun wandering around the hut, examining some of the things that rested on shelves and small tables. In a corner of the hut she found a few amulets and talismans, some parchments, colored stones, and other odd artifacts.

"Look, Oron."

"What?"

She held up a small amulet; it was bronze, and designed in the shape of the seven-pointed Star. "He must have been dealing with Mosutha."

"I suppose so."

"Do you—? Oron, do you think it's possible that Du-ubas was hired by Mosutha? To tell him about the villages?"

Oron shrugged. "It's possible."

"He lived here in the Valley."

"Well, I've just killed one of them, and now I want to kill the other one."

"He told me—" Uira came over to the table and sat down. "Oron, he told me that Mosutha is a barbarian. The tribes hated him, and now he lives in the mountains. Three days from here, across the river."

Oron was unfamiliar with the Nevga when it flowed any farther north than the area of his village. It was possible that Mosutha lived in the mountains beyond it. But, "Eat," he told Uira again.

"I will, I will. . . ."

Chewing on some of the cheese, Oron rested his elbows on the table and watched the girl. There was compassion in his gaze. "You were frightened, weren't you?"

She eyed him carefully. There were nervous hints of emotion in her face, the light dance of her fingertips on the tabletop, and the still-white pallor of her cheeks. "Yes."

He set down his cheese and rested his hands on the table. "We'll go back now," he told her. "Go back to their camp."

Uira glanced out the open door; the purple and scarlet sunlight of dusk had darkened what she could see of the yard, and had drawn heavy lines on the door. "Tonight?" she asked him.

"We can't stay here."

"I don't think any harm will come to us."

"There are things," Oron replied quietly, "all around. . . ."

Uira eyed him sympathetically. "Things," she murmured. "You have killed him, Oron. The things are here no more."

"Maybe." He reached for the wine.

Uira tore a piece of bread from the loaf. "What—?" He looked at her.

"What was it, Oron? The vampire. That you fought outside."

He swallowed thickly, held the wine bottle between his thick, rough fingers. "It was . . . foul," he told her. "It read my secrets."

They built a fire in the hearth and lay on the floor of the hut, relaxing on the furs and blankets they'd found.

"It looked like Esa," Oron admitted to Uira, as they lay there.

She was stretched out beside him, examining the bronze amulet she'd found. "Your woman?" she said to him; a question, although she knew it was true.

Oron grunted. "But I was not a warrior of my tribe. I hadn't passed the test yet, before Mosutha's dogs destroyed my people."

"You are still a great warrior."

He didn't answer her. Uira, looking at him, saw the troubled expression on his face.

"What is it, Oron?"

He sighed heavily. "I am a criminal."

Her brow creased. "What crime could you have done? You have only—"

"I killed my father."

He didn't look at her as he said it, but still he felt the pressure of her reaction. He would recognize the feeling in her eyes; he heard the slight noise in her throat. Killed his father. Such a thing was unthinkable.

Finally, she asked, "Why?" in a trembling, wondering voice.

"He forced me to slay him. I hated him, but I would not have killed him, yet I did."

"Why, Oron?" She moved closer to him.

"I desired Esa. My father desired her. He was a warrior; he had the right. I did not. Esa and I were together and my father intruded. We argued, and he drew his sword. He did not have the right to draw his sword, yet he did. What else could I have done? If I drew my sword, it was a crime—I was not a warrior, and he was my father. Yet if I did not draw my sword, I could not defend Esa. What could I do? He attacked me; I had to draw my sword. I never wanted to kill him, but he made me. The anger possessed me, and I slew him."

She said nothing to him for a prolonged, silent moment. Oron, in the shadows of the hut, lay brooding, feeling as open and vulnerable as if he had torn out his heart and placed it in Uira's hands. Uira, warmed by the fire in the hearth, touched his arm with light fingers.

He faced her, scowling.

"Did you," she asked him, "kill him to save Esa from him?"

"Yes."

"Do you feel that the gods will punish you for this?"

"No," was his grim answer. "The gods do not know who I am. I have never called upon them, they do not know me."

Uira moved closer. "You are a great warrior," she said to him tenderly.. "You did what any man would have done."

He wanted to believe her, but he wasn't certain that he did.

So he lay there for a long time, pride battling with memory, wounds reopened, thinking on the matter. Uira did not speak more. After awhile, Oron tilted his head to look upon her and ask her a question.

But she was asleep. Her hand still rested on his arm,

her face lay nestled in the sprawled foam of her hair, and her peaceful face seemed content to be asleep. She was beautiful.

He did not waken her. He lay there, thinking to himself, struggling. Gradually he fell asleep, too, unaware that he did so.

When he awoke in the morning, he did not know if he had had any dreams, and he was unable to recall any phantoms or vampires that might have visited him in the night. The hut was dimly lit; dawn had not yet lifted itself to the small window by the door, and the fire in the hearth had fallen into a warm glow of red embers.

Uira's head was on his chest, her face close to his. When Oron opened his eyes he looked directly into her stare.

They studied one another deeply.

"Are you afraid?" he whispered to her.

"No, Oron. I am not afraid." Her voice was very quiet and calm.

His arms moved around her; tightened upon her. Uira pressed herself to him and unlengthened her body along his. She brought her mouth to his; watched his eyes. Oron kissed her and held her even more tightly.

Together, they were not frightened by what had happened to them, and together they felt strong. Esa was distant—and perhaps, indeed, she had been turned into a vampire by the robed henchmen of Mosutha. Adrum was dead. Their villages were dead. Their lives, up until this perplexing moment of half-wakefulness, were dead save for memories of death, slaughter and fear. They were aliens to their pasts.

And they were alive.

As they moved and made love, the warm sucking

sounds they created and the soft kisses they shared and the moans of pleasure they raised were loud complaints against the shadows and the sorcerous icons and the blood and the dirty oil lamps of the shaman's hut. Neither of them spoke. They came awake and alive as they made love, but they did not speak, though they shared eyes and read one another's thoughts and touches the way lovers do in moments of passion.

Oron had seen animals mating in the wild, and he had seen animals of the village, domesticated animals, mate openly in the paths of the huts. He had slain a wolf, and he had seen wolves mate. He had slain men, and now he was a man mating with a woman. In some deep manner, he did not understand it; in a deeper, more glorious way, he comprehended it instinctively, without thought. And all the tribal customs and all the tribal laws of marriage and mating and domesticity meant nothing to him now, in his passion. For it was a strong thing, a testament and a glory, for him and for Uira both—young animals trapped in a hut and trapped by suffering, freeing themselves the way dogs of the village and wolves of the wild freed themselves. A secret as secret for them as was any sorcery or any magic steel or any flaming death, any screaming birth.

They removed their clothes and settled beside one another, and touched one another with stroking fingertips, feeling the awesome power of one another's touching. They kissed—kissed one another's mouths, kissed one another's hair, kissed eyes and cheeks. They laughed and they breathed. Oron kissed Uira's arms, he kissed her breasts, he pushed her breasts together and kissed her nipples, and was happy when she sighed heavily with pleasure. He kissed her stomach, he felt the smoothness of her belly and ran his hands

105

around the firm muscles of her thighs and the deep softness of her buttocks. When Uira moved and rolled, Oron was enthralled by the slow tumble of her large breasts, enthralled by the patterns the light made when it slid over the curves and shallows of her body.

She touched his muscles, kissed his arms, licked his chest, kissed him with moist kisses and trailed her lips along his fingers, purred, moved her tongue in the hair of his chest.

When Oron moved his hand between her thighs and felt the wet thickness of her vulva and stroked her hair, Uira moaned and hunched her hips, and Oron felt a thrill deep inside him. He was a man and a wolf and a god, and he was giving pleasure and sharing life. With an eager hand Uira pulled on his hard penis and stroked him, cupped his scrotum and tickled him, rubbed her legs along his.

She lay back and Oron sat beside her and stared at her wondrous body. He pressed his hands along her belly, felt her thighs, buried his hands in the remarkable softness of her breasts. He gazed into her eyes and felt a magic light of life move from her eyes to his.

Uira opened her legs and Oron lay atop her, careful not to hurt her, and though they were awkward they did not know it. In their minds they were recreating the natural ballet of all living things, and they were happy in their awkwardness, happy with their desires.

Uira held his penis, long and thick, and pushed it inside her, and Oron sucked in a breath. Lights filled his brain. It seemed to him that he was somehow more than a man, and certainly more than an animal. When he began to rock between Uira's legs she moaned and pulled his face down to hers, rolled her hips, kissed him, then stopped kissing him and held him close, pulling him down to her. They fell into a steady movement, the rhythm of passion, and tremendous strength surged through Oron, a desire for everything.

The smacking sounds of their lovemaking, the weight collecting deep inside his loins, the slapping sound of Uira's breasts, the dull sunrise light of the room, the pull and feel and elemental eternity of his mind soaring— Uira gasped, Oron breathed deeply and shuddered as he came; Uira let out a little shriek and hugged him tightly, digging her fingers into his back. When he was done he lifted himself up a little and stared down at her. The warmth of what they had done filled him wholly, and the shining glow of her face told him that he had done a great thing, a good thing, that he was a man and she a woman, and that they were mates.

Mates.

It occurred to Oron that somehow Uira might be Esa; but he knew she was not, and he knew that she was his woman now. He wondered about the gods that had stolen Esa from him so that he could have Uira.

It was a very wondrous thing, Oron decided, as he stared down into Uira's happy, damp face. He was glad that he had done this, for her and for himself. Vaguely, tired though he was, a thousand pictures floated in his mind, and he realized many things he had not realized before.

He lay his head upon her wet breasts, she moved her arms around him and whispered something. He did not hear it. Very soon, Oron fell asleep.

When he woke up again, it was daylight outside and he was lying beside Uira. He opened his eyes and saw her staring at him; she was smiling.

He answered her smile.

Uira laughed, and Oron laughed.

They hugged one another, happy and victorious,

man and woman, and lay down and made love once more.

When they finally left Du-ubas's hut, much later, it was to walk to the small stream that crossed the field just beyond the fringe of woods. There, they bathed and filled skins and bladders with fresh water. When they returned to the hut they filled some satchels they found with goat meat and venison and slung them on their backs, took up their water, and left to return to the camp of the slavers—went to destroy Mosutha, and to free Esa, and to free the captive people of their tribes.

A wolf and his mate. Oron and Uira. A warrior's daughter and her warrior mate.

They entered the forest, and Oron felt more full of life than he had ever felt before. He could kill. He could live. He could love. He was a man.

He was Oron, the Wolf.

PART II

THE SORCERER

Therefore they shall do my will
To-day while I am master still,
And flesh and soul, both now are strong,
Shall hale the sullen slaves along,

Before this fire of sense decay,
This smoke of thought blow clean away,
And leave with ancient night alone
The stedfast and enduring bone.

—A.E. Housman,
"The Immortal Part"

7

Deep within his fortress, standing within the protective circle of his sorcery, Mosutha faced the smoke that rose from the center of his brazier and listened as the voice of the smoke told him, "You have an enemy, magus."

Mosutha was intrigued. Filling his palm with blood from a bowl, he flung drops upon the small fire in the center of his circle. The flames ate the blood hungrily; the coals sizzled on the iron grate and pungent, pink-colored fumes rose and collected above the fire, swirled and held in the semblance of a distorted face. A demonic face, which looked down upon the magus.

"Tell me further, spirit of Hell, lest I touch you with my iron knife. Who is this enemy?"

"He is of the Blood of the Sword. He is a hero, born of the line of the First Hero. He is a boy, and he hates you. Your soldiers have slain his village. He is a wolf in the skin of a man; he is a god wrapped in human flesh."

"Such a thing cannot be! How was he born?"

"The stars," answered the demonic visage in the smoke, "watched his spirit and birthed him in the wild. His future is not long, but he is an old hero. He is a boy, but he has killed his father. Such is a sign that he is new; not of the old ways."

Mosutha wiped his greasy face, wiped away the sweat that was collecting around his nose and upon his chin. "Tell me his name."

"He is called Oron, son of Aksakin, of the lineage of Taïsakul."

"Taïsakul!" Mosutha went cold to his bowels. "Such a thing . . . it cannot be!"

The smoke demon began to dissolve, its suspension upon the hearth controlled by the weak catalyst of the blood-mist. Quickly the barbaric sorcerer hurled more blood onto the grate. The face returned; purple and evil.

"Tell me more! *More!* I must know of him!"

"He has slain Du-ubas."

"How do you know this?" Frightened, Mosutha nearly shrieked the words. The barbarians of the valley all had feared Du-ubas, and known him for a dark power.

"I was there in the last of the sunlight. The haunted trees of the woods screamed silently, the shadows quickened, many haunted spirits flew away when Oron's angry sword slew the shaman. The air shrieked and demons leaped upon his shade."

Mosutha gave the matter a moment's consideration. He had an enemy, indeed. "Where is Oron now? How will I know him?"

"You will know him when you face his sword."

"Where is he now? *Tell me!*"

"He hunts you, sorcerer."

Mosutha thought swiftly. What more could he need to know of this enemy, this nonentity of which he had had no suspicion? He asked of the smoke spirit, "How many more lives needs the Demon God before he will aid me in my great magic?"

"Ernog is ancient and hungry. He needs rivers of blood. A human, he has slept in Hell for longer than your kind has walked the earth."

"Then he shall *have* rivers of blood! Can Oron die?"

"He can die. He will die. The stars mark him. He was born to a doom."

"Then I shall slay him. Will he die by sorcery?"

"Aye, battling sorcery."

"Then I shall slay him."

The voice said no more. Dissipating, the fumes vanished and became no more than incense mists wafting into the air of the magus's tower apartment. Mosutha, deep in thought, added no more blood to the grate.

An enemy. . . .

He knew that his orders to bring captives from the villages of the Valley would provoke retaliations by the dogs but that was why he had bought the mercenaries.

He needed time to plan and think.

He set down his bowl, placing it on the stone at his feet, and took up his iron wand. Walking around the inner border of his circle, Mosutha paused at each station, at each angle where the points of the great seven-pointed Star drawn within the circle touched its circumference. At each station the sorcerer lifted his wand and from a pocket of his robe cast a bit of salt upon the floor. Calling out, he dismissed the guardian powers of his sorcery, banishing the elemental invisible things he had called forth for protection during his ceremony.

"Be you gone now, phantom of Ishtritis, named by me and conjured from me, and dismissed now by me in the Name of the Star!

"Be you gone now, phantom of Osrogeh, named by me. . . !

"Be you gone now, phantom of Thet-Humah. . . !"

Even before Mosutha had concluded his ritual there came a loud pounding on the wooden door of the chamber. The sorcerer cursed lowly and yelled out, "Stay back! The strengths are unleashed!"

The knocking desisted.

"Be you gone now, phantom of Semoth Sibdis. . . !"

When he was finished with the dismissals, Mosutha completed his ritual by sprinkling purifying wine upon the grate and around his circle, closing the Gates against any intrusion outside his control.

"By the nine of the gods, and by the seven of the Star, and by the five of man, and by the three of the three spirits, and by the one unity of cosmos, I bid all elementals and demons, all shades and things, begone from here! and molest me not at all, and answer no commands other than those by my own voice and will and gesture!"

He offered a brief prayer to Ernog, the destructive foulness, then crossed from his circle and went to his door.

"Who is there?"

"Wizard, it is Hanmor. Open your door to me!"

Mosutha did so, lifting the heavy beam bolt as though it were weightless. He pulled open the door, and the rushing current of air that followed swirled the incenses of the room, driving away the stench and fogging the brilliant candles that stood lit all around.

Hanmor, the mercenary chieftain, sniffed the air with an expression of disgust. But there was more than disgust in his voice—a trace of superstitious uncertainty, perhaps—when he addressed his employer.

"Riders have returned from the south, Mosutha. They report the slaughter of five villages and their return with slaves. They are three days from us."

"This concurs with what my spirits have told me."

"Indeed. . . ." Hanmor regarded Mosutha doubtfully. "Then perhaps we should sit now and discuss my payment and the gold you promised my men. For when they deliver these barbarians to you, we will be gone from this hellish place."

"There is time enough to discuss our bargain. I must attent to many things."

"I want to talk about it now. Let your many things wait, spirit-chaser."

The threat implicit in the chief's voice did not sway Mosutha in the least, but he decided nonetheless that perhaps it was time to discuss with Hanmor promises he had made to him—and to make clear issues that heretofore had been assumed.

"Shall we talk over wine, chief?"

"That would be good. Men make matters over wine."

"Good. For I have worked up a thirst. . . ."

Hanmor glanced about the room; ever the alert sword, he anticipated the squeal of a shadow or the betrayal of some demon hidden behind a curtain. "Indeed," he commented gruffly. "Worked up a thirst. . . ."

From her bed of pillows and silks Sarit, Mosutha's mistress, arose as the sun went down. She lay quiet, listening to the dim-carrying sounds of the fortress and, nearer to her, the noises of one of Mosutha's man servants at work in the anteroom just outside her sleeping chamber. Apparently he was setting out her evening meal. Sarit did not move. Unrelaxed, she remained in bed, curled and tense, thinking deep thoughts. Only when the servant beyond her door rang the small bell to rouse her did she sit up and swing her long legs to the floor.

"Mistress?"

"Enter." She told him to do so, even though she was nude. It had never embarrassed her to let any of Mosutha's acolytes see her without clothes. She enjoyed the freedom she felt when she was nude, despite the coolness of her mountain home and the fine robes and clothes of her wardrobe. She was beautiful, and she liked the fact that she was beautiful.

The robed, white-faced young man in the doorway bowed low and waved a hand behind him. "I have set out your food."

Sarit slipped on her sandals, stood up and stretched. She was a slim, well-proportioned young woman, and in the dim light her white flesh stood out ghostily against the shadows and against the darkness of her long hair. "What mood is he in today?"

"I do not know. He has been upstairs in his chamber, at work. Just before coming here, I heard that some of Hanmor's riders had returned. They had seen the slave caravan."

She did not seem interested. "Is the water warm?"

"Yes, it is warm."

"I'll bathe before eating."

The acolyte bowed and turned, and Sarit followed him into the anteroom.

Like all the rooms of the fortress's buildings and towers, the anteroom had been carved from the interior of the mountain. Mosutha and his people lived inside a rude, honeycombed series of structures that had existed on the mountain, and within it, for thousands of years. A natural spring higher up fed into the buildings of the fortress at certain points, and in this anteroom a small bathing pool had been built, utilizing the water flow. Kept warm artificially by an ingenious system of channels hollowed beneath the brick-built pool, it was one of the few luxuries to which Sarit looked forward upon awakening every day. Now, as her servant set out a clean robe for her, small jars of oils, and a number of drying towels, the mistress of the sorcerer kicked free her sandals, mounted the edge of the pool and slid slowly into the water.

It was indeed warm, and Sarit appreciated it as she tantilizingly lowered her body, a little at a time, into the comfort of it.

Relaxing, she paid no attention to the robed acolyte, who returned into her sleeping chamber and began lighting torches and cleaning food trays and wine goblets. Having sold himself into the service of Mosutha in return for knowledge, the acolyte did what was required of him in return for his instruction. He performed his tasks quietly and efficiently.

Sarit floated to the center of the pool, stroking her arms lightly in the water. With closed eyes she let her thoughts travel where they would, and she sought to push away any intrusive imaginings or remembrances.

She paid no attention to the quiet acolyte busy with his chores in the next room.

Neither did she hear the slight tread of footpads that soon scraped behind one of the tall arras hanging against the wall, nor did she sense the eyes that lingered upon her from their hiding place there.

"As soon as my men return," Hanmor reminded Mosutha, "I'll expect them to be paid. And then my army and I will quit this place."

Mosutha told him, "It is right and proper that you should expect them to be paid when they return."

Hanmor's response was blunt as, in a snide voice, he corrected himself. "They *will* be paid when they return."

"Of course."

"I do not trust you, sorcerer. Let me be frank about that."

"I would not expect you to trust me, chief. I do not

trust you, either. But both of us are strong men. If one of us possesses a stronger weapon than the other. . . . Well, nevertheless, we are both strong men, and—"

"My sword is as strong as your deviltry, Mosutha."

"—and, realizing that, we shouldn't forget the bonds between strong men are only as strong as their weakest link."

Grunting, Hanmor set down his wine cup. He lifted a paw of a hand and stroked his thick, dark beard. "What weak link?"

"Our mutual distrust."

"You can remedy that by surrendering your gold to me when my men return."

"I have said that I would do so, chief."

"And I have said that I do not trust you."

Perplexed for a moment, Mosutha studied the warrior. Then he grinned, purposefully amused. "It's good that you are a soldier, Chief Hanmor. I doubt if you possess the skills for hardier work."

"Don't mock me, spirit-chaser."

"Then don't threaten me. What do you wish of me? Proof of my gold? What if I showed you a mountain of gold?"

"I would think that you had created an illusion."

"And if I handed you a sack of gold coins, even at this moment? Would you trust that?"

Hanmor stared at Mosutha, looked away, and took up his wine.

"I will tell you what illusion is, warrior. Illusion is the gold you hold in your hand, just as it is the life you breathe every moment you suck in air."

"You play word games. I came here to talk—"

"You play word games, Chief."

Hanmor growled angrily, slamming his wine cup to the table so that it spilled drink onto the wood. "I want gold for my men, wizard!"

"And you shall have it."

"I came here to talk about that, not about—illusions, not about *breathing!*"

Nor did she see the slight, parting ripple in the arras as the hand that belonged to the eyes carefully, silently drew aside one edge to study the beautiful woman a moment more.

Sarit pulled herself along in the water, swam to a towel, and used it to wipe the perspiration from her face. The water was quite warm. As she returned the towel to the stone and splashed into the water again, she felt a breeze.

She looked up.

And saw the arras rippling. . . .

Sarit observed the drapery very closely; suspiciously. Someone spying on her? It had never happened before. She knew that none would dare do so, none would dare to spy on the mistress of Mosutha.

Keeping an eye on the arras, she splashed in the water, beginning to lave herself—

The cloth moved.

Sarit backed to the edge of the pool. "Who is there?"

No sound. No movement.

"Someone is there! *Speak!*"

Footsteps behind her, as the acolyte entered the room.

"Damn you, speak! *Who is there?*"

Suddenly the arras billowed into life, dull footsteps slapped on the stone behind it, and a winding curve of movement slid horizontally along the hanging as the hidden spy ran for escape.

"Gold," Mosutha said, holding out his hand.

Hanmor got up from his seat, moved from the table, and crossed the room to the sorcerer. He looked at what Mosutha held in his hand, reached out, and took it in his own fingers.

"No need for trickery here," the wizard promised the mercenary. "This belongs to the treasure I discovered here, when I made this mountain my home."

It was a beautiful object — ancient, true, but gold, pure gold. A small scarab, the replica of some hideous insect-creature, carefully worked from a ball of purest gold.

"Cursed?" Hanmor inquired worriedly, looking from it into the sorcerer's eyes.

"What is a curse? It was hidden here, lying in wait for whoever unearthed it. I have little use for gold; what I need, I conjure — or steal. Gold is for such as you, still trapped by material things."

"This is but one piece. How much gold is in this 'treasure'?"

Mosutha grinned. "A lakeful."

"What do you mean, a 'lakeful'?"

"When Ernog, the demon, owned this mountain at the beginning of Time, he dwelt in a lake of gold. This mountain rests atop it — or where it once was. I will not tell you how to reach the gold. But I will tell you that for a thousand years Ernog's slaves worked the gold and turned the lake into a treasure of trinkets, such as you hold there. Do you know where you stand, Chief Hanmor? Or are you a man of small imagination? Where you stand, in this very room, but thousands and thousands of years ago, Ernog once stood. Before the seasons changed, before the stars changed, before the oceans and the lands changed, when these mountains were but the heights of other, more massive mountains, Ernog stood where you now stand. An elemental giant of the cosmos, trapped on earth."

"I think you lie." Hanmor did not seem overly impressed. "I think those stories all are lies."

"You hold the gold in your hand. Ernog's gold. What is a curse, Hanmor? I worship Ernog's spirit, and I will free his curse upon the Valley. You hunger for his gold, and you will spend his cursed gold in the cities of the east."

Hanmor examined the piece in his fingers, shook his woolly head, but thrust the scarab into his pocket. "Tell me about this lake of gold. For my men."

"It is no longer a lake. It is a cave of gold—trinkets such as you have there. Gold ornaments the size of seeds, and golden chairs the size of this room—large enough to seat demons." Mosutha laughed cruelly at the expression on Hanmor's face. "When your men return, chief, I will show you the cave of gold. But you must shield your eyes. The glare will blind you!"

Hanmor grumbled, "I would see it now."

"Ah, he does not trust me."

"I would see it now, priest."

"I have promised you gold when your men return. I promised you nothing else. You and your men are hungry, chief. That does not mean you are stupid. Do not threaten me."

Leaping, the servant threw himself upon the arras. With the screaming sound of ripping tapestry the curtain flew free of the wall and billowed to the floor. Standing motionless behind it, dagger up in a defensive posture, crouched one of Hanmor's mercenaries.

Frightened, Sarit pulled herself from her bath and kneeled upon the stones. She pulled a towel around herself to cover her nudity from outside eyes.

The acolyte stepped close to the soldier, who

growled and bent back, pressing himself against the wall while hefting his dagger dangerously.

"Give me the knife, man."

"Go to hell, dog!"

"I will take it from you."

"I'll spill your guts, priest!"

"Give me the knife. . . ." The acolyte moved forward.

"Let me go," the mercenary warned him, "or I'll slice you in half! Get back!"

Keeping the soldier in sight, the servant yelled back to Sarit, "Tell the man in the outer hall, my mistress. Have him inform the master."

Trembling, Sarit backed across the floor to do so.

It triggered the desperate mercenary into a rash act. Lunging forward, knife up, he threw himself against the acolyte and brought his blade down swiftly.

Sarit screamed.

The mercenary howled in agony. His knife arm was bent back as the servant caught it in his right hand, while his left gripped the soldier's throat and pushed his head severely to one side. Gurgling, the mercenary fought for balance, then escape. There was a loud crackling sound, like the striking of a hard stone against a second, as the soldier's bent arm burst from its socket beneath the acolyte's superhuman strength. A moment later, as Sarit stared, the neck was shattered with a great snapping and popping noise, and the soldier's head bent around so that his bearded chin rested saggingly between his shoulder blades.

With a gesture that showed no effort on his part, the acolyte took hold of the corpse by its hair and hurled it to one side. The body skidded scrapingly along the stone floor and bumped into a wall.

He turned, eyes bright, and moved to Sarit. Bowing before her he said, "I will summon Mosutha." And he crossed the room, leaving Sarit alone, dressed in her towel and shivering, staring at the corpse of the mercenary—whose dead black eyes met hers with a soulless, frightened stare.

". . . and I have said—" Mosutha ceased and turned, facing the door of the room. "What is it?"

The acolyte bowed and entered. Never looking to Hanmor, he walked to Mosutha, bent his head low and whispered in the sorcerer's ear.

"You have just done this?" Mosutha asked in a shocked undertone.

The robed man nodded.

A cruel expression filled Mosutha's face. "Lead us." Turning to Hanmor he said, "You will come with me."

Concerned (but not showing it) the war chief followed with heavy footsteps as the acolyte and his master exited the room and proceeded quickly down a stone corridor, took a stairwell to an upper floor and hastened down the lamp-lit hall. In the upper passage Hanmor passed two of his men loitering in a small chamber, throwing dice. He snapped his fingers and they left their game to hurry after him.

In her bathing chamber, Sarit had pulled on a robe and was standing, calmer but still distraught, by the small table that her evening meal was on. She had poured herself a goblet of wine but was not drinking.

Mosutha strode past her and walked to the corpse that lay against the wall. Behind him, when he entered the chamber, Hanmor stopped abruptly in his stride and growled at what he saw. His two men lined up beside him, and their hands moved toward their swords, for they sensed an eruption nearing.

Mosutha studied the corpse, turned, and faced Hanmor. "He was spying on Sarit."

"Was he?" Sweat had broken out on the war chief's red face, and no pretense could mask the tension in his voice.

"By your orders, I assume."

Hanmor did not answer.

"Do you think it a good thing to set spies upon your host, chief? Do you?" His voice was terribly quiet, low and dark with a promise of intense hatred.

"Mosutha, if he spied, he took it upon himself—"

"What was his plan?" the sorcerer asked, crossing slowly—slowly—to Hanmor. "To spy, only? To kill, perhaps? To study, and then strike if I did not deliver *gold* to you and your men?"

Hanmor's eyes blazed with fury, his hands curled into fists, but he restrained himself from striking out.

One of his men was made of quicker temper. Frightened and unnerved, as he stood amidst the escalating tension, his hand, lurking near his sword, naturally fell to the hilt at the first dark intimation in Mosutha's tone. It was an unfortunate move. The sorcerer glimpsed it from the corner of his eye and instantly jumped to defend himself and Sarit.

"Die!" Mosutha shrieked. Throwing out a hand to the man, he closed his fist and threw his arm high above his head in a powerful gesture.

The mercenary had no time to utter a sound; no cough, no gurgle, no whimper escaped his lips. Even while his fingers closed around the hilt of his blade his feet left the ground as, in answer to the sorcerer's gesture, his helmeted head abruptly ripped from his shoulders and flew in a red blur to the ceiling. A trail of gushering blood, hanging rootlike as a mist in midair, followed the head skyward; the helmet crashed against the stone of the ceiling with a loud knock.

Hanmor threw himself to one side, and his second

man did the same. Sarit, stunned, stood where she was, staring in disbelief at the spectacle. The acolyte, guarding the entrance door, did not move.

The head dropped to the floor, bounced slightly and rolled still in the widening pool of gore that spouted from the body's broken neck. The corpse, still fidgeting from the shock of the attack, fell gradually on weakened legs to crumple backward to the floor, landing with a splash.

Mosutha stared evilly at Hanmor and moved quickly to the open door as Hanmor, outraged but very wary, turned to watch him, anticipating further evil.

Sarit, finally reacting, covered her mouth with her hands and fled the room for the shelter of her sleeping chamber.

At the door, Mosutha lent Hanmor a deadly, stark glare. "Speak to me *no more* of gold or warriors!" he thundered. "Speak to me *no more,* or you will command an *army* of corpses! Distrust?" he screamed, voice rising with powerful emotion. "You dare to speak to me of *distrust,* animal? Speak to me *no more!*"

Then he turned and left the room, disappearing soundlessly down the outer hall. Leaving Hanmor to stare at the two fresh corpses he once had called men — beneath the stern guard of a slim young man with white eyes who, like his master, possessed a far stronger weapon, it seemed, than a mere sword of steel. . . .

8

They buried Adrum in the light of the dawn. Oron dug the warrior's grave, on the spot where he had died. And while he and Uira, by necessity, had to leave the corpses of the others where they had fallen, they lay her father to rest in the forest. Oron thrust Adrum's sword into the earth at the head of the grave, which is the way warriors' resting places were marked (and woe be to the one who stole such a sword). And though it was a habit to speak words to the gods upon the death of a comrade, thus helping to guide his spirit across the Sky River into the Shadow Land of Mist, Oron did not offer any words. Rather, Uira did so, whispering her prayer to the high ones, forestalling any attack upon her father's shade by the goblins that loved to harry the newly dead.

When she was done saying what she said, she looked at Oron and he nodded silently, grimly. She had spoken good words for a man who had been a warrior first, and all else second.

But it came to him that he had not buried his own father, nor had he buried Ilgar, his chief. Oron, honestly, had his doubts that burial meant anything at all. Death was death, life was life. One dealt with the present, and if death came as a result, then one dealt with that.

But he knew that he should comfort Uira in some way, and so he told her, "He was a strong warrior, your father."

She sighed heavily. "He was a man first. He never fought unless someone attacked him. He loved the forest, and the sun, and he loved hunting and he loved to fish. He preferred those things, rather than to kill men."

When they moved on, across the camp and into the forest, Oron saw that Akrim had been slain, as he had feared. But he did not see any sign of Host's body, although it was always possible that his corpse was lying somewhere out in the trees. Oron knew that he would never see any of the men of this camp alive again.

They traveled north, and before noon sun reached the place where Mosutha's soldiers had made camp on the night of the raid. Oron studied the bodies that lay there; already a day and a half old, they were beginning to decay, and were crawling with insects and vermin. A horrible stench hung above the camp, but Oron nevertheless scrutinized the bodies. Yet nowhere did he spy the body of Hukrum, his uncle.

No doubt he had been recaptured. Perhaps he had been wounded. Still, Oron believed his uncle was yet alive. As the Wolf well knew, the desire for vengeance keeps the life-blood flowing, strong and with a purpose, against even great foes.

With Uira following a step or two behind him, Oron led the way into the forestland—land that was unfamiliar to him. Gradually they drifted toward the northwest, for that was where the Nevga flowed, from down out of the mountains. Following its bank was their quickest and easiest path.

They paused in the afternoon to fish and caught three fat trout, skinned them, and cooked them over a small fire. As they sat watching the flames, Oron on one side and Uira on the other, the young woman studied her man.

Oron felt her stare and looked up.

Uira asked him quietly, "Were you thinking of Esa?"

"Yes. . . ." He moved his eyes away.

"What were you thinking, Oron?"

He did not answer immediately, but when he did, after a moment's thought, it was in words that did not surprise Uira. "I was thinking—that Esa is no longer my mate. I am no longer her mate. You are my mate."

"That is true, Oron."

"But still, I must save her."

"Yes."

"I must free her. She, and all the others. But I must free Esa because even if she is not my mate, I still remember her. My heart still loves her."

He looked at Uira uncertainly, afraid that she would be hurt by his honesty.

But she told him, "I understand, Oron. My father is dead, but I still love him, although he can no longer be my father. You love Esa, although she is stolen, and although you and I are mates."

He considered that, and saw that Uira had described the matter succinctly. But another problem presented itself to him. "I don't think you should go all the way to Mosutha's fortress," he told her.

"Why not?"

"What if you were killed?" It had never been the policy of his tribe to allow the women to fight, although many had learned how to do so.

Uira smiled generously to him. Rising up, she moved around the fire and sat beside him, placed a soft hand on his arm. "And what if you were killed,

128

Oron? Either way, one of us is without a mate. Mosutha and his men have done us both the same injury. Are you afraid that I can't defend myself? Think—my father was Adrum, I carry his knife, and he showed me how to use the knife."

"You can kill?"

"To defend myself, yes. To help you kill Mosutha and free Esa and the people of the Valley, yes. I can kill."

Oron was reassured to hear it. "Then we fight Mosutha together."

"That is just how it should be."

They settled down to eat their cooked fish, then took up their northward trek. They spoke little, moved silently, and ate from apple trees or berry bushes when they passed them.

The bank of the wide, rushing Nevga was rocky and steep, with great trees and undergrowth pushing down the slopes. Knowing that eventually the caravan of the slavers must reach a point where they would cross the Nevga, Oron had not bothered tracking the wagons through the forest. Following the river, they could regain their lost day. And if they found the slavers on the riverbank they could devise some scheme to take advantage of it. Oron was not particularly inclined to repeat his error of the night of his capture. Opportunities would present themselves, and any one of the plans revolving in his mind might serve to outwit the dogs.

As dusk came down, Oron climbed a tall tree to spy, as well as he could, farther up the river. Uira waited below. She was alarmed when he hurried down with the news, "There is a camp just beyond."

"Soldiers?"

He shook his head. "I couldn't tell. The light is too dim. But there are fires. . . ."

They hurried through the darkening forest, moving as swiftly as they dared, watching for the lights of the low campfires. As the day finally died and night wholly obscured their passage, Oron picked his way cautiously through the underbrush, listening keenly, making sure that Uira was close behind him. Suddenly, he paused.

"What is it?" she whispered. "Fires?"

"No. Listen. . . ."

Silent, she perked her ears, but could discern no noise.

"Again," Oron whispered, moving into the forest.

"What is it?" Uira prodded him.

Not answering her, he crept on for a few moments, breaking carefully through the trees, only to stop again. Cautious. Still, no sign of the fires, but, "Do you hear it?" Oron whispered.

"No, I—" But then it came to her. Uira felt a nervous wave ripple down her back at the sound. "Oron, what is it?"

"A man," he told her, listening carefully, watching ahead. The distorting effects of the trees and distance had not thrown him. "It is a man, screaming."

"Gods. . . ."

They hastened on, the sounds of the shrieks becoming more and more distinct to them. Then, dim orange lights wavered through a far stretch of the forest, and Oron prowled, silent as the wolf he was, through the thinning foliage that led to a flat upon the riverbank ahead. He crouched at the edge of the forest, staring, and waved a hand to Uira. Noiseless, she knelt beside him.

In the darkness of the night they saw half a dozen fires, their heavy plumes of smoke rolling up to the clouds. Far beyond they could see the wide black expanse of the swollen Nevga, and beyond that, a stark gray wall of mountain. Around the fires on the bank men stood in a loose group—barbarians, by their clothes. Perhaps twenty-five or thirty of them. And in the center of them, mounted upon a pole thrust into the earth, hung the screaming man.

A robed man. His clothes were torn from him, his arms tied above his head, and feet tied tightly to the base of the pole. He was moaning, now. But as one of the barbarians lifted a flaming torch from the fire, the man's moans rose into a scream, and he shrieked in agony as the heat of the torch was passed across his belly and down his legs.

"One of Mosutha's men," Oron realized. "And they're killing him slowly. . . ."

Uira turned her face away; her fingers sank into Oron's arm, digging tightly. The screams ended in a long, painful trail of sobs. Uira looked up and saw the man with the torch moving away from his victim. He bent to one of the fires and reheated his torch.

Slow torture. . . .

"They'll kill him," she said to Oron.

He grunted, not apparently disturbed by the fact.

"We should stop them," Uira urged.

"I know that." The thought had come to Oron that the dog might be able to help them. Du-ubas had only been troublesome, but this man was more intimate with Mosutha—and that meant he was important. "He could tell us things," Oron admitted out loud. He rose from his cover.

Uira said to him, "Don't kill any of them."

He looked down at her.

"They are our people," she reminded him. "They are afraid, and angry."

"They are men," Oron told her. And then, in a wise insight, "Yes, they're afraid. Because they have no

131

leader to bind them. They have no Adrum, no Ilgar. Men without leaders . . ." he jerked his head ". . . they do that."

Uira, surprised by his comment, smiled at him, anticipating his intentions.

Oron grinned back at her, and then boldly stepped out from the forest and marched toward the riverbank. After a moment, Uira stood up and followed him.

At the first sound of his approach the barbarians at the fires turned to confront him. Their hands lifted to their belts. Instantly Oron read their minds—for weren't their thoughts the same as those of his people on the morning of the banishment? He was alone, an outsider, a stranger. He was, therefore, an enemy. Mosutha's raiders had shattered the ever-tenuous bond of mutual respect that had grown up in the Valley. Survivors had reverted, in the backlash of the storm, to the most rudimentary of social accords. Oron was a potential enemy, not a potential ally or brother or anything else. He knew that he must use words to cut as keenly into their minds as his sword could cut into their flesh.

He paused a short distance from their fires and allowed them to study him, even as he watched them. He recognized none of them. But he held up his right hand and asked them, "What tribes are you from?"

No one answered him, but a few heads jerked to attention at the sight of Uira, who quietly approached Oron from behind and stood facing them by his side.

Oron asked them again, "What tribes are you from? Or do you all come from the Tribe of the Deaf?"

One of them barked a harsh laugh in response, but a large warrior there—young, balding, with tattered skins for clothing and a long blade on his hip— stepped forward and proclaimed, "We are of many villages that no longer exist. I was of the tribe of Nor."

"I knew one of your brothers," Oron told him.

"And who was that?"

"Kosun the Ax-Maker."

"And how did you know Kosun?"

"He was taken captive. So was I. He was killed by Mosutha's soldiers when the men of Adrum raided their camp."

Now a second stepped forward to stand by the first. "I know this one," he spoke. "He was with us in Adrum's camp."

"Who are you?" asked Oron.

"I am Sathen."

Oron recalled him—not by his name but, in the lights of the fires, by his face and build. "You were there," the Wolf agreed. "You argued with Akrim when Adrum died. You wished to run away; you refused to fight."

Sathen's mouth curled in a derisive sneer. "You speak words," he retorted, "to anger me."

"I speak words to shame you before our brothers. I don't understand why warriors of the Valley, whatever their tribe, would run from their enemies or refuse to fight their enemies."

"You're a pup," Sathen growled. "Pups play and fall into traps. You have no—"

"I am a warrior," Oron told him, his voice betraying a waning patience. "I am Oron, the Wolf, of the tribe of Ilgar the Moon-Hunter. My people were slaughtered and burned by Mosutha's raiders. I have tracked his soldiers, I have fought and killed many of them. I will kill all of them. Sathen, give me a good reason why I should not. Give me a good reason why I should not revenge the destruction of my tribe, my people."

The others on the riverbank seemed content to

listen to this exchange in silence. Sathen did not answer Oron, so the Wolf deliberately brought the others into the argument.

"What of the rest of you?" he called to them. "Are you afraid to fight, like this one? I do not believe that. I believe that you would like to fight Mosutha's dogs, if you could find them. Is that the truth?"

He was playing a dangerous game. The large, bald warrior growled to Oron. "You are a boy. You cannot shame us. We know what we are. You have fought and killed, so have we all. Look you, we have fished in the river, and see what we have caught." He nodded behind him, to the man on the pole.

"You are poor fishermen," Oron chastised them, "to think that one fish can feed the wrath of thirty warriors. Why catch one fish, when it can lead you to a school of fishes?"

"They have moved across the *river!*" Sathen yelled at Oron, as if that were the decisive factor.

"I know that," was his answer. "Listen to me. This woman is my mate." He held a hand out toward Uira. "She is the daughter of Adrum, as you know, Sathen. She is brave, her father was brave. Adrum knew that Mosutha lives in a fortress in the mountains across the river. Uira, his daughter, has told me this. My village has been destoyed, my chief has been killed. Am I going to let a river and a mountain stop me in my wrath?"

Thirty faces, red in the firelight, soiled, sweating, wrathful, stared at him—and Oron could sense their pounding blood at the deft slicing of his words.

"I am alone," Oron told them, "with my mate. I am going to cross the river and kill Mosutha. If you wish to fight with me, come with me. If you would rather not fight your enemy, then I will fight him alone. But I see thirty men with one enemy to share among them,

134

when across the river is a fortress of enemies. And I tell you now that your anger against Mosutha and your anger against this man you torture is an anger that is a sword with two edges. One edge may hurt your enemy, but the other edge may hurt you. You have let your anger dull your blades. Would you rather torture this man than let him lead you to Mosutha?"

"We cannot trust him!" the bald warrior countered. "He has fire in his hands! He is a wizard!"

Oron grinned, baring his teeth. "Have you asked him to help you?"

Several of the warriors guffawed loudly.

"Ask him," Oron told them, and when none responded. "Man!" he called. "Can you hear me?"

The victim on the pole weakly lifted his head. "I . . . hear. . . ."

"What are you called?"

"Saldum. . . ."

"Saldum, you are one of Mosutha's men, are you?"

"Yes-sss. . . ."

"Saldum, these warriors will kill you before morning-rise. If you promise to help them, they will not kill you. But you must lead them to Mosutha and use your fire to help them kill Mosutha. Saldum, do you promise to help them?"

Saldum's glaring eyes burned for a moment. "What is death . . ." he whispered hoarsely ". . . to me?"

"What is Mosutha to you?" Oron called to him. "Are you a man, or are you a slave to Mosutha? If these men kill you, Mosutha will not care. If you help us, you will live. That is better than dying, and these men are not as cruel as Mosutha."

Saldum, hanging awkwardly in his torture, lisped dryly: "They are . . . cruel. . . !"

More harsh laughter, and Oron snickered himself.

"Help us, Saldum."

But the man's head fell weakly to his chest and he did not respond.

Oron made another bold move. He walked forward, straight toward Sathen and the giant who stood beside him. When he reached the giant, Oron looked him in the eyes and proclaimed, "What is your name?"

"Thos," the warrior replied, regarding the Wolf guardedly.

"Thos, I will not draw my sword. I will not draw against a warrior of the Valley. Will you let me pass?"

Thos was cautious. "You will free him?"

"Yes. He is weak, he is dying. Give him water; let him speak. If he betrays us, you can kill him, and I will say no more. I will go away from you."

Thos did not answer. For a tense moment, Oron eyed every face there. None made a motion against him.

So Oron passed by Thos, moved past Sathen, crossed beside the fires and, drawing out a knife, he cut free Saldum. The acolyte of Mosutha dropped like a dead weight, and Oron grabbed him and lay him on the ground.

"Uira. Get some water."

She passed through the camp, under the watchful eyes of the gathered warriors, and from her pouch spilled cold water onto Saldum's face, dripped it onto his gasping lips.

Oron sat by one of the fires, listening to the heavy sound of the Nevga as it moved behind him in the large emptiness of the night. Beside him stretched Uira, asleep, and across from her lay Saldum, exhausted—but in pain, and afraid that should he doze off he would once more be victimized.

Oron did not pay him much attention, but the Wolf

kept ever alert of the warriors who stayed awake with him. Sathen was one, Thos another. The rest of the barbarians, trusting to the vigilance of their comrades, either gave in to sleep or made conversation at other fires.

It was an uncomfortable assortment of men. The tilt of a head, the posture of a body, the grunt or the sigh late in the early morning, told all. There was slight trust here, and very little sympathy. Oron, in his banishment from his tribe, had learned one very valuable lesson that was now reinforced upon him: Every man is alone. Invisible ties bound him to every other man and every other woman, and possibly to every other living thing in the world, but still, when it mattered, he was alone. And aloneness meant solitude, it meant strangeness, it meant that an emotional dance of greeting, sharing, testing, and balancing must be endured whenever one living thing met another. Trust, however, was not so much an issue. Oron did not care tonight whether or not these men trusted him, for trust (like love, he sensed) was an uncertain thing, changing with the breeze, dependent on custom or familiarity, and pertinent only when necessary. But balance was important. Weight, strength, dexterity, agility in mind and body, attitude and commerce, insight and understanding: balance was all. No man could be master of himself or a leader of others if he did not understand balance, if he did not first and foremost strive to maintain a rigorous balance of all things.

Oron had come to realize that.

He considered how greatly he had undermined the balance of his tribe when he had slain his father, and how Ilgar, with his justice, had sought to restore that balance.

And it occurred to Oron that Mosutha, the sorcerer, had unbalanced things terribly by waging war upon the barbarian villages of the Valley. That balance must be restored, and quickly: Restored by vengeance, bloodshed, and more war, until a moment of new balance presented itself. And it would be at such a moment that decisions must be made. The new balance must be recognized; the vengeances must then cease, and the war must then end. The earth must be returned to balance. The Valley, and attitudes and tempers must be righted.

At that future moment it would take a leader of insight and strength and skill to impose that new balance, that new order, and Oron wondered if he would be the leader.

He wondered then what made him so concerned with leadership. He was alone, a man without a name other than the name he had chosen for himself. Why then should he lead men? Because he had always admired Ilgar? Because the thought of leadership and decisiveness—and balance—had always seemed to be within him? He wondered. . . . Sometimes Den-usutus had spoken of an old doctrine, a doctrine of continual return, a pattern to the death of bodies and the reinstatement of souls. At birth (he had told Oron one night) souls of those once dead returned to life; the one who was born passed his days thinking he was himself, but in truth he was this old soul come back, which itself had been an older soul, and so on, into the past. All these souls were in fact one great soul, born in a land of continual darkness and portioned out to all living things. And there were other great souls, and there was one mighty soul of all which commanded even the gods. . . .

Oron at the time had thought Den-usutus mad, or at least impractical. But now he wondered. The deep things in him had to have come from somewhere.

What had made him choose the sword over the plow, long before he had even understood the difference? There were many mysteries, and light did not disperse all shadows at once. . . .

But such things began to smack too closely of shamans and woodland vampires, insubstantial and (therefore) untrustworthy and unbalanced things. He was of the sword.

Straightening himself where he sat, Oron yawned and stretched, then pulled free his knife and poked at the coals of his fire. As he did so, he heard Saldum stir. He glanced over at the acolyte and saw the man's white eyes staring at him. His body was prone, and a tense, veined hand, glossy with perspiration, was curled beside his face, like a retracted talon ready to strike.

Oron said nothing.

Staring at him, Saldum whispered quietly, "I thought you meant to hurt me with the hot knife."

"No," Oron replied quietly. "I did not."

Saldum's lids drooped over his eyes slowly, and then he stared again at Oron for a prolonged moment. "Ah," he muttered, and said no more, but closed his eyes to sleep.

Oron lifted his knife from the fire, drove the point a few times in the dirt to cool it, thrust it into his belt. Feeling other eyes upon him, he glanced up into the shadowed faces of Sathen and Thos, on the other side of the fire.

"Shall we kill him?" Sathen asked Thos, loud enough for Oron to overhear.

"The robe?" Thos replied.

"Uh."

"No. Not yet. Let the boy have his way. There is time."

Oron asked them carefully, "If he is so powerful,

then how did you overcome him? How did you capture him?"

Thos told him, "He was in the river. I told you we landed him, like a fish."

"Why was he in the river?"

Thos shrugged his big shoulders. "He told us that Mosutha's soldiers had dunked him."

"Why?"

"As a sacrifice. So that their crossing would be safe."

"And when you took him," Oron continued, "and tied him to the post, didn't he hurt you with the fire in his hands?"

"No, he did not."

"Don't you wonder why he did not?"

Thos's brow creased. "No," he admitted. "I did not. But we are many and he is one. He did not hurt us."

Oron told him. "He was abandoned by his people—by his tribe. He must hate them now, as much as he hates us. Perhaps he wanted to die. He is an enemy to his people, Thos, more than he is to us. Do you understand that? That means he is a weapon for us."

The giant mulled it over for a few moments. "perhaps—" he began.

Sathen interrupted callously, "Don't listen to him. Oron is a boy. What does he know?"

Oron grunted to him, "I remember a coward who would not fight, even with his enemy eager to make him die."

Sathen quickly got to his feet. In the darkness, by the orange light of the low fires, Oron saw his hand slip quickly to his sword hilt. "You continue to—"

But he stopped short, gasping, when Thos's huge hand suddenly grabbed him by the belt and forced him back down to the ground. Sathen croaked loudly, fought free, and shot the giant a murderous glare.

Thos was not at all intimidated. "Keep silent," he warned Sathen. "The boy has spoken more truth in one night than I have heard you grumble in two days. I am not a fool, and neither are these men. Remember who you are with, and remember who found you lost in the forest. Oron is a warrior. Treat him with the respect a warrior deserves."

Oron smiled to himself. Thos's surprising outburst was the last thing he had expected, and it was a victory for him. He had broken whatever solidarity kept these men together, their kinship of fear, of isolation. Thos, he intuited, was the loosely accepted leader of these rogues—and he had just won Thos to him.

Though Sathen grumbled, he made no further display of his temper. He slouched away from Thos and settled against a log some distance from the fire, and pretended to sleep. The dawn was just beginning to gray the dark treetops of the forests far to the east, and the first early calls of birds carried thinly through the air above the low, dismal roar of the Nevga.

Thos stretched his huge arms and yawned heavily. Slipping down against his log, he rolled to one side and without a word to Oron, or to Sathen, he wrapped his arms around his chest and dozed off.

Oron watched him, and watched Sathen; he glanced at Saldum. As the dawn gradually and patiently rose to light more and farther treetops, he stood up and walked to the edge of the riverbank and looked down the long slope into the wide stretching Nevga.

Quietly, deep inside him, he felt a stirring in his soul, as though—banished from his tribe, an outlaw in a distant forest—he had somehow, in some strange way, come home to a river, a dawn, and a cool awareness of his kinship with other warriors, other men. A

cool awareness, a foretaste—almost disquieting, nearly unnameable—of his destiny.

As though prearranged, Oron sat beside Saldum,
with Uira off to his right: the three of them confronted by thirty warriors on the opposite side of the
smoking fire pits. Oron thought again of balance, and
of what a dangerous balance this parley presented.

Food had been eaten; tempers reined. The thirty
were now sprawled or sitting on the riverbank, paying
attention to Saldum. The acolyte had dressed himself
in the robe that had been torn from him the night
before, and he was addressing the warriors—his
enemies, his torturers—with words of strong pride and
even stronger equanimity.

"I would slay you," he told them fearlessly, eyeing
Thos directly, "if I felt the need to, despite the fact
that I am ill and weak. I owe my life to Oron the
Wolf, and because I owe him my life I swear
allegiance to him. I am his man. I am indebted to
him. He has said he is alone; I, too, am alone—
betrayed, and with a vengeance. He does not need you
and neither do I. But because he has chosen to join
you, and because I owe my life to him, I will swear
before him my oath of allegiance. I am a sorcerer;
nothing that I can do will alter that, because my
powers are my own. But because the soldiers of
Mosutha sought to kill me, I now hate them, and I
hate Mosutha, and I will aid Oron in his hate. If you
move against Mosutha, and if you move with Oron,
then I will move with you."

Not waiting for any response from them, Saldum
turned from them and faced Oron. He held out his
left hand, palm down; on the back of his hand was
burned a brand: the mark of the seven-pointed Star
encircled by a triple ring. "Wolf," he said to Oron,

"will you loan me your knife?"

Not understanding the sorcerer's purpose, Oron did so. Saldum crouched beside a fire pit and, holding the knife in his right hand, he warmed it over the hot coals. When the tip of the knife was smoking he stood up and aimed the blade at the brand on his left hand.

"I do not lie to you," he announced to Oron. "I am your man, now, and I hereby renounce any fealty to Mosutha, who branded me with this mark and made me swear myself to him and him only. If I lie, let this stab be my death."

To the astonishment of the collected warriors, and to Oron and Uira, Saldum, who had feared Oron's blade just last night, pressed the knife into the skin of his hand and proceeded, methodically and with no outcry of pain, to outline the branded mark. When a circle of blood surrounded the Star, he returned the knife to Oron, saying, "I can feel no pain when I do not wish to."

Oron understood—understood why Saldum had screamed in agony last night. A man betrayed by those he once trusted may want to harm them through himself, just as Oron had contemplated slaying himself in the first hours of his banishment.

Deftly, Saldum tore the branded circle of skin from his hand; it came loose with a wet ripping sound. He turned toward Thos and held up the bloody patch of skin. The back of his left hand was a raw pink wound dripping red.

Saldum threw the patch of skin at Thos.

"Burn it," he instructed the giant. "Throw it on the coals, let it blacken and burn. If I do not die horribly, then I have not lied, and I will not die. Let Mosutha's sorcery slay me if I lie. I am Oron's."

Wary, Thos stood up and stepped to the fire pit. He dropped into it the thin patch of skin. It fell upon the warm coals and smoked instantly, sizzled, and sent up a charnel stench as it burned black and curled like a piece of damp parchment.

Saldum did not die.

He did not cry out, he did not cringe or crumple over, he did not die.

A cruel, self-satisfied smile lit his thin face, and he displayed it proudly to Thos and the warriors. Turning to Oron, he said, "It is done. Let us now move to destroy Mosutha. I will lead you, Wolf of the sword. And let the sorcerer die in Hell. . . ."

9

"He is too powerful, too shrewd to trust," was Mosutha's opinion. "And if I indeed have a second strong enemy approaching me, I do not care to deal with this viper in my nest."

Sarit listened to him, saying nothing. They were alone in one of the tower rooms; wholly alone. There were no servants outside the door, no guards in the hall or beyond the drapes, and all spirits had been banished.

"I must move carefully," Mosutha continued, speaking half to himself. "For even a dead viper contains poison, and a wounded viper has the anger of three." Absently, the fingers of his hands worried the Star emblem he wore on his chest.

Aware that she might incur his anger for interrupting his thoughts, Sarit nevertheless knew that her entire security rested upon the magus, and she wanted to show her concern for him. "Can you win his warriors to you?" she offered. "Will that—?"

"No, no." Mosutha shook his head, still preoccupied with his own thoughts. "Hanmor's crime against me has only made them side with him more stongly. Even now, I do not doubt, he speaks to his retainers. He will tell them that they are trapped here, that I am their truest enemy, that I have much gold for the taking if I can be slain. I must doubly guard myself, but I must leave an avenue open." He thrummed his fingers on the basalt tabletop, paused, and looked sternly at his mistress.

"I will have need of you, Sarit."

"I am yours."

"You must aid me."

"Tell me what to do," she promised him, "and I will do it."

"When I hired Du-ubas—the fool—to keep watch for me in the Valley, I gave him an element of strength, a Star. I did not tell him how to use it, for I presumed that if he were intelligent enough to discern its purpose, then he was intelligent enough to gain my tolerance of him. I have learned that he has been killed by a barbarian of the Valley."

Sarit sucked in a nervous breath. "Slain? What barbarian could kill him?" Of barbarian stock herself, she knew how superstitious the tribespeople were.

"One of the dogs. . . . That is not important. What matters to me is regaining the element of strength, for with it I can trap Hanmore and allow him to slay himself. It will be elementary. He is greedy and in some ways very stupid. With the Star, he will call down upon himself a powerful doom, and his men will be delivered into my hands."

"How can I help?" Sarit asked him.

Mosutha leaned across the table and reached out a hand. The woman placed one of hers in his. "You must retrieve the Star," he told her. "It must be done quickly, with no time to waste."

"But I cannot cross the river in less than—"

"I do not mean for you to travel by foot," Mosutha corrected her. "Your spirit will travel and do the deed; you will be perfectly well guarded here, and it can be accomplished in only a few short hours. Are you willing to do this for me?"

Guessing what might become of her if she were to refuse, Sarit was amenable. "Tell me how to do it," she answered the sorcerer, "and I will gain the Star for you."

He sat back, a satisfied smile on his face. "We will do it," he told her, "now. Already the day is nearly here, and I must offer sacrifice to the Demon. But this afternoon we will burn incense, Sarit. It will empower you, and release your spirit speedily. I have done it many times, to converse with the elder things of the Void. It is harmless—although you may find the pleasures rather . . . intoxicating." He smiled.

Nervous, but wanting not to show it, Sarit replied, "Let me do it for you. I am afraid that I'm not much use to you, and I want to be. I want to help you, Mosutha."

He leaned forward and stroked her hands. "With this, you will aid me in a very great way. I have a serpent in my midst and another crawling up the road. The Moon of Isfotis draws closer. If I am to cast my wave of hell upon the Valley, it must be soon—and I can broach no arguments or interferences."

She nodded to him, thrilled by his talk of such power. When Mosutha spoke this way, Sarit loved him greatly—because Mosutha was, in every way, Power. And not a barbarian, but wise and much learned.

She rose, glided to him and bent over him. "I will help." She held his head and kissed his bald pate, stroking his chest with her supple hands.

It had taken them a day to cross the Nevga. Trees had been felled to provide support for the wagon-cages, which were floated across the river. The Nevga was a black river; swollen, grim, rushing and roaring like a huge inland sea unleashed, ever in the shadows of gigantic mountains and ancient forests. Some said monsters dwelt deep in its belly, and that spirits of the dead hovered in its mists, eager to trouble any who came to its shores. Like the gods, it was a turbulent titan, isolated, and cold. The first men had been formed from the cold clay and icy mud of its banks.

The four hundred prisoners were in twenty wagon-cages—for three cages had been lost in the crossing, tipping over in the flood, their trapped captives shrieking as they were smashed against rocks and drawn down, suffocating, into the freezing water. Two horses had been lost, and their soldiers. Midway through the enterprise, the four acolytes of Mosutha had drawn lots to cast one of their number into the icy river: Saldum.

But he had survived.

Those who had crossed spent the night drying out by large fires on the opposite shore. The acolytes had lifted blasphemous prayers to dark deities, and the soldiers had feasted on what food they had brought along. But because food had been lost in the crossing, two horses were killed and their stripped meat roasted over flames. The meat was lean and tough, but it was belly-filling.

In her cage, Esa slept. Crowded with the other women, she sought to escape her fate by slumber. Her clothes were ragged. The straw of the cage, as with all the cages, stank with offal and vomit and urine and sweat. The girl had stayed awake—terrifyingly awake—during the fording of the river, but following that she slept through the night, and through most of the next day, when the wagons were drawn away from the river and pulled onward in their slow, arduous journey up the mountain. Esa had come to realize that she would never see Oron again. She had come to understand that she would die. And so she began to change. Withdrawn, realizing these things, she no longer wished to live. She wished to be quit of a world that gave all power and meaning to a thing with a barbaric name that lived in the mountains, sent killers to the tribes, slew people she loved, and cut through the long rope of custom and history and habit. Esa no longer wished to live.

But Hukrum was restive. Oron's uncle had not given up. Fearful in his belly of the robed men, and apprehensive of his future, he was kept alert and alive by his one driving emotion: vengeance. The world had changed; monsters ruled now, and evil. Soldiers, not warriors, owned the world, and the world was vast. Sorcerers could kill and rape and demolish, reduce ancient villages and strong warriors to burning piles. The stars, to which shamans had once turned for knowledge, now held secrets only for white-faced men in robes, men with fire in their hands. Yet though the world had gone mad, Hukrum had not. Where Esa, the woman-child, had made herself forget that she had ever lived a life other than her life in the stinking wagon-cart of the slavers, Hukrum not only remembered, and remembered in detail, but lived with the hot coal of revenge in his heart.

Oron.

The blood-murderer.

His nephew yet lived; or, if he did not live, then Hukrum had to make certain that Oron was dead.

Through the nights in the forest, trapped in his cage—and the day crossing the river—and the half day moving into the mountains, all during this time Hukrum planned and plotted. He must escape. He must return beyond the river and find Oron, and kill him. The world was not so changed that justice was ended. The gods would punish him if he did not kill Oron. His brother's shade would slay him in the next world, if Hukrum did not avenge a blood-crime in this one.

He worked. Lying, day after night after day in his cage, as though he were asleep or exhausted, Hukrum used a small bit of metal from one of his boots to slowly and carefully weaken two of the wooden bars of his cage. The other prisoners with him knew what he was doing. They did not help. They were afraid they might be discovered, if many of them were found lying or kneeling by the bars. Occasionally soldiers would pass by the cages and examine the bars, to see if they were weakened or cracked, and to see if anyone had worked against them. When this happened, Hukrum pushed straw against the poles, and none ever discovered his handiwork.

Unexamined freedom is a path to self-destruction, just as strength can be a shield for weakness and weakness, sometimes, a mask for certain strengths. Hukrum did not know these things, not had he ever given them a thought. He had been free and he had never considered the fact. Now, trapped, he used the weakest parts of him as a strength to gain freedom. He cared only for himself and for his freedom, and for the lust in him.

By midday, as the slaver caravan made its way up into the mountains, Hukrum had managed to weaken two of the bars to such an extent that, with a push, they would break open. He replaced his piece of metal in his boot, and waited. . . .

Half a day—and Oron, with Thos and the other warriors, had fashioned themselves two rafts for crossing the Nevga. Uira had helped. Not strong enough to fell trees or tighten vines, she had aided by cutting the vines and fashioning them into ropes, and by chopping down tall, thin saplings and fashioning them into guiding poles.

At noon they finished their rafts and were prepared to slide them into the river. But the men, low on food, forestalled crossing immediately and entered the forest to hunt. While they did so, Oron, Uira, Saldum, and Thos remained by the rafts.

Oron, because of his temperament, because of Saldum, and because of his knowledge of Mosutha, had taken charge of the group. Thos, gruff, independent and with a mind of his own, had nevertheless during the construction of the rafts made himself Oron's right-hand man. It was not that he was subservient to the younger man, but Thos seemed content for the time being to stand back and see how Oron would handle authority. The giant was not hungry to lord it over others, for he knew that he could always do so. Oron felt the same way, but both men recognized that the men needed direction, and so Oron had stepped to the fore. The true leader (Oron knew) was a catalyst, just as the chief of a village was a catalyst, and someone who ruled by group assent, someone who had earned the right through respect for his strength and intelligence.

As they waited for the hunters to return, Oron and Thos discussed these things.

"All is barter," Oron told Thos. "All is based upon trade. These men agree that I will lead them, and in return I lead them well. When I cannot do that, I have failed in my barter. They hunt food for us; in return, we lead them well, and we make each man the leader of his own job."

Thos nodded, agreeing, but Saldum, who had helped with the raft, put in, "It is not always that way. I have been in the east. There is no barter there. Men work for money, there is no loyalty."

"Then if they use money," Oron replied, "that is

151

their barter."

"But they do not know their chiefs. Their chiefs live in big cities or in fine houses. The chiefs and the rulers are different from the people. They have made themselves so. Men are unequal, there."

"As with Mosutha?" Thos asked him. It was a cruel question, and Saldum recognized the point to it; but he answered frankly:

"Yes; as with Mosutha. When men sell themselves to someone who is not their equal, then they court their own misfortune. Mosutha is a powerful sorcerer, but he sees no one as his equal. He can bring harm, he can destroy. That is where his power rests."

"Then he must be killed," was Oron's opinion.

Thos laughed loudly. "There are many leaders in the world!" he reminded the Wolf, slapping the young barbarian on the back. "Will you kill all of them if they do not agree with you?"

Oron did not smile. "I would not kill them for not agreeing with me," he told the giant. "But if they do not treat me as a man, if they barter with me unfairly, then they deserve to die. If they take without giving, if they do not know justice to treat a man or a woman as they themselves would be treated, then they should be killed. Ilgar, my chief, was a fair man. All before him were equal. All had skills, all had voices, and none was better than any other, although all were different. If I am a leader, it is because I can lead—that is my skill—not because I am better than other men."

Thos's eyes narrowed and he studied Oron for a long moment. "You have a gift," he said after a while. "You see things clearly, whether they are in sunlight or in darkness. But others do no see things that way."

"Then they must learn," Oron said.

Saldum added, smiling obscurely, "or you will kill them?"

Oron grinned frankly at the sorcerer.

The hunters began to return with their bounty. Some had felled fowl, others had gathered fruit. Three, together, had slain a deer and carved it up. Only Sathen returned with nothing.

Thos was outraged.

"Do you not know how to hunt?" he growled at the man. "Do you not know how to pick and gather? Are you a fool?"

Sathen kept his distance from the giant but shot back, "I am not one of you! I am not crossing the river!"

Thos bellowed at him. He demanded to know why.

"Oron is not my leader," Sathen replied snidely. "I do not travel with the slave of a sorcerer! I am free! I will not go with you!"

Thos drew his sword and levelled it at Sathen. He was a good distance away, but all there knew that if the giant moved, Sathen would not have time to escape the thrust.

"Viper," Thos charged him coldly. "You will go. You are one of us, and you will learn that you are one of us."

Oron said nothing. Sathen was poison, he knew that, and he would have preferred to leave the dog behind. But it would do no good to argue with Thos in front of their men, so he did not interfere. Yet when a poison infects a body, it is better to remove the poison, not keep it in and hope that it will become part of the body.

"You are one of us," Thos said again, louder than before, challenging Sathen. "And you will come with us. Dog."

Sathen did not move, but only stared at the giant.

The fortress had been built into the side of the

mountain, upon a wide plateau. This plateau, by unknown demonic hands, had at the beginning of Time been fashioned into a courtyard. It was as wide as any barbarian village and flanked on both sides by tall walls that extended from the mountain to the edge of the plateau. Tall poles with lit torches atop them lined the walls, and in the center of the courtyard was a wide circle—as wide as six men stretched head-to-feet—with a huge seven-pointed Star in its center. Mosutha knew that sorcery had been worked in this courtyard by giants of the ancient days, and that huge flying demons had been able to spot the Star in its circle from the clouds.

At the end of the courtyard, carved out of the mountainside, was a gigantic idol of Ernog, as tall as the tallest tower of the fortress. Ernog sat, flanked by two rows of buildings, with hollow eyes and horned bald pate, staring down upon the courtyard and, beyond the courtyard, into the endless forests and lower mountains that led to the far Nevga River itself. Huge idol. Carved of rock. More ancient, perhaps, than the Nevga herself. An idol of a demon-god, one of the first on the earth, built long before men had ever been fashioned from clay and mud and infused with the flame of life.

On both sides of the idol a series of wide stairs led up to the fire pot that Ernog, in his squatting cross-legged posture, held in his hands. This fire pot burned with an endless flame, and into it living victims had once been hurled. Fed by oils dumped into it by Mosutha's acolytes, the flames of the pot roared and leaped as an inferno, washing the rock visage of Ernog with heat and smoke.

Mosutha made obeisance to this idol three times a day—at morning, dusk, and at night. And every night when he raised his prayer to Ernog he watched where the moon in the dark heavens made its quick circuit. The sorcerer measured that moon, month after month, as he had done scrupulously for nearly a year. Soon, that moon would wax full, and it would shine on a certain night directly between the horns of Ernog's statue: the Isofodis Moon. On that night, Mosutha would cast into the flaming fire pot cartload after cartload of barbarian victims. They would scream, their bodies would writhe and burn and pile, smoking, to the rim of the fire pot. More would scream as they were slain upon the arms of Ernog, their blood drooling down the arms and legs to collect in the basin at Ernog's feet.

Flames, and blood.

For on that night, when the wagonloads of men and women were slaughtered, Mosutha would shriek his mightiest prayers to Ernog, he would bathe in the pool of blood, and he would call Ernog's spirit up from Hell to rule the earth.

And Ernog's spirit, a vast shadow of gas and heat and death, would rise from its pit in Hell and cover the world, while Mosutha, dressed in robes of gold and reborn by the blood and the flames, would rule the lands of men from this mountain fortress as the most powerful sorcerer since the arch-demons of the Dawn.

This afternoon, as his dozens of acolytes lined up before the courtyard walls, and as Sarit watched from the steps that led from the main tower into the yard, Mosutha made his prayer. The sky was cloudy. The huge visage of Ernog stared down at him, and in the wide courtyard of the plateau Mosutha the wizard was a small insect before the mountainous idol.

He stepped into the circle of the Star and burned incense at an altar, lit flames at each of the seven points of the Star, lifted his arms and bowed thrice to the demon, then, in a screaming devotion to the cloudy skies, to the flaming fire pot, to the titan of evil, Mosutha swore his pledge.

Mosutha, the first man in four thousand years to enter this mountain, walk the fortress, revive the prayers of evil—to try, willfully, to resurrect upon the earth the powers of Hell that had commanded the lands at the beginning of Time. . . .

"O Ernog!" Mosutha's voice lifted in the courtyard, and it was a pitifully small, frail and shallow voice—the voice of a man, rebounding between the walls of the courtyard like the mewing of a child lost in the vastness of a forest. "O Ernog!"

But is was a sorcerer's voice directed at Hell—and Hell heard. . . .

"O Ernog! The time approaches! Grow angry with mankind! Resurrect your power! Bring upon the lands your smoke and flame and anger! Rise up from Hell! The Moon approaches and I know you grow strong! Invest me with your strength, O Ernog! O evil from the birth of Time, come up from Hell and reign with your glory and your darkness and your sorcerous wrath!

"Reign, sorcery! Reign, Ernog! And make of mankind again dust and nothing! Turn back the wheel of time and lift back the veil of eternity, O Stars, O Moon, O Ernog of Hell! Lend me power, O Ernog!

"Reduce man my enemy to blood and smoke! And let sorcery reign upon the lands and the villages and the cities of the men of swords and laws and tribes! *Reign, Ernog! Reign, sorcery! Reign, Mosutha!"*

As the soldiers gathered to move out with their wagons and force the first rough path into the mountain steepness, Hukrum made his move to escape. With a grunt and a lurch he rolled against the bars

156

and broke them. He pulled them down from their recesses at the top of the cage and dropped them to the ground.

The gap left by the two bars allowed Hukrum to pass through, but only by grunting and stretching the bars on either side to the near-breaking point. His bulk crashed through and in a furious moment Hukrum fell to the ground—even as the wagon jumped forward—and scrambled for freedom.

With cries and yells the others in the cage followed him, pouring out in a mismanaged wave of legs, arms, heads—

"Prisoners! Prisoners have broken free!"

Instantly soldiers on horseback galloped to the wagon, and the caravan was thrown into utter confusion. A chorus of demonic screams rose from all the other prisoners. Soldiers drew out their blades and slapped at the bars of the cages, trying to quiet the frenzy. Twenty horsemen surrounded the shattered cage, ran down the escaped prisoners, and battered them with the butts of their swords, forced them to return.

It was over quickly. Those who had managed to gain freedom had not gone far. Forced back against their cage and surrounded by drawn swords and dancing hoofs, they were pushed back in.

All save one.

The robed acolytes had hurried to the cage, eager to slay any who resisted recapture. The prisoners, weak from lack of food, and dispirited, offered little fight. Slapped, beaten, pushed, and thrown, they crowded back into their cage whining, growling, and licking their wounds, as new poles were quickly fashioned and put into place.

All save one.

And one of the acolytes noticed.

As the wagon was repaired and the caravan began its trek again, that acolyte held behind. He hid himself behind a tree and watched, patient and angry—watched the thick bushes and large rocks that crowded the slope of the mountainside. A prisoner was hidden there, and the acolyte knew it, so he waited, patiently, for the man to show himself. . . .

Sathen went with them.

Oron led one of the rafts and Thos the other. With Oron came Uira, Saldum, and the cowardly Sathen. Uira and Saldum crouched in the center, while Oron and the warriors braced themselves along the sides of the raft and variously shoved across the current with their poles and managed rudely to steer. Where rocks jutted above the foam of the quick Nevga, their poles were necessary to fend themselves away lest they smash.

The current pushed them swiftly westward, but nothing could be done about that. They would land where they would land, then search along the opposite bank for the direction taken by the slavers.

The afternoon darkened with the gloaming storm clouds that were moving in. As the rafts bounced and jostled on the thick waves of the dark river, sprinkles of rain began to fall, and hardier winds blew upon them, driving them farther to the west.

"Lie back," Mosutha instructed Sarit. "I will light the incenses."

Nervous, she did so. Her bed was in a closet, a small antechamber connected to Mosutha's larger apartment. Comfortable in a silken robe, Sarit closed her eyes and sought to calm herself, as Mosutha quietly made his way to the several incense braziers placed about the room. Each one he filled with powder and lit, intoning a chant as he did so. Very soon the room filled with a thick haze of smoke; it had a pungent, sweet odor to it.

"You will feel yourself beginning to drift away," the sorcerer told Sarit. "Concentrate on the sound of my voice. I will not make the journey with you, but I will be here and I will feel you. You can tell me what you see. I will instruct you. It will not take long."

Sarit was very pleased that Mosutha trusted her enough to send her spirit on this journey. He might have done it himself, and more efficiently, but she knew that he was testing her, in a way. Surrounded by enemies, it would be to the sorcerer's advantage to have as many strong allies as possible with him. Sarit could become his ally, as much his ally as his paramour, if she was strong enough and learned quickly enough.

"What do you see?" Mosutha whispered to her.

She opened her mouth to speak; her eyes were closed and her voice was very quiet. She thought that she was still resting in the chamber, but as Sarit made to speak, she realized that she was not in the closet, and no longer on her bed. She did not feel her mouth moving, nor recognize the voice that came as her own.

"I see light," she replied softly. "I am light. I see a bright thread."

"Follow it," were the sorcerer's instructions. "Follow the thread."

Feeling as insubstantial as a ghost or a vision, yet aware of herself, Sarit did so. The moment she told herself to follow the thread, it seemed that she almost became the thread: a bright white light. All around her was darkness. Then the darkness separated into dimness, and vague impressions.

"Where are you, Sarit?"

"I am in darkness. . . . No. I am free. I am above

the trees. I am looking down at the river."

"What do you see?"

"I see two rafts. They are damp, they are shadows. There are men on the rafts, with poles. They hate you."

"Who are they?"

"I do not know."

"Is it raining?"

"Yes. Raining. . . ."

"Let the rain dampen you, glide down softly with the rain. Hover with the mist. Find out who these men are."

She did so, but felt herself becoming very heavy. "I will fall into the river," she whispered, frightened.

"You will not fall into the river. Hold on to the white light, it will not let you fall into the river."

She hovered above the rafts.

"Who are they?" Mosutha asked her.

"They are barbarians. They hate you. They are hunting for you."

"What are their names?"

"They are speaking. It is difficult to listen. The rain makes me feel too wet to hear them clearly. One of them is called Thos. He is a large man. On the other raft is Saldum, one of your acolytes. He hates you; they tried to harm him."

Mosutha was surprised at this knowledge. "He has abandoned me?"

"He wants to see you die in flames. Wait. . . . He is speaking to a man whose strength makes a strong aura. The man is named Oron."

Mosutha let out a slow hiss.

"There is a woman with them. Wait. Her name is Uira and she has a secret. . . . I can feel the glow of her secret."

"What is her secret?"

"The Star . . . the element . . . it is in her belt."

"The Star?"

"She has stolen it from Du-ubas."

Mosutha grunted. He moved from his seat and grasped Sarit's hand. "She has the Star? You are certain of this?"

"She knows that it is powerful, but. . . . Wait. There is a man with them. He hates them, he glows red."

Mosutha squeezed her hand powerfully. "Help him," he ordered Sarit, his mind suddenly racing with determined tension. "They cannot have the Star!"

"He is pushing the raft with a pole."

"Tell him to lift the pole."

"How can I do that?" she asked in her quiet, nervous voice.

"Make him lift the pole and strike the woman. He will take the Star and leap into the river."

"How can I make him do that?"

Mosutha glanced around the room. Quickly he took a torch from the wall and lay it in Sarit's hand. "Do you feel this?"

"It is very heavy. . . ."

"It is the pole. Lift it."

"I am lifting it. I am striking the woman."

"Dog!" Oron howled at Sathen.

The coward was as shocked by his action as Oron was; the hate in his heart seemed to have erupted by no plan or device of his own. There was a mad light in his eyes.

Uira shrieked and tried to back away as the pole fell with an air-smacking sound and crashed into the logs of the raft at her feet.

Quickly Saldum threw himself toward Sathen.

But Oron got hold of him first.

From the other raft. Thos yelled something.

Sathen tried to escape. He dropped to his knees, released the pole, and drew his sword. "Give me the Star!" he shrieked at Uira.

Oron growled and grabbed his arm. The sword shivered in Sathen's grasp and almost sliced Oron's leg.

"There is violence. I am not strong enough."

"But the Star? The Star—?"

Oron nearly ripped Sathen's arm from its socket. The sword dropped with a clatter to the riverwashed logs of the raft.

Thos was screaming from the other raft.

Saldum, angry, lifted his hands and grabbed hold of Sathen.

"You will not—!"

Instantly, the acolyte shrieked, as fiery pain grew up his arms and burst in his head.

Gasping, Sarit sat up in her bed. She choked on the thick incense fumes; her pale body was coated with sweat. "It broke . . . it broke!" she sobbed.

Mosutha held tightly onto her arm. The torch slipped from her hand and fell to the floor.

"Saldum!" she shrieked.

"What? What?"

"He touched me. I felt pain! The light. . . . I came back!"

Quickly, Oron picked up the sword. Grabbing Sathen by the throat, he stared into the man's eyes. "Dog—!"

Sathen screamed, "The St——!"

Then the blade slipped through his belly and Oron

tripped him over the edge of the raft, into the foaming black waters of the Nevga. A trail of blood and intestines spread quickly on the waves. Sathen, still alive, screamed terribly and tried to swim, floundering in the water.

Frozen, Saldum sat in the center of the raft. "Mosutha. . . ." he groaned.

Uira crouched beside him and rubbed his hands and arms, which were cold as ice.

"What happened to him?" Oron asked the acolyte.

Breathless, Saldum told him, "Too sudden . . . Mosutha tried to grab him. I don't know. . . . What—what is the star?"

Oron shot a look at Uira, who understood. "It is something," she told Saldum, "that I stole from the hut of Du-ubas, a shaman."

"Du-ubas?"

"I killed him," Oron told the acolyte.

Uira removed the Star, the amulet, from inside her belt and showed it to Saldum.

"Gods of the gods!" he breathed. "Do you know what this is?"

Behind them, in the water, Sathen shrieked insanely. Oron turned, all faces turned, to see, far out in the river, Sathen—ripped—shrieking—his body lifted far into the air by a long, dripping head. Yellow eyes. Jaws drooling blood. In the mists it looked like a wet, moving tree limb, gigantic.

"A serpent!" Oron breathed.

The screams ceased abruptly, and Sathen's shattered corpse was drawn back under the waves by the yellow eyes, the long neck.

Saldum held the amulet in his hand. "Do you know what this is?" he repeated in an astonished tone. Looking up into Oron's eyes, he said, "This belongs to Mosutha! It is ancient! He wishes to call up a demon, he wishes to unleash Ernog upon the world! And this amulet is the demon's! It is Ernog's! It is older than man! We can *destroy* Mosutha with it! We can destroy him, Wolf! By the very power he wishes to control, we can slay Mosutha himself!"

On the opposite shore, far up on the bank, where the land sloped rockily up into the mountain steepness, dusk settled and Hukrum carefully came out of his hiding place. He had waited a long time, until all was silence, until the wagoncarts had disappeared far, far up the mountain.

He was alone, and safe.

Now, running from behind the protective boulders and shrubs, he hurried down the gravelly way toward the far shore—toward the river, and his nephew.

He heard a noise behind him. Growling, Hukrum turned, doubling up his fists. Some animal? Another escaped barbarian?

"Fool," said the robed man.

Hukrum screamed, tried to run, stumbled, and got up. He could not believe. . . . He tried to run.

"Die," said the robed man, lifting his arms.

10

"It is a lake of gold," Hanmor told his three retainers. "Hidden, somewhere, inside this fortress. Or deep below it."

They were young men, all of them, and they listened carefully to their chieftain, displaying confidence and self-righteousness.

"Our raiders will return in two days," Hanmor continued. "Maybe less. I want that gold before they return. Otherwise, I know the sorcerer will cross us."

His retainers appeared uneasy.

"His power disturbs you?" Hanmor asked them. "I know what you're thinking. But there is Mosutha, there is his mistress, and there are no more than twenty-five of the robed little devils floating around. How many of us? Sixty here—and, let us assume, at least half the men of the slave-caravan, who still live, if they're men at all and know how to defend themselves. If you're taken by surprise it doesn't matter what got hold of you, whether it was a sword or whether it was some kind of rancid magic. Remember that. These bastards die just like everyone else. But it won't serve our purpose to just kill and steal. I don't want *any* of our men to die, although the stupid ones will blunder. But these little bastards in the robes—kill them. Other than that, we're wolves in the forest. Understand?"

His men grunted.

"Now find it," Hanmor ordered them. "Find the lake of gold. Or the secret place where he keeps all the gold he has. It's a room or a cavern. Find it, tell me where it is. Then we'll start running it outside, moving it into the forest."

The three slapped their chests and, without a word, hastened out to begin their work.

Hanmor the war-chief sat alone and silent, emptied his cup of wine, and stared at the gold scarab amulet in his hand. . . .

Trust, and strong weapons. Indeed. Words. Words.

Hanmor was tired of words, and tired of sorcerers. He was hungry for gold, hungry to avenge the deaths of two good men. And hungry for the deaths of all sorcerers. . . .

Night.

So that none, in a fit of doubt or fear, might escape across the river while the others slept, Oron and Thos had the rafts speedily dismantled when the opposite shore was gained. Then small fires were lit and two sentries posted at the perimeters of their small camp to watch and listen for anything untoward.

All were exhausted. The sentries would have to be alternated frequently, for everyone deserved his share of rest. But now, as the watchers stood just outside the light of the campfires, and as Uira and the men slept off their fatigue, Oron and Thos, tireless, sat up listening to the story Saldum told them.

"The fortress you go to raid," he explained to them, "is a very ancient temple. It was created thousands and thousands of years ago by demons and brutes—unhumans under the direction of Ernog. Ernog is a mighty demon. He sleeps now in Hell. But just as the gods can be called down by men, so too can demons be called up, and this is what Mosutha intends to do. Mosutha hates the people of the Valley. Long ago he was a shaman—to what tribe, I do not know. But he was banished for trying to work strange magicks. He traveled—far, far south, into the swampy regions of Kostath-Khum, beyond even where the mighty Serir divides the world in half, where its waters plunge down falls as large as the Nevga, where the waters of the river empty into a basin to create an ocean that stretches forever, to the stars."

Oron had never heard of such a river; he had never heard of such a land as Kostath-Khum.

"It took Mosutha many years to journey there, and for many years he lived with the devils of that land, and learned their magic. He told me, and his other acolytes, that he discovered there the secret of the ancient demon-gods. They had once ruled all the earth, and the gods battled them. When the gods defeated them, they then created human heroes on earth and tribes and societies. That is where all of us come from. But some of the early men stole away from the gods and lived with demons, and kept magic alive. There is good magic, and there is evil magic. Mosutha discovered the secrets of these old sorcerers, and with them he will call up Ernog's spirit from Hell. With Ernog, Mosutha can destroy the Valley. Perhaps he can destroy the world."

"The world is very big," Oron pointed out. "No one can destroy the world, except the gods. Perhaps."

"Ernog is very old and very powerful," Saldum assured the Wolf. "The world is huge. I have heard that the world is so big that no man, no matter how fast he traveled, could journey around the world in his lifetime, even is he started walking when he was a babe."

Oron didn't believe him. "It can't be that big," he disagreed. "When things become too big, they fall apart. Why doesn't it fall apart?"

Saldum chuckled at the comment, because everyone knew that the world rested on gigantic mountains a thousand times larger than the mountains surrounding this valley. But Thos was becoming impatient. "Tell us more about Mosutha," he grunted. "How to kill him."

"His sorcery," Saldum told him, "is very strong. You must understand about sorcery. The shamans of the tribes do not know about sorcery. They do not know about magic. Men use magic and sorcery for the same reasons they use swords and knives—for protection, to get what they want, for vengeance, to hurt people. The brain that uses a sword can also use magic. But men are new and swords are new, and magic is very old. It succeeds because it is old, just as swords and men succeed because they are new."

"You use magic," Oron said to Saldum. "How do you make it happen?"

"There is outer strength and there is inner strength," Saldum told him. "You, Oron, and you, Thos, are strong outside. But you could not succeed with your strength outside if you did not have strength inside. Yet you concentrate your thoughts upon your outside strength because you were raised as hunters and warriors. I was born to be a shaman and a magus. Because I hungered to know wide things, I wandered, and when I met Mosutha he promised to teach me such things. He taught me about inside strength. I have outside strength but it is not as great as yours, Wolf, or as great as Thos's. Yet my inside strength is greater then yours. Your hearts are strong; my mind is strong. You know the world that surrounds you, the forests and the rivers; I know the forests and the rivers, the stars, and the beings that dwell within me. Each of us has a world within him, and if you choose to explore it, it is the same as exploring the world around us. There is fire there, and the mind can be as strong as steel. If you attack me with your sword, Oron, I can stop you with my mind. That is sorcery: the mind, the inside strength, which is as strong or stronger than outside strength. Your sword is as strong as a mountain; my will and mind are as strong as the force that caused the mountain to be. You use steel; I use magic."

Oron considered this for a long time. He was intelligent, insightful, aware; he had common sense. He wondered if he could learn these things.

"You could," Saldum assured him, "but you must learn from men like Mosutha, who know these things and use them for evil. You must speak to demons, if you use these things; you must send your spirit away from your body and bring it back; you must deny your body many things to make your mind great and strong. Would you do this?"

Oron replied firmly, "No, I would not. I am a man. I have my sword."

"And I am a man, Wolf," Saldum reminded him. "And here is my sword." He held up his hand, and was silent for a moment. His hand and forearm glowed with a blue radiance, which eventually ebbed and vanished.

Thos swore quietly.

"Yet there are things I will not do," Saldum told Oron and Thos. "I will not call up demons or spirits of the night or of the ancient grave, because they can eat your naked soul if you are not careful. I am a man, not a demon. Mosutha has become a demon. They have eaten his soul, and he is damned."

"His demons will not protect him when I kill him,"

Oron said certainly.

"No. They will not. But you may have to fight his demons to get to him."

Thos was becoming impatient again. As entertaining and instructive as some of this was, it veered from the point. He would worry about demons when he faced them. When he did, he would gut them or throttle them, the way he would any animal. But for now, he wished to know solid things. "How far from here is Mosutha's fortress?" he asked Saldum.

The acolyte held up a pair of fingers. "Two quick days. Into the mountains, and up. You cannot see his fortress from here; it is well hidden. But it is there."

"And is it protected by demons? Or are there more soldiers?"

"More soldiers. Mosutha hired the army of a mercenary chief named Hanmor to raid the villages and bring him captives."

Oron did not know the name, but Thos swore efficiently and crudely. "Hanmor! He is a dog from the south," the giant explained to the Wolf. "A madman. He used to harry the barter trails, until he was driven out. That was two summers ago."

"He has been hired by Mosutha," Saldum told them. "He has at least a hundred men under him there, more in the caravan."

Oron grinned evilly. "Something less than that," he commented with pride. "I emptied the guts of several of them."

"I lopped off a few heads, too," Thos growled. "But Hanmor's a bastard, Oron. Born of a she-viper and a dog, and he's cunning."

"Perhaps," Saldum mentioned.

"How do we get into his damned fortress?" Thos wanted to know. "Is there a secret way?"

"None," Saldum reported. "There is an open

plateau before it, which is protected by tall walls. Beyond the walls are the sides of the mountain."

"Then we climb the mountain," Oron interjected, "and jump in."

"It'll be something like that," Thos agreed. We'll use fire to burn them out."

"You will need a lot of fire," Saldum warned them. "It is a large fortress. As big as the Nevga is wide."

Thos's brows lifted and Oron let out a low whistle. Was Mosutha a giant, indeed, to possess such a large fortress and mountain? Surely Saldum exaggerated.

"And," Saldum told them, "there is a cave full of gold beneath."

"Gold!" Thos's interest was instantly roused. "Can we steal it?"

Saldum grinned at him. "You could try," he answered. "But you would die in the attempt. There is a foul curse on it. Only strong sorcery—or the death, perhaps, of Mosutha's magic—would let you near it. Nevertheless, it is gold. . . ."

Gold. . . .

In the middle of the night, the first of Hanmor's three recruits discovered the cave of cursed gold. Armed with the sword at his side and his sizzling torch, he wandered through the closed damp bowels of the mountain fortress, breathing damp rank air that threatened to extinguish his torch, it was so heavy and thick. He followed first one corridor, then another, circling around maddeningly, he discovered, when he began marking walls with a piece of soft stone to help him with his way.

At last, he came to one of the many converging tunnels deep below and found that he'd circled around again. This time he took the path other than the one he had previously marked with his stone.

He was surprised when, within just a few moments, the tunnel floor led steeply downward. The earth beneath his feet became so slippery that he nearly skidded and fell. Thrusting his torch forward, he saw two things: first, that the steepness led to a wide, roughly hewn series of stone steps, and second, a quick movement just ahead of him. A quick glimmer of shadow or light just outside the reach of his torch's brightness.

Animals, he thought. Rats, or serpents, or bats, this far down. Perhaps, even, a wolf or a dog of some kind, trapped down here, very hungry—and maybe transformed by sorcery, or age and illness into something more than an ordinary wolf or dog. . . .

He drew his sword for protection, shifting his torch from his right to his left hand. Proceeding very cautiously down the stone steps, he held the torch before him and moved it around and around, so that anything in front of him would reveal itself to the firelight before it had a chance to surprise him.

He saw no more moving shadows, however; no more glints of light. But at the bottom of the stairs he came upon a vast tableau that stole his breath and started his heart racing.

Gold!

A roomful of gold. A cavernful of gold. Ornaments . . . chairs . . . crowns . . . trinkets . . . armbands . . . spears and weapons . . . and sceptres and chains—all of gold, purest gold, brilliant gold. The light of all that gold, reflecting back at the recruit from the shining brightness of his torch-flame, dazzled him and momentarily blinded him. He stepped into the cavern, partly feeling his way, and looked about for a sconce or some cleft in the rock wherein to place his torch.

He felt something moist at the back of his neck.

Dripping.

Reacting, he turned around quickly, pivoting on his boot heel, and brought up his sword.

He screamed.

His sword sank into something insubstantial, and he was thrown back against the cavern wall as the wet cold slipped swiftly up his sword arm. He dropped his torch; it rolled, breaking into a thousand flaming coals on the earth.

By the fragmented light of that torch, he saw his sword, still in his hand, turn instantly into rust, and saw the flesh of his arm dissolve until only gray bone protruded from the sleeve of his leather jerkin.

He screamed again, screamed even as the wet cold, jellylike, jumped upon him and in the darkness covered him over, sucking and dripping.

Oron heard the shifting of the latest sentries, and knew by them that fully half the night had passed. Still, he could not sleep. He was excited by too many things, and too many imaginings and emotions kept him awake and alert.

He was the Wolf, and he was a leader of men. He was battling sorcery, an enemy so impossible that barely a week ago, he had never dreamed of such a thing, such an enemy, such a world. So much had happened, and so quickly, that he had begun to doubt himself, to doubt that he really was.

Yet, as he thought, trying to relax so that he might sleep and rest, Oron remembered strange things that Den-usutus had told him, long ago (it seemed now). Not about sorcery, or monsters, or demons, but about man. About the tribes.

And it seemed miraculous to Oron, when he considered these things now, that man and the tribes of man had ever come about. Certainly it was as miraculous a thing as demons and sorcerers. The people, Den-usutus had told him, at the beginning of Time were not as we know them now. They had no weapons and they ate little food; they fought amongst themselves and made the gods angry. So the gods had scattered the men and women they had created, sending some to the south, dispersing others to the east, forcing more into the far northlands where there was only snow and ice. Man, thought the gods, by this stern measure would either die out or learn to survive and prosper.

Man prospered. Because they were forced to do so by necessity, the early tribes had learned to help one another, and they taught one another things. To help communicate these things from one generation to another, men developed languages and learned to draw signs on animal hides and carve on rock. They created stories, whereby the truth might be passed on, no matter how fantastic the truth might seem. They built huts, they worshiped the gods and made sacrifices to their gods, they developed clothes as ornaments and, in colder climates, as protection from wind and snow and rain. Women learned to do their share and men learned to do their share. Not always had men been the hunters and women the cooks and raisers of the families; in some tribes women were esteemed as hunters and warriors, while in others some men were good at making clay pots, painting strong signs, and talking good stories.

But as these early tribes progressed and taught and learned and shared, differences invariably appeared. When the tribes became large, they fought within themselves and fractioned. This was the genesis of the two great ancient tribes of the old Nevga River Valley. The tribes had early learned that metal weapons were stronger than wood or bone or stone weapons. They

learned of copper and tin,
iron and then, by experime
learned that they could fashi
different kinds of weapons. S
one weapon, others another,
tribes named themselves afte
while others retained their
bears or wolves or deer.

Even though they w
almost begrudgin
(from Ilgar) to
trust them
they wo
thrill
of

The People of the Ax had l
axes and small, deadly hatche
As their tribe expanded, they came into conflict with
the People of the Sword, who had learned that the
knives they made could be developed into longer
knives, huge heavy knives with long reach and heavy
thrust. Ax and sword both could be used for cutting
down trees, killing animals, slaying enemies.

Great wars had happened. The forests had blazed
with fire, the Nevga had run deep with blood. Heroes,
born, had battled, conquered, created, died. In the
east, men built large nests called cities. In the forests,
the people lived the way they lived since the old days.

As Oron lay there, thinking about these things, it
seemed to him a powerful and a good thing that the
early men had developed weapons and tribes and
laws. He was glad that his tribe was descended from
the People of the Sword. For although those old tribes
no longer existed, there was something good and
strong about heritage; the history of one's people. A
heritage meant a past and, because of that, a future.

He considered this—the heritage of his people in
laws and clothing, in huts and steel. Perhaps men who
became magicians had such a heritage for their ways;
that was why they had such strength, too. Even
though they were evil and had developed their
strengths inside, they were not so different, actually,
from the men who had developed strength outside.

...ere wrong, and evil, Oron felt an ...g respect for them, as he had learned ...o respect strong enemies. Oron did not ... He could not comprehend, really, why ...ld deny themselves certain things—like the ...of the hunt, or the love of a woman, or the laws ...a tribe—in order to hunt down some sun inside them when there was a perfectly good sun already hanging in the sky. But, considering the fact that they must have a heritage, he began to understand how someone like Saldum could be so strong, when his body did not seem strong and he did not know how to use an ax or a sword.

It was intriguing.

Still, they were his enemies. Oron, a man of the sword, and Saldum, a sorcerer. Perhaps one sorcerer and one sword could become comrades, in times like these, but different laws and heritages and tribes would prevent more than that from ever happening. It was almost unfortunate. Oron reflected that no one path, whether by tribe or sorcery, could guarantee that a man was free from evil or recklessness. Mosutha was proof of that, as were his own father and uncle.

Well, then, that was why the gods had created death. That must be why. To cleanse the earth of all foolish, evil people as well as good ones. One worked with what one knew best; the gods did not care. If one made a fatal mistake, then that was the end of him, whether he was good or evil. If one could kill, then one survived. If men could agree and decide on a balance, then it wasn't necessary to kill. Life was not difficult. Truths were simple, if unspectacular.

It was strength that sometimes seemed unjust, and thoughts that seemed sometimes to turn common sense into a wild maze. One learned and dealt with what one knew; one had senses and instincts. The animal seldom died because its instincts failed it; it died because it was ill, or too slow.

Oron fell asleep. As he dreamed of the old days, and the People of the Sword, and dreamed of an ancient wolf howling longingly in the snows of the ancient Nevgan forest—a wolf alone, his ancestor, a wolf with a sword—he lay beside Uira and wrapped an arm around her, and slept.

He did not hear the next changing of the sentries, and he could not know that as those men traded places, the tired going to sleep and others, tired, taking their watchful places, each man looked down upon the sleeping Wolf with respect in his eyes. For laws and steel and tribes can only do so much; it is up to each man and woman to learn for themselves what truth is, and respect—judgement, and balance. And these men, renegades, of many villages, wolves themselves, looked upon the boy warrior and saw in him the strength that once had dwelt within themselves. Another clue to leadership that Oron had yet to learn: A man can only lead when it is the strongest part of him that leads the strongest part in others. Otherwise, his leadership will dissolve, his strength will prove a lie, the rule will corrode from within, and his men will turn upon him.

And even sorcery cannot protect against that. . . .

Unknown to them, dawn was rising high across the mountains and the trees of the world, far above and outside. Yet where they stood, it was the deepest of night, the most ancient of hells.

They saw only the bones of their comrade, and his rusted sword, and the leather and bronze of his armor eaten away in portions as though some powerful acid had feasted there.

"Gold, yes," spoke one, nervously, "but guarded by—"

He grunted, lurching.

His companion, dropping his torch, jumped back and screamed.

Invisible, it took him, dropped him to the ground and dissolved the flesh of his face, burned away the bubbling muscles of his bones, the skin of his writhing body.

The other screamed.

Ran.

Threw himself up the slippery stairs and ran, screamed, shrieked. . . .

Dashed himself against a wall, fell, stared down the tunnel he had taken.

It was there—but he saw only darkness, a glimmer of reflected gold, and heard wet slurping sounds.

"Gods of the—*gods*—!"

He ran on, stopped once to vomit, his throat and stomach burning painfully, and ran on, ran madly, not screaming now but panting, a thousand eaten bones pursuing him, wet cold slime inching up him, his heart pumping, draining sweat, until his slapping feet emptied upon cold air.

He screamed as he fell, stomach jumping, rank fumes biting into his face.

Then all was darkness, and there was no hint to show him where he fell.

Except for the sharp pain in his left hip, and the hot wetness drooling down his forehead.

Deep in a pit, deep into muck and old, un-breathing, swampy waste.

No light to show him what it was that moved toward him, clicking and belching, in the darkness.

No light to reveal to him where his broken leg broke through the shattered and torn skin.

No light—no light to explain to him what it was that suddenly covered his face and head and smothered him like a warm wet pillow, made his eyes pour from their sockets, made the skin of his scalp dissolve like running vomit, made the strong bones of his skull snap and spatter like a hard nut beneath the weight of heavy stone jaws. . . .

She lay, sweating, breathless, a woman suffocating in a warm rain and damp fog.

"Help . . . me. . . ." she whispered.

Beside her, Mosutha slept.

She could not breathe. She was not dreaming. She had fallen asleep, and had awakened again, out of control, in a rainy mist high above the river. The sickening smell of sweet incense was in her brain; she could not repel it.

"Mmmm-sutha-ahh. . . ."

He slept on.

Her fingers dug into the pillows of their bed.

She was suffocating.

As she dreamed it, lived it, she sought to hold on to the white thread that was her life. But she was out of control.

She could not breathe, and she was dying.

"This is Hell," she thought, as she floated above the river. "this is why Mosutha is master of Hell. I am within myself, all is dark, I will be this way forever. This is Hell . . . this is Hell . . . I am the demon of Hell. . . ."

Frantic, her fingers dug into the cushions, lashed out, groped, sank into the flesh of Mosutha's back.

He yelped, and rolled over to strike her.

But he stopped, his hand half-lifted, and looked into her widened eyes and sweating face.

"Help . . . me . . . Mmmm-su-thaaah. . . ."

"Sarit! What have I done?"

He gripped her arms strongly. "Sarit . . . Sarit!

179

Where are you?"

She could barely hear him. "I am . . . fog . . . rain. . . . Helpppph . . . !"

"Return! Do you see the white line? Sarit!"

"I love you! I want . . . to help you! Do not let me sink!"

"Sarit!"

"Do not let me—!"

"Sarit! *Sarit!*"

Her hand dug into the cushions, her eyes stared up, "I am too weak! This is Hell!"

"Sarit! I am here! Feel me!"

I am in the waves! I am in the—!"

"Sarit!"

She lurched. Her body lurched, then fell slack.

"Sarit!" Grabbing her, Mosutha felt her damp flesh, wet with perspiration. He touched her forehead; it was flaming hot.

"Sa-*rit!*" he screamed.

She had been too weak. He had not known. He wished to strengthen her, she was his woman, his mate, he had wished to—

Dim light at his window.

How had she sunk back?

Ernog, *no!*

Yet she was—dead. . . .

The white life of her gone. Her body, dead.

Her spirit, trapped, overpowered, beneath the Nevga. Where, unheard by Mosutha, it screamed, and screamed, and screamed, as it was attacked by sliding things. . . .

She had been too weak. She had wished to help, she had wished to—

But she had been—

"Sarit!"

She had been too weak. . . .

11

Dawn.

They breakfasted on fish caught from the river and on fruit they'd brought with them on the crossing. They spoke little—Oron, Thos, and Saldum not betraying the things they had discussed last night. Uira was silent. Occasionally she and Oron would converse lowly, privately, but since the two of them had come upon these renegades the young woman had tended toward reticence. Oron wondered why.

"I'm listening," she told him in a quiet tone, as they walked along. "I'm listening, and thinking, and remembering. Planning. . . ."

"Are you afraid?"

"Of what we're doing? No. Oron. Not afraid. And . . . that frightens me, a little. Perhaps I should be afraid, but . . . I'm not ready to be afraid. I feel like I'm a ghost. I'm not afraid, but there are strange things in me. I feel . . . very close to you, when we don't speak much. Almost as though I can read your thoughts."

"You . . . understand," was his comment.

"Many things," Uira told him. "Many things. . . ." And she turned her gaze from him to the high wall of forest that rose about them.

Oron looked at it, too—the forest, and the misty

gray pastel of the mountains. He thought again on how large the world must be, and how powerful Mosutha must be. For they had crossed the river, and now when Oron looked upon the forests and mountains on this side of the Nevga, he thought of them as Mosutha's forest and Mosutha's mountains, Mosutha's sky, Mosutha's world.

The morning sun was cool and clear when they came upon evidence of the slavers' crossing: logs discarded on the bank, remnants of fires, picked animal bones. And farther up the bank—

"A corpse!" called one of the men.

Oron stared sharply as Thos and the others began making their way toward it. They gathered around, staring down, then parted to let Oron take a look when he came up.

"Erith and Corech!"

Uira asked, "Did you know him, Oron?"

"It is my uncle! It is Hukrum!" He dropped quickly to his knees and examined the body. It was barely a day dead, if that. Yet there was no mark or wound upon it.

"He is dead," Oron announced gravely. He stood up again, telling Thos and Uira, "He and I parted in anger. He blamed me for a crime, and swore death to me."

Uira understood, remembered, but said nothing. Thos, unconcerned about family rivalries, remarked that it was unfortunate that Oron's uncle couldn't have lived a little longer, for he could have told them things. "He was captured?" the giant asked.

"Yes. And he must have escaped. . . ."

"But he wasn't slain by steel," Saldum commented. The acolyte peered closely at the body.

Thos watched Saldum, but Oron interpreted, "You mean . . . one of Mosutha's dogs slew him with magic?"

"Aye, I mean exactly that." The acolyte bent to the corpse and passed an open hand over the face and chest. "There is still the atmosphere of sorcerous fire here," he explained. "The art was done to this man."

The collected barbarians grumbled apprehensively.

Saldum lifted his hands to his face and rubbed his nose and cheeks—a gesture of tiredness and deep thought. "Do you," he asked Oron, phrasing his words carefully, "wish to know what your uncle learned?"

Oron's gaze was troubled. "You can speak to his shade?"

"He is freshly slain. His spirit, wounded by sorcery, hovers close by. I can return it to his body. I will not," he emphasized, "conjure to use his spirit foully—that is damning. But I can—"

"Bring him back to life?" Thos asked, astounded.

Saldum faced him calmly. "No. I cannot do that. But I can force his spirit back into his body for a short time. It will be painful for him, and he may become difficult to control. But if he knows things, he may reveal them."

Oron showed his teeth. "My uncle was not a man to help others," he said. "He was my blood only by accident. If it will cause him pain—"

"Great pain," Saldum assured him.

Oron gave it a moment's consideration. He saw the look Uira lent him, but nevertheless ordered the sorcerer, "We need to know whatever we can. Do it."

"I will need your help, Wolf. Yours, and Thos's, and one or two others'."

They did as Saldum instructed them. Using their swords, two of the warriors carved a wide circle into the ground and filled it with dry scrub. Inside the circle Saldum dug a seven-pointed Star, fashioned so that its points just touched the circle's diameter. Then he told Oron and Thos to place Hukrum's corpse,

183

spread-eagled, inside the circle, the head toward the top of the star, arms and legs stretched out. "Drive heavy stakes into the ground," Saldum ordered. "One at each wrist and ankle, and one at his throat. We must bind him securely."

The barbarians muttered loudly at this desecration of a dead warrrior, but Oron and Thos did as Saldum told them, breaking strong limbs from trees and driving them deep into the ground, securing Hukrum's lifeless gray flesh to the wood with tight leather thongs.

Saldum watched them silently. Uira hovered near the acolyte, but the others stood well back. When it was finished, Saldum asked to borrow Oron's knife. With it, he cut free the armor from the corpse's chest, then carved a second seven-pointed Star upon Hukrum's breast, as though he were making a tattoo. The acolyte returned the knife to Oron and borrowed flint and steel. He lit the dried scrub in the trough-circle. The flames jumped up quickly.

Saldum gave the flint and steel back to Oron. "Now stand away," he instructed. As the barbarians moved back, Saldum approached the head of the corpse and, positioning himself behind the flames, lifted his arms, spread them wide, placed his hands into the flames and withdrew them.

Uira gasped.

In Saldum's cupped hands danced a small ball of fire. This the sorcerer breathed upon, until its consistency seemed to change from pure flame to a waxy glowing ball, a shimmering orange and yellow sphere.

He hurled the ball into the air, directly above Hukrum's corpse.

The colored flame-ball fell slowly, drifting to rest upon Hukrum's chest in the center of the star tattoo. As it touched the gray flesh, Saldum yelled out a single word:

"Sethid-hu-uhmm!"

The corpse jerked from the ground as if stricken, fought at its bonds, and uttered an ear-piercing, agonized, and utterly hellish shriek.

Positioned around the plateau, the acolytes of Mosutha each pounded regularly and dully on crude skin drums, hammering out a low, coarse rhythm that did not vary, that thundered like the collected heartbeats of a dozen unsatisfied giants.

In the center of his circle, upon the altar that rested there, Mosutha had stretched out the nude corpse of Sarit. It had been coated with oils, its hair decorated with pungent flowers, the lips and eyelids and nipples and nails painted with staining juices.

Mosutha stared at the corpse, and tears flowed down his cheeks.

All around him sounded the pounding of the drums—his anguished heartbeat intensified and magnified by the agony he had suffered. . . .

"Sarit," he whispered, as the tears dripped from his face.

There were two oil lamps on the altar; one at Sarit's head, the other at her feet. These Mosutha lit with a gesture, waving his hands over them so that they sprang to life, firing up instantly.

"Sarit," the wizard whispered quietly. "May your shade now know peace. You served me loyally and you loved me, and I loved you. Daughter of my spirit, lover of my flesh, changeling soul; I did love you, as you loved me, but I could never forget, my Sarit. O lover, I free you now from my magic. Beloved one, I swear that all I do I will do in remembrance of your name, for you were with me through the many long years of love and anguish and turmoil. I free your spirit now, and return to you memories that I took from you when I changed you. Love sustained you, O Sarit. I free your soul now from this body. Fly away, true spirit, and return to what you were before I raised you and trapped you, O daughter of lame Osrith!"

He lifted his face to the skies and raised his arms. "Free her spirit from my command, O Things that Watch and Guard!"

Swiftly, then, the sorcerer swept his sleeved arms over the oil lamps. The breeze of his movement caught the flames, and a line of fire jumped across the altar and across Sarit's pale, beautiful body, joining the lamps. In a moment a shield of dancing fire covered her over, and Mosutha screamed out once more, "Fly, true spirit, I trap you no more! Free her spirit from my command, O Things that Watch and Guard! *Aeior!*"

The flames rose into a tall column. Sarit's body, untouched by the fires, nonetheless was reduced instantly to its skeleton, the flesh withering in a moment, the bones browning and streaking. And within the tall column of flame appeared a strange figure—sinisterly human, but a pale and almost transparent creature of unearthly beauty, with burning eyes, red mouth, and the figure of a woman, the appearance of a sylph or an elemental.

"Fly, now!" Mosutha ordered it. "I have freed you, and you are Sarit no more, but your true self!"

The thing hissed within the column of fire and slowly faded as the flames of the pillar shot toward the sky and evaporated. Upon the stone altar there remained only the browned, distorted skeleton of a deformed, hunchbacked peasant woman. . . .

The drums beat, beat, beat out their pulse, guiding the freed spirit on its way.

And deep beneath the Nevga only the waters flowed. The entities there no longer harassed Sarit's confused, human spirit. The dead body, freed of its magic, burned, and the true spirit, beautiful in itself, vanished and knew no more pain.

"I . . . am . . . *dead!*" Hukrum's corpse shrieked, as it thrashed at its bonds. "Gods, *gods,* set me *free,* I am in *agony!*"

Saldum showed no expression. He did not seem alarmed or terrified. He lifted his hands, not touching the ring of flame, and announced to the corpse, "I have brought you to earth again! Your soul is damned, man of the tribes! I will free you, I will release your shade if you will—!"

"*Save me!*" shrieked the corpse, writhing and bending. "I am burning! Oh . . . *gods!* I am being tortured! I feel my bones! My brain is afire! My shade is heated on coals! I vomit dust!"

Oron stepped forward. Maintaining his distance from Saldum and the flames, he nevertheless came close enough to yell, "Hukrum! Can you hear me? Do you know me? It is Oron!"

"I am *dead!*" howled the corpse. "What flames are these? Shadows come at me! What hell do I see before me now!"

Oron snarled at Saldum, "He does not know us! He cannot even hear us!"

Saldum cast him a brooding glare. "It is true. The sorcery has touched him too deeply. His spirit must have been very weak, indeed. His shade is mindless."

"Destroy it," Oron told him, disgusted. "It can do us no good. Send it back to where it was."

"Yes," Saldum agreed gloomily. "Yes. . . ."

"I am in flames!" shrieked the corpse, fighting against its bonds. "What am I? Where am I? Gods

. . . *gods* . . . protect me from those . . . *things!
Aie!"*

Saldum quickly circuited the flames, throwing loose
dirt upon the fire to suffocate it as he did so. That did
not seem to affect the screaming corpse in the least,
but it allowed the acolyte to step nearer. Kneeling
above the howling dead man, Saldum made motions
with his hands, and from the star on the chest there
rose the many colored ball of flame. It lifted up,
glistening and sparking, and Saldum ordered it (in
some strange tongue) begone. It did so, as though by a
will of its own, evaporating or disintegrating into a
trail of black smoke.

As the flame-ball died, Hukrum's corpse ceased its
mad shrieking and relaxed upon the ground—the tattoo on its chest blistered into a hideous hard scab.

Oron looked grimly to Thos. "Bury it. Have some of
the men bury it."

The giant, very shaken by what they had done,
nodded and pointed to a few men.

Oron stared at Saldum, but the acolyte was walking
farther up the bank. He sat down heavily in the dirt,
lifted his arms to his raised knees and sank his head
low in exhaustion. Oron went to Uira who, trancelike,
stared at Hukrum's corpse, even as some of the warriors gingerly grasped it and dragged it off toward the
hole that was being dug. Uira jumped when Oron
touched her shoulder. She stared painfully, deeply, into his cool eyes.

"It was terrible," she whispered to him. "Screaming
like that. . . . Where was he?"

"He was dead," Oron replied starkly. "Dead . . .
and damned. Uira—"

She swallowed thickly, and a mist of fear and terror
coated her eyes.

"Do not think on it," Oron warned her. "That was

188

Hukrum . . . not us. Not your father."

She moved abruptly, throwing her arms about him. She did not weep, but she hugged her lover tensely, holding on to him to remind herself that she was still . . . alive, and in reality.

Oron held her, pulled her close to him, and was a little surprised to find that, despite his outward calm, his arms were shivering as he held Uira to him. . . .

"It has been long enough," Hanmor declared, "to go down a hole and come back out of it, and they have not returned."

The soldier standing before him, though disturbed by the implications of that, was more nervous (at this moment) of his chief's temper, than he was of uncertain, shadowy, sorcerous things.

"Do you trust your sword arm?" Hanmor asked him.

He was a young man, blond-headed—a headstrong bully from the far north. "I trust it, Chief Hanmor."

"You don't want to have your balls cut off, do you, for refusing me?"

"Tell me what to do, my chief. I'll do it."

"Then go down there," Hanmor grumbled. "Get down there, see if you can find them, any of them, or the lake of gold. Take a torch. There's a door behind that tapestry. That's the route the other three took, and they haven't come back that way. They either found something and ran off with it, or they didn't make it back. You understand me, don't you, pup?"

"I understand completely."

"If you run into anything," Hanmor warned him, "make it back here. Don't get yourself killed. I want to know what's going on. If the other three are dead, I can't afford to lose another good man. Just get your ass back here. But bring me something back, if you can. Anything. Gold. I must know if it's there. If it's not—"

The young blond soldier smiled. "Then we stab him?"

"Into little pieces," Hanmor grumbled. "And we feed him piece by piece into the mouth of one of his own hell-spawned demons. Now get going."

The soldier slapped his chest, bowed his head briefly and stepped back, then moved to take down a torch. "This tapestry?" he asked. Hanmor nodded. He swept it aside and looked back a last time. "I'll return, my chief . . . with gold."

"Come back with your life, gold or no gold. I can't afford to lose any more men."

The young fellow smiled and stepped briskly behind the arras.

In Sarit's chamber, Mosutha mechanically piled all her things into a heap on the floor, and four acolytes gathered them into chests, filling them up one after another, and locking them. Clothes, jewelries, bed things, ornaments she had made, pictures she had drawn, cushions she had sewn. . . .

When the final trunk was sealed, Mosutha surveyed the denuded room wistfully. He had saved only one robe, a pair of slippers, some jewelry—memories. He nodded to his disciples. Each took up a large trunk, lifting them effortlessly. The sorcerer led the way from the chamber and down the hallway, down a series of stairs until, deep within the fortress, he came to a large iron door. It opened at a word from him, creaking on old stone hinges, to reveal naught but shadows and shadows within shadows, and cold darkness.

Unhesitatingly, Mosutha advanced, followed by his four acolytes. As the last of them passed through the open portal the great door swung shut behind them, closing with loud reverberations, like the din of a groaning dragon.

They lit no torches nor carried illumination of any kind. With Mosutha leading them, the brilliant-eyed sorcerers made their way familiarly deep into the lower bowels of the ancient, demonic fortress.

Oron led the way up into the mountains, taking charge of the passage through the forest. He said nothing as he moved, and his silence conveyed concentrated awareness, not particularly of the path he took, but of the troubling events that had been suffered so far. Thos, who followed Oron, could appreciate that, but only Uira, who followed close behind them both, could read Oron's mind and understand wordlessly what must be pulsing within him as he somberly, grimly, and determinedly cut the way forward for his men.

The world—Oron's world, their world—had been demolished, and it was not the physical violence that was the most harmful, because that could be dealt with tolerably. But the emotional violence, the deep violence that wounds brain tissue and heartbeat. That was another sort of violence, and far more scarring. It changed life in midstream. It disrupted, brought forth questions that one short life could not answer, and made a mockery of all things that had been held good and strong and true by oneself and those around one. The tribes, the villages, the laws, the intimate lives that were lived and had been lived, generation by generation, sharing knowledge and expertise and genuineness: these things, wiped out, and for no reason. Not even, in the wildest fancies of imagination, for any reason of the gods. The gods did not care. What did it mean? The effect was only to hurl people back into the maw of raw existence. It could not even be called Life, for Life has value, substance, continuity, and when those things are dashed, there remains only existence, and the primordial beginning again, the senseless but practical and necessary rebuilding of the heart and the mind, the values and the genuineness.

And now had it happened? Caused by a sorcerer? A sorcerer who somehow had unleashed a power that, like the power of storms or earthquakes, destroyed whole villages, dismembered lives, demolished all hopes? It had changed all of them, this destruction. It had wiped out what they had once been, wiped out all of it—save for the tenacity, human, to continue existing, existing only by the rawest and most practical methods: by thought, with food, for emotions.

The suddenness of it. The senselessness of it.

Uira realized, and she knew that Oron realized as well, that even if they confronted Mosutha, even when they met this sorcerer, even if they slew him, even if they did that, there would still be no explanation for it. Whatever Mosutha's motivation, it would not be enough. It could not rationalize the destruction—not in a way that was comprehensible to human beings that had built lives, slowly and carefully over many long years, only to have them reduced to rawness.

It had changed Uira in ways she did not like. And it had changed Oron, too. He was strong, he had always in some sense been alone, but he had been changed, now. He had become a leader, but he would have become a leader anyway. But he was grim and hardened, and not in the same way that the life of the tribes hardened a man. He still trusted—Uira knew that, for he trusted her with his heart. But otherwise, he trusted only what he knew, and he would not let that trust any longer extend to dreams, or ideas, or wonders. He could no longer trust his starry nights in the forest, not trust the mountains, nor the stars, nor the river, nor any animals. Uira sensed that. Oron could only trust himself now; his sword, his brain, and eyes, and heart. And it was not good that he should trust only those things. Especially if he was a warrior, and a leader of men.

But Uira knew that she trusted only those things now as well. .

And, she decided, that was why sorcery was evil. Because it reduced men and women to being only animals; sentient and little more: reduced people to being no more than existence, awareness, tension, when it was true—untrustworthy, but true—that people were more than that and had to be more than that.

Killing Mosutha would not be a release or a vindication, but would only trap them more so in this . . . existence. Yet it would have to be done. They would have to kill Mosutha so that they could remain alive, so that they could exist in the trap of life. But that was all the sorcerer's death would insure: that they would continue to exist, raw and harmed, aware, in a world that remained only a shadow of their world.

Mosutha's death could not guarantee them a return to their humanity, to their hearts, to their minds. Those things were gone, burned with the villages, shattered with the death-screams of warriors and women, animals and babies.

Sorcery, Uira realized, as she made her way through the forest, was a very evil thing indeed, because it was not spiritual; the evil destroyed the spiritual. And it had made her, and Oron, and all the rest of those with them, really no better than the shrieking corpse of Hukrum staked and bound to the earth—a corpse screaming madly against things he did not understand, haunted by things he once had been. . . .

* * *

There was a deep well at the very bottom of the fortress—a well, dropping down forever, a hole that Mosutha had discovered one time during the long sojourn of his first lonely years in the place. He had placed a small barricade around it—a stone wall only five bricks high—after making sure that nothing foul came and went by route of it. It was only a well, and if once it had been alive or had been the path of something alive or hellish, it was that no longer.

He ordered his acolytes to drop into this well the chests containing the things that had belonged to Sarit. They did so, and none of them heard how the chests fell, for no sound of their striking bottom ever came to their ears.

Mosutha began the long path back, through damp corridors of solid stone, up stairways that had been reduced almost to sheer pathways—presumably by the passage, ages agone, of demonic things now lost to Hell.

They were nearing the upper levels of these passageways when Mosutha paused in his steps and held up a hand. He said nothing, neither did his acolytes make any sound. But to them carried, after a moment, the noise of approaching footsteps, and soon upon the sound the dim light of some torch or oil lamp.

"I suspect—" Mosutha whispered, then said no more.

He cautioned his acolytes back into the tunnel while the sorcerer himself held to the opening that led into the main corridor.

The footsteps came more loudly, sounding brisk, and the light of the approaching torch was like that of the sun, so bright was it in the utter darkness of the underground.

Mosutha drew in a long, slow breath—a hiss—and

lifted a hand, holding it up beside his head. The fingers were spread clawlike, the knuckles white, the nails talons ready to strike and rend.

He came around a bend, and the full light of the torch burst upon Mosutha like the flare of a comet deep at night.

"Gods—!"

He fumbled for his sword. Mosutha's hand lashed out, caught the soldier's throat, and pushed his head back. The torch fell to the ground and crumbled into a scattering pattern of flaring coals. The boots scraped on the stone earth, the arms reached to fight Mosutha's impossible strength.

And it was over. With a loud ripping and breaking sound, followed by the sloppy wet noise of exploding blood, the head was torn from the shoulders. Loudly, the armed corpse slumped back against the corridor wall, slid, and crashed to the ground.

"Take him," Mosutha breathed harshly, "and feed him to the thing that protects my gold." He stared at the head in his hand, did not recognize it, but gripped it by its long blond hair and, carrying it as he would a package, quickly moved down the corridor, heading for the upper levels of the citadel.

Hanmor was drunk and becoming drunker. Two wine vessels, emptied, lay broken on the floor of his chamber, and the war-chief was well on his way to adding a third to them. His senses were dulled and his reactions very slow when his door was slammed open with a crash. He stared up instantly, pushed back his chair as he got to his feet, and nearly stumbled. His hand went for his sword—then stopped. Looking in the sorcerer's eyes, Hanmor instantly understood that reaching for his weapon would do him little good.

So he leaned forward and rested his bear paws on

the table. He felt his legs shivering uncontrollably inside his breeches. Nervousness. . . .

Mosutha stood, lit by the one bright torch of the room, half in shadow, tall, lean, incredibly sinister. A robe of shadows topped by a half head, white, with yellow eyes. A demon.

"Fool!"

He said it, and it struck Hanmor like a hurled curse. The war-chief ducked, reacting, before hearing the complete word, on the impulse that a death sentence had been returned against him.

But Mosutha said no other word, and made no gesture other than to lift his right arm and display, in the harsh light of the one bright torch, the severed, still-dripping head of the blond young soldier. He let Hanmor stare at the trophy for a prolonged heartbeat, then cast it forward. The head struck the flags of the floor with a squishy sound and rolled, precisely with the noise of a thick wooden ball rolling upon flat stone.

Hanmor choked something in his throat.

Mosutha sneered and held his hand raised. A bright flame appeared upon his fingers and burned for a few intense moments, then vanished. When it was gone, Hanmor saw that the blood and cruor had been cleaned away from the sorcerer's hand and arm.

Mosutha stepped forward. One pace. His shadow quivered on the flags.

Hanmor made another sound in his throat and began to fall back, but he was drunk, unsteady, and his lurching motion failed and died out. He remained leaning forward, tilted, sweaty hands on the table. He was incredibly frightened. His stomach felt bloated and cramped and he became squeamish. Hanmor knew that he was going to vomit. Just as he knew—suspected, sensed—that Mosutha, by some trick, was producing this sensation of fear so alien to the chief. . . .

Mosutha announced to him, so quietly that an outside breeze would have drowned out the words, "I intend to let this continue no more. Chief, you have—"

He stopped at the sound of footsteps in the hall behind him. He did not turn, but kept his burning gaze full upon the war-chief.

Hanmor knew that the sorcerer intended to kill him.

The steps paused, and Mosutha heard the rustle of flowing robes quiet behind him.

"What is it?"

"Master, the caravan has returned. They await your presence outside."

Mosutha, not moving, stared terribly at Hanmor, as though deciding whether or not to slay the chief before going down to inspect his victims.

Hanmor felt his stomach rumble volcanically inside him, and knew that if Mosutha did not move soon—very, very soon—he would vomit a bellyful of wine upon the table. Very soon—

The sorcerer turned briskly on his heel and faced his acolyte, then went out. His man followed.

The torch sizzled, and Hanmor stood as he was, his stomach gradually, very slowly, calming down until he no longer felt that he would vomit. When that had passed, he sat down—reaching behind him blindly for his chair, pulling it forward a bit, settling his bulk into it. The wood creaked. His leather boots scraped loudly on the stone.

He did not look at the severed head.

Instead, Hanmor placed his hands out before him on the table and studied them. His hands. Large, hairy, battle-scarred. They were shaking uncontrollably. They had never shaken like this in his life.

He was fearless. He had been born fearless, his father had told him that. He did not know what fear was, did not know its effects on the human body. Hanmor had no comprehension of the vomit that had wanted to escape him, of his full bladder that had wanted to explode, of the gas trapped in his bowels that—comically, ludicrously, actually—would have erupted from him, had Mosutha held his pose one moment longer. Hanmor's head ached, his heart raced, and his hands were trembling. All because of fear.

He was afraid.

Mosutha had done it to him.

He was terrified, and it was new to him, and Hanmor could not even think properly, so confused was he, so lost in this new, wild maze of a strange emotion.

He was afraid.

And Mosutha had won.

The sorcerer had the stronger weapon, and Hanmor understood that now, and he was afraid. He became filled with revulsion—at himself—and then with anger. Incredible anger. Incredible wrath, at the man—*was he a man?*—who just a moment ago had stood, a shadow with a white head, at that doorway, on that floor, staring with the stare of a demon, quivering with the strength of hellish nature.

Wrath: Fear turned to insatiable anger.

Hanmor stared at his shaking hands. In his mind's eye, in the hurry of an instant, he envisioned himself groveling like a maniac, then leaping up like a fire storm, all heat and wrath, steel and blood, a bear, a giant, a monster, a demon himself, a warrior.

And, suddenly, he began to laugh. Uncontrollably.

He laughed.

He looked over at the blond head lying on the stones and it was a ridiculous head, it couldn't speak, its eyes were wide open, it was gray and red and black, it wanted to be alive, it wanted to speak, but it couldn't. It had dropped from its body.

Hanmor laughed, howled with mad glee, and could not stop himself from laughing, laughing, laughing. . . .

12

Dusk was heavy upon the forest, the shadows growing, the coolness coming down, when Saldum said, "We are near."

He had moved toward the front of the procession and now was standing just behind Oron, pointing to something obscure in the distance. Either his eyes were keener than the Wolf's, or he was familiar with what he saw.

"What is it?" Oron asked him.

"A warning. We enter Mosutha's territory."

Oron's strong eyes could not make out what the object was, so obscured was it by its distance, the crowded forest, and descending night. But Saldum did not object when he began walking toward it, so Oron assumed that it was not deadly. He loosened his sword in its scabbard, however, as he advanced.

There was a corpse lying just off the trail. It had been nailed to a log with wooden spikes, its throat slashed and the torso and head mutilated. Oron grunted when he saw it.

Behind him, Thos muttered darkly, "That's—what?—the sixth, seventh one since we found Hukrum?"

"Seven," Oron answered. "Could they all have been killed trying to escape?"

"No," Saldum told him. "I would say that they were offered as sacrifices to the spirits here. Appeasement, if you will. Just as I was offered to the river. Mosutha casts a long shadow. . . ."

Oron looked him in the eyes, and Saldum met his stare frankly. "There are more, Wolf." The sorcerer nodded to the object up ahead.

Advancing, Oron made certain that Uira stayed close by him. The light of day was disappearing quickly, although a strong moon had risen to lend them light. But that could prove to be a handicap as well as an advantage. The forest was thinning rapidly as they ascended the mountain, and Oron feared that they might easily be detected from Mosutha's fortress if they advanced boldly across naked rock in the moonlit night.

That thought slipped to the back of his mind, however, as he approached the "object" Saldum had pointed out. It was not a single thing, but three—three more corpses. And not even corpses any longer, but skeletons, hung upside down high on posts, with only the merest wisps of dried flesh still evident. It was as though the wind had eaten them. One of the skeletons had already lost a skull, arm, and leg, and the skull of a second creaked slightly in the breeze.

"Killed by Mosutha?" Oron asked Saldum, unable to disguise the loathing in his voice.

Saldum shook his head. "Not directly. These were among the last of his previous captives, taken from the east. He sacrificed them, but he did not slay them. Some . . . angry spirit of Hell . . . did that. Feasted on them."

An attack of strong emotion gripped Oron, and he tensed. The animal "must" came upon him; the instinct to suddenly run, scurry, move with silent leaps and gliding motions, to find what he would find and rend it with his hands and teeth and feet. To destroy the thing that had destroyed life in this manner—that might perhaps destroy Esa.

But just as quickly, the vital power and vision passed from him, and he was left only with an image: a woman's face, disturbed in his memory by the swift passage of events and fears, but the face of . . . his woman?

Esa. . . .

Oron took up the trek again, and Saldum and Thos, Uira and the others noticed the subtle alteration that had visited their young leader's temper. He had become more . . . wolflike.

Uira held close to him as they moved on, past the skeletons, and stepped into a stony clearing that rose very sharply before them.

"You are thinking of Esa?" Uira whispered to him.

He grunted. "Yes. How can I not?"

Uira touched his shoulder. "We will save her, Oron, if we can."

He glanced at her and saw something like a smile trying to form itself on her lips. He attempted to smile in response but didn't succeed very well. Oron's mouth moved jerkily and he managed only a failed sneer, an awkward grin.

His men moved silently behind him, as quiet as the growing root, the sleeping stone, extremely cautious because of the warning corpses and Saldum's sobering words. At the height of the sharp slope Oron paused and crouched, and for the first time beheld the destination of his long quest. Beside him, Uira gasped. Saldum stepped beside the Wolf to announce in a low, grave tone, "There is the fortress."

It was revealed sharply and distinctly for them by the strong moonlight: a tall series of towers and square buildings and ramparts carved directly from the mountainside, settled upon a low, wide plateau flanked on its sides by tall walls and, at the end of the plateau, in the center of the collected buildings and towers, a huge statue; a gargoyle or demon frozen in stone. No bigger than Oron's fingernail, from this perspective, and gigantic because of that. It was obvious that Mosutha's fortress was still quite distant, that it would take fully another half day, at least, to reach it.

Oron judged the best route for approach. He could not tell how the slavers had managed to reach the plateau, for the way seemed perilous for wagons and horses. If there were a passage for the wagons, however, Oron did not want to take it. But if they moved slightly to the east, and advanced then behind those boulders and kept as much as possible within the protection of the thinning forest, they would be shielded. The morning sun, rising in the east, might strike that side of the mountain as it rose and push shadows to help obscure them, and that would improve as the day went on. From the boulders, Oron saw, they could strike westward toward the fortress by climbing up the side of the mountain. If they continued to make use of the shadowed rocks and the clumped areas of trees and scrub, it would be possible for them to very nearly reach the fortress without detection. Surprise, to whatever degree, was a factor.

Musing thus, Oron turned to Saldum. "If we have need for . . . sorcery, or magic," he said, "to help protect us—"

Saldum lifted a hand. "I have already considered one or two methods. They are simple contrivances, but effective. Tell me your plan and I will aid you. But don't take that way to the west—there, in that stony canyon." Oron saw it, now. "That is how the wagons pass. And remember, Wolf, we must work quickly. I told you of the Isfodis Moon. It is soon . . . perhaps tomorrow," he glanced into the sky "for it waxes full and strong."

Oron looked back at his men and announced to them, "We will rest here for the night. The fortress is less than a day off. The mountain will hide our advance, but we'll need our strength. No fires—but I want every man well rested by dawn tomorrow."

"What about sentries?" Thos asked him. "We'll need lookouts."

Saldum offered to act as guard. "I will be up for the duration of the night," he explained. "It will be necessary for me to do so. I must enter into a trance and gather strength to me. Do not be worried, Wolf, I am aware of what goes on around me when I do this. But sleep would only fatigue me more. I must journey inward."

Oron glanced at Thos, but the giant made no comment.

"Do it, then," Oron told Saldum. "I'll be sleeping lightly, anyway. They'll make enough noise if they try to come against us here."

Saldum nodded. Below, the warriors found places to stretch out and rest.

Esa was not asleep. She had not slept since the moment the fortress had come into view.

She suffered their arrival silently and almost objectively, as though she herself were not present, as though what happened occurred to others around her and to another Esa. The carts were led into the open area at the top of the mountain and more soldiers appeared and surrounded the cages. One by one, the captives were let out and chained together. Occasionally one of them was singled out and led away separately. Esa wondered why, since she could not see very clearly from her cage. But the other women with her made remarks about illness and disease, and it struck Esa profoundly that those who had not fared well on the journey were being led away to their deaths.

The release of the prisoners—their escort in single file by the soldiers, chained together, across the plateau to the rocky buildings—continued slowly and agonizingly for most of the afternoon. Frightened as she was, Esa—dissociated as she was—nearly nodded off a few times. But whines and shrieks, growls and savage outbursts from angry male prisoners, kept her alert. She wanted to see what was going on, but at the same time she did not want to.

She began feeling extremely nervous and anxious, however, when the wagon directly next to hers was emptied of prisoners. One sick, coughing man was led away by a soldier—dragged away, literally—too weak to protest. It was while these prisoners were being released that Esa heard the voice for the first time. A strong voice with a strange hollowness to it— "That one. He is not to be with the others." —and Esa looked up, saw a second prisoner dragged away, and in the same moment stared upon the man who had spoken the words.

Tall. Lean—lean to gauntness. Bald, and dressed in a dull, flowing black robe. Deep eyes that seemed to glow. He must be Mosutha.

Mosutha. . . .

The soldiers came to Esa's cage, unlatched it, and took out the first of the women.

Esa watched Mosutha. He was standing only a short distance away, flanked on both sides by a number of acolytes, other men in robes. His stare was centered on the open end of the cage, and as each prisoner was brought out Mosutha studied her, judged, and nodded in one direction or another.

There was a slight breeze blowing. It whispered at the hem of Mosutha's robe, causing the black cloth to move in slight, dry ripples. That, for some reason, seemed to fascinate Esa, in her despondent, spirit-emptied state. She glanced up again and looked at the face of the sorcerer.

Mosutha saw her.

Something happened with his eyes.

Immediately Esa was filled with fright. Mosutha stared at her, studied her, held her with his eyes, and she could not move. She felt as though she were made of clay and straw. Her feelings were drained; the breeze on the plateau touched her blond hair, brushed it against her cheek, and she did not feel it, although she knew it happened.

Then Mosutha looked away, and Esa breathed again.

But she kept her eyes on him. Mosutha never looked at her again, however — not until she, the final prisoner, was dragged from her wagon.

Then he approached and, once more, fixed her with his deep stare. Esa trembled, her legs weakened, and two soldiers grabbed her roughly under the arms to stand her up. She was not able to meet Mosutha's yellow gaze. He touched her, reached a damp cold hand beneath her chin and lifted her face toward his.

As though overhearing a voice from a depth, she heard him say, "This one. Take her up."

And his face disappeared. Esa felt herself being dragged by the soldiers. She could not move her feet, could not move her head. She could not cry, although she wanted to. All the things she had kept repressed for the days and long nights of her captivity reached for escape, but they would not come free. She could not scream, she could not cry, she could not even muster her ebbing strength to make a token effort at resistance.

She knew that she should, because it was not good to go to one's death without selling one's life as dearly as possible. Yet she was too empty.

She was led into one of the buildings, dragged up an endless series of stairs, variously pushed and pulled down a number of long corridors, placed in a room, and dropped on a bed. The soldiers left her. Weakly, Esa sat there, and it occurred to her that she should find some means of killing herself, to save herself from being tortured.

But there was no time. Momently two others entered the chamber: young men, bald, dressed in robes. They said not a word, and although they did not appear men of much strength Esa felt such an effusion of extreme power emanating from them that, regardless of their bland appearances, she knew it would be useless to resist them.

They undressed her. Not roughly, and apparently with no intention of doing her harm. When she was naked, one of them led her into an adjoining room, a large room that—incredibly—held a pool of water in the middle of its floor. Esa was walked to the pool and encouraged to step into it. The water was warm. She wanted to cry as she sank down into it; the water brought life to every ache and scratch and cut she had suffered, but it also laved her swollen and bruised flesh, seeped into her muscles to bring an incredible sense of refreshment and awakening.

The robed man produced some jars for her— "Oils," he said—and some towels, and set them beside the pool. His companion soon returned and set upon a chair a long flowing robe of silk. This one disappeared again and returned as Esa, reluctantly, fearfully, pulled herself from the water and toweled herself dry.

The second man placed a tray of food and a goblet of wine upon a table and motioned for Esa to sit. Holding the towel tight around her, she hesitated.

"Our master means you no harm," the first man said to her, quietly and convincingly. "You are a very fortunate woman. Dress in the robe. Eat. Do not fear poison or any harm. You will not die here."

She was starving. And she did not want to remain nude any longer before these two strangers. She walked to the robe, undid the towel and set it aside, then slowly and carefully pulled on the robe. It caressed her body softly, reminding Esa of how alive she yet was.

Then she ate. Ravenous but wary, glancing peripherally at the two men in the room, she took them at their word. Even if the food were poisoned, she would at least have a mouthful of it before she died. And she was craving for something solid and nutritious.

She ate, and drank. She did not die.

The two robed men stationed themselves at the door of the chamber and watched her as she ate.

When she was finished, Esa pushed her plate and goblet away, held her hands in her lap, and stole a look at her guards. "What . . . what should I do now?" she asked in an almost childish voice.

"Wait here. Occupy yourself. Our master will arrive soon." They grinned at her reaction to that statement. "You will not be harmed," they reminded her. "You will be well treated. You are extremely fortunate, barbarian woman."

Esa stood up. Uncomfortable beneath their eyes, she did not know what to do. But she was curious as to where she was, so she walked to a window. It was unlatched, although the shutters were closed. She opened them, and looked out over the sill.

Below her stretched a wide garden of trees and bushes and, beyond them, the plateau. The wagon-cages were gone, no soldiers or prisoners were in view. The place was desolate, and only early moonlight, cool and brilliant, showed upon the stone.

Esa wondered if she should throw herself from the window. A cool breeze washed up from the trees, fragrant, rippling her robe against her breasts and breathing upon her face and hair.

It almost reminded her of the cool river winds that had come to her in the village.

Stricken suddenly with sadness, she turned to close the shutters, and glanced again at her guards.

They were not there.

Esa gasped.

Before her, silent, alone with her in the chamber, stood the tall, gaunt, yellow-eyed sorcerer who had destroyed her village, killed her aunt, demolished her life, fed her, bathed her, dressed her. . . .

Mosutha.

Hanmor's men were extremely agitated. Collected in the great audience hall on the first floor of the fortress's main building, they were fed food and wine by Mosutha's acolytes. They watched their words, speaking as they ate, but no words were needed to convey what was on their minds.

Gold.

Gold, and escape.

Hanmor observed his men closely and he did not like what he saw. Over a hundred men just come from an exhausting, twelve-day campaign of butchery, crowded now into a warm, torch-lit feasting hall. They were gorging themselves on food and drink. Mosutha knew what he was doing when he'd ordered these men well fed and watered upon their return:

they would be useless for several days, bloated, tired, weighted down. Certainly in no mood to cause trouble.

Hanmor's brow furrowed deeply, and he began to drum his fingers quickly on the table. Narrowly he watched Mosutha's acolytes. They seemed too polite, too attentive and servile. Emptied cups were replaced promptly with full ones, finished trays removed, and plates piled high with steaming meats set in their places. Was it the sorcerer's intention only to make these men slothful and fat for several days? Or were they being lulled into quiescence and contentment, to be slaughtered in the middle of the night?

The war-chief considered it. With the return of his men, he and his army meant nothing to Mosutha. Surely a man with the magical powers the wizard held at his command could destroy the entire troop without much effort. Had he only lured Hanmor on with the promise of treasure? Had Hanmor himself been a fool to sell his men in the first place into the services of such evil? Last winter had been harsh for the mercenaries; many of them had died, few had gotten through the season without falling ill, discontentment had run high. Hanmor was their leader and it had been his duty to find employment for them, and the mercenaries spent gold as quickly and easily as they spent other men's lives. The bargain had seemed a good one, and Hanmor had thought himself the equal and more to any pale, yellow-eyed devil dressed in robes and amulets. But had he been wrong?

There were deaths, cruel and unfair, damning deaths, to prove how wrong he had been.

His mind clicked and worked and imagined, until it became a certainty to Hanmor that this feasting hall would soon be a blood chamber, a sepulcher, before the night was out — unless he took measures to prevent it.

To his right and left sat loyal retainers, men who had not journeyed on the slave campaign. Hanmor knew them to be as alert and chary as he was; he could rely on them.

Pouring for himself more drink, Hanmor waited until one of the slowly circling acolytes passed on behind him, then whispered into the ear of the man at his right, "There are a hundred-and-fifty of us in this room, and we are weaponed. I do not trust the sorcerer. He may try to harm us, while our men feast. Keep your eye on his dogs. Choose one, and watch him. If he looks to betray us—if he leaves the room or seems to make any kind of sign—tell me. We will move against them."

The man heard and understood.

"Tell the one next to you. Alert all of us who have been here in the fortress."

Then Hanmor leaned to the man at his left and commented quietly, "I do not trust this sorcerer. Mark you, there are a hundred-and-fifty of us in this room, and we have our weapons with us. Settle your attention on one of the acolytes, and if he seems to act strangely or make any kind of sign or signal. . . .

"You are lovely," Mosutha complimented Esa.

She backed away from him, watching him carefully.

"Ah, you are frightened of me. Understand me, woman. I am a power, yes, but I am a man. I have loved. There was a woman I loved—you remind me of her. Indulge me. There is something in your eyes, your bearing, your face. . . . I created that woman, made her in an image, the thought of my love. Now you arrive, a barbarian woman, a slave, my enemy. . . . And what are you? but the image of that woman I loved. The shadows move strangely, do they not? Do we ever know ourselves, or our destinies?"

"Don't . . . don't hurt me," Esa mumbled. She was terrified, and sought to move farther away from Mosutha.

But he reached a hand out to her shoulder. "I could hurt you easily," he assured her. "But I have no wish to do that. Comfort me, barbarian woman."

"What are you going to do?" Her voice rattled; she knew that she looked into the face of the man who had slain her tribe, burned her village. . . . "And what will you do with my people?"

"Do not concern yourself with them."

A fire lit Esa's eyes. "How can you look at me?" she asked Mosutha hotly, anger welling up in her. "I am a barbarian! I am a barbarian . . . *wizard!*"

Mosutha grinned condescendingly. His hand moved from her shoulder to lightly touch her cheek, finger her hair. "You are foolish," he whispered to the woman.

Esa began to say something more, the fear and anger building up in her.

Mosutha's hand suddenly ceased its caressing; his fingers locked upon her straw-colored mane and pulled her head sidewise. Esa gurgled.

"Foolish!" Mosutha yelled at her, and painfully twisted her head in all directions. "Foolish!"

Esa raised her arms to scratch him, and kicked out with her legs.

Mosutha grunted, let go of her hair, and grabbed her robe at its neckline. Sarit's robe. His fingers tightened on it, he pulled Esa toward him, then thrust her away. The robe tore open and Esa fell from the sorcerer.

She stumbled, fell, sprawled to the flags. One arm and thigh struck sharply on the stone. Her body, long, white, and lean, was stretched full.

Mosutha hissed as he stared down at her.

"Foolish. . . ." he breathed, and moved toward her.

Oron awoke from his slumber. He was not alarmed, and no instinct in him had alerted him to anything deceptive in the night. He simply awoke. He did not move, but opened his eyes where he lay, stretched out, beside Uira. He listened to the soft sounds of her breathing.

He watched her. In the brilliant moonlight she was painted gray and silver, her beauty accentuated by the shadows and the brightness. Glancing down her body, Oron noticed the star amulet; it had slipped partially from her belt.

He did not bother to touch it or replace it. But, eyeing it, he wondered. Could it destroy Mosutha, as Saldum said? Could Oron himself use it to kill the sorcerer, or must it be used by Saldum?

He bent his head a little and settled his sight on the acolyte. Saldum sat, legs crossed one upon the other, arms at his sides, and hands clasped in his lap. His eyes were closed; he gave every appearance of being asleep. Oron did not doubt that he was. But still, there was a strange—

The acolyte's eyes opened, staring straight into Oron's.

And Oron felt the whisper of a chill feel its way down his back. Still he did not move, did not reach for a weapon or sit up. But he returned the sorcerer's stare, and it came to him that there was no meaning in the acolyte's gaze—only his eyes, wide open, looking upon Oron as though he had overheard something and glanced—as though he had overheard Oron's thoughts and, curious, had opened his eyes to see.

Oron took in a long, slow breath while Saldum's eyes closed once more, and the sorcerer resumed his pose of sleeping. The moonlight painted him in black shadows and silver highlights, and he seemed serene, at peace, a man in the night.

Oron gazed at the acolyte for a long, long time, wondering why the eyes had opened, wondering if Saldum had read his mind. . . .

"Stand up," Mosutha ordered her. His voice was calm but cold and threatening.

Esa, frightened, curled her legs protectively to cover herself.

"Stand up!" the wizard screamed, the anger erupting from him as abruptly as a storm.

Esa tried to crawl away. Tears of pain, fright, and agony swelled in her eyes, and her elbow knocked hollowly on the stones as she pushed herself away from the black-robed madman.

In one move, Mosutha had her, grabbed her by the hair and yanked her up, so that Esa was on her knees. She struggled, lashing out with her fists, but Mosutha knocked her arms aside. He stared down at her, eyes burning; Esa truly thought she could see the smoke of hell fires clouding his black pupils.

"You foul me," Mosutha hissed at her. "You disgust me, do you know that? You are not Sarit! You are a barbarian and nothing will change you. You are a pig! No, you are lower than—"

Esa whimpered; Mosutha yanked hard on her hair.

"—than a pig, aren't you? *Aren't you?*"

Esa sobbed.

"Admit it," Mosutha urged her. He cackled a laugh. "Nod your head up and down, barbarian woman, if you are lower than a pig, if you are lower than a dog." Brutally he shook her head from side to side, up and down, until Esa screamed from the pain.

"I thought so," Mosutha breathed. "I thought you were lower than a she-pig. You will show me how low

214

you are, barbarian woman. Are you a virgin? I suspect you are a virgin. I see no tattoo on your wrist, so you must be a virgin. You belong to no big strong warrior? Or was it a lover? Were you in love with—"

Esa sobbed hysterically, her face tightening, fingernails digging into her naked thighs and drawing blood. "Stop it . . . *stop it.* . . !"

"—in love with some dog of a warrior, no doubt? And I burned him to ashes, didn't I? *Didn't I?*" Mosutha howled viciously, forcing Esa's head back.

With her head bent back she promised him through clenched teeth, "My lover is a wolf and you did not kill him, you could never kill him!" And she threatened him with that fantasy that had tormented her every minute since the attack on the village, every moment since she had tasted freedom and then been dragged back into captivity, "You could *never* kill him, my lover is Oron the Wolf and he will—!"

"*What?*" Mosutha actually fell back a step in his astonishment.

Esa's face filled with fright.

"*Who* is your lover, barbarian woman?"

She was terrified now. What did Mosutha know? How did he know of Oron? Had something—?

The sorcerer gripped her by the cheeks, forcing Esa's mouth open in a humiliating contortion of wrenched lips and bared teeth. "*What name did you say?*"

"Ohhr . . . *Oron!*"

Mosutha's eyes glowed with brilliant intensity. "You lie," he whispered. But he glared into her eyes, and even without the use of sorcery he could tell when or not a woman was lying.

He is a hero . . . he is a boy, and he hates you. . . . Your soldiers have slain his village. . . . He is a wolf in the skin of a man. . . . He is a god wrapped in human flesh.

215

Reacting as violently as though the woman had been a demonic power, Mosutha shoved her away. Esa, weak, fell to one side, slumped and sprawled, whimpering. The wizard's stare tightened, and the obvious formed in his brain. Quickly he strode across the chamber and with his fist struck a small gong. Immediately, the two acolytes entered.

"Bind her," were his instructions. "Hold her here, but do not harm her. It is your lives if she is harmed or wounded in any way." Mosutha shot a stern look at them to make certain that they understood the finality of his command. "She is far more than a woman. She is far more than any spirit or demonic thing. She is a weapon, and a weapon against an enemy. Do you understand?"

Rather disillusioned that their master should put such emphasis on the life of a mere barbarian woman, the two answered with one voice, "We understand, O *isilla*, and swear by the Star that it shall be as you speak."

Mosutha nodded stiffly to them. Not looking back at Esa, he exited his chamber and hurried down the outside corridor, hastening to his workroom.

As one of the acolytes came past, gliding carefully around the tables of feasting warriors, Hanmor motioned to him, and the man stepped near.

"I wish to speak with Mosutha. Where is he?"

"I do not know. But he does not wish to be disturbed."

"Summon him."

The acolyte's features did not move; he did not smile disdainfully, but his eyes flickered secretly in response to Hanmor's voiced intemperance.

"You will not summon him?" The war-chief's aggressive tone alerted those retainers close by him; they moved in their chairs, hands ready to grip swords.

"Why for do you wish to speak with the Master?"

"We made bargain. My men have returned slaves to him, and he is to pay us in gold. I want the gold now."

Hanmor made sure that this reminder was pronounced in a thunderous voice. In response, a number of those warriors who had made the journey looked up from their plates and cups, their minds instantly on their payment. So, too, did the chief gain the attention of those acolytes close by. Their eyes fell on him, lidded, and each of them tensed slightly, with a presentiment of conflict.

The acolyte addressed replied patiently, "Perhaps you should wait until morning for—"

"I want the gold now, so my men and I can ride free of this hell-hole."

A direct provocation. The acolyte slowly, slowly nodded in agreement. "Let me see," he suggested, "what arrangements have been made for the payment of your men."

Hanmor sneered at him, "Let me go with you, to find out what arrangements have been made." He shoved back his chair and got to his feet. Immediately, five retainers did similarly.

The acolyte glanced briefly to his comrades in the hall. None moved to leave with him, but the intelligence was shared with each of them. The barbarians had shifted the balance, made a move upon their gameboard. A countermove was appropriate.

"Follow me," the robe advised politely, "and we will inquire of Mosutha just—"

"Just get me gold," Hanmor growled at him impatiently. "Take your arrangements and shove them up your ass. We've done our job and we want to be paid for it."

"Of course," the acolyte replied. "Of course. . . ."

13

Mosutha was furious. *"What* does he want?"

"His payment, Master." His man held well back, standing by the opened door of the chamber.

Mosutha was in preparation for a ritual. "Then lead him to the gold," he said coldly, eyes burning through clouds of incense smoke. "Take him. Take his men. Down there. Lead them into the room, allow them all the gold they care to take—if they can manage to do so."

The acolyte bowed briefly and made a sign. "It shall be done, Master."

Quickly, with a rustle of robes, he was gone, and Mosutha returned to his ceremony, feeding incense into his brazier, shaking blood onto the coals, making his signs, calling out. . . .

Tell me now where Oron is. . . . Fly on the wind and find him. . . . Tell me how he approaches my sanctuary. . . .

"Get the men," Hanmor ordered, when the word was relayed to him. "Half the men. I don't care if they're so drunk they can't walk. Gold'll sober them up. Get them here. Now!"

It was done: the news relayed to the feasting hall and the announcement made, yelled out beneath the very noses of those acolytes present.

"Gold, you dogs! Our payment awaits us! Half you men, come with me! Orders of Hanmor! We get our gold and ride from here!"

Those sober enough upended chairs and tables to make for the exit door. Others, too drunk to participate, lifted cheers of greed and called for their companions to do a good job hauling the chests and coffers. Very shortly, then, half a troop of men were thundering through the corridors of the mountain fortress, eager to pile their belts and arms with gold . . . gold. . . .

"I'll wait here," Hanmor proclaimed, when the great iron door was opened. "The rest of you men station yourselves all along the route. Pass the gold back, man by man, until it gets to me. I'll pile it here. I don't want anyone pocketing anything for himself. We divide the spoils later."

At his command his men filed past him, following the acolyte deep into the bowels of the fortress. Hanmor watched them, listened to them, his temper on edge. He wanted this done and his men away from here by dawn—down the mountain by dawn, with the wagons full of gold. Cursed gold, maybe, but gold, nonetheless. . . .

"Call out!" he yelled down into the corridor. He could scarcely see the first man inside, who stood down at the end of the tunnel where the way took a corner.

"All here!" sang the chorus of echoing answers, one by one, feeding back to the war-chief.

Two acolytes came down the hall, approaching Hanmor. Seeing them, the chief rested a hand on his sword hilt in a guarded movement. The acolytes held back; they wanted no part of this, but they were intrigued, knowing what doom was about to befall these headstrong barbarian animals.

Hanmor grunted at them, "What are you thinking, heh? No—I know you won't answer me. Slime. You think we're fools, don't you? You think we're easily duped, don't you? You think we can just be bought to do anything, isn't that it? Scum. . . . I'm a warlord, and my men are strong and honest bastards. You fools walk around in your robes with your stupid eyes and you never say anything. It disgusts me. Slime. . . ."

The acolytes stared at him.

It itched at Hanmor, boiled at the core of his guts. Slimy dogs in robes, never saying anything, never sat down to take a good honest—

He yelled into the corridor, "Call out! Have they reached the gold yet?"

"Not yet! We're all accounted for!"

Hanmor glanced back toward the acolytes. "You bastards think—"

But they were gone.

Spoke the demonic voice of the blood-misted smoke, "He is near, sorcerer; hasten with your ritual. The Wolf has a heart full of hate and a small army of men, and there is a ring of power about him; sorcery raised by spells. Hasten, sorcerer. But do not provoke the cosmic tides against you, for the Wolf is armed, his heart is iron, and his throat is full of blood, and he is the chosen of the gods."

Crouched upon the bed that had been Sarit's, Esa, cold, frightened, but humiliated and angry, lay down on her side and faced the two acolytes. They stood across the room, watching her. Esa noticed a small oil lamp resting on a table beside the bed. Its glow was not strong, but it was burning. She closed her eyes to feign sleep.

The acolytes remained as they were, observing her.

In a few moments Esa pretended to be deep in slumber. She began to grunt and moan, moving her hands nervously as though fighting off some dream phantom. The acolytes were suspicious. Esa began to murmur words. "No . . . don't . . . stop it, please . . . I don't want—"

One of the acolytes started across the room.

Esa heard his approaching footsteps and acted even more erratically, beginning to toss on the bed and throw her arms about. "Help me!" she cried, apparently awakening.

The acolyte, cautious, paused, then came nearer.

Esa opened her eyes and stared at him. "Help me!" she screamed. "It's upon me!"

He was close, now, and he lifted a hand palm out, spreading his fingers to sense what psychic manifestation must be near. He felt nothing.

"It is upon me!" Esa shrieked, sitting up in the bed and jerking her arms, shrieking as though under a terrible attack.

The acolyte said to her, "Woman, there is no thing—"

She moved—threw herself to the table, picked up the oil lamp and hurled it at the acolyte, all in one sweeping effort. The robe jumped back, but Esa's action was still too sudden for him. The lamp struck his chest, spraying hot oil all over his robe and face. Instantly the acolyte was aflame. He screamed in agony and dropped to the floor and rolled, as a curtain of fire engulfed his chest and head.

His companion moved immediately, bounding across the room. Esa jumped from the bed and crouched by her fallen victim. She fumbled to retrieve the gold-hilted knife in his belt. Oily flames jumped at her.

The second man was too quick for her. Pouncing, he backhanded Esa with a vicious, wide slap that sent her skidding on her bare buttocks. Swiftly he wiped his hands upon the face and robe of his brother, putting out the flames. Then he moved again toward Esa.

"*Barbarian—!*" His voice cracked in his throat. Furious, the man lifted a fisted hand and waved it at Esa.

She screamed as the force of that fist, which never touched her, struck her and slid her farther along the flags. Moaning, Esa struggled to get to her feet, to run—"

"*Get up!*" the acolyte yelled at her, pulling up into the air with his hand.

Esa felt herself yanked to her feet, jerked a short distance from the stones, then dropped again.

"Whore!" the robe screamed at her.

Again she was victimized by an incredible concussion, a forceful blow that never directly touched her. Forced backward, awkwardly pushed by a current of real power, legs skipping, arms flying, breasts bouncing ludicrously, Esa was smashed against the wall. Her head knocked painfully on the rock.

The unwounded acolyte, holding her by his current of will, came close and growled, "We must keep you alive, so you'll stay alive, little whore-woman! But you'll cause no further problems!"

Grabbing one of her arms, he pulled Esa along the wall to two chains that depended from the ceiling. There were gyves fastened to the ends of these chains, and these the acolyte hastily secured around Esa's wrists, yanking her arms painfully over her head.

He left her there and returned to his comrade, helped the man up and walked him, moaning and partially blinded, to the door.

While Esa hung, breathless, the pain and the fright of it all fluttered wildly in her belly. She felt the wine and food she had eaten quicken nauseously in her, and she was afraid she would spit it all up.

But she hung there, bruised and pained and humiliated, small tears rolling down from her eyes. Hung there, wondering if, indeed, Oron had been killed. Wondering if, indeed, he would ever find her, ever. . . .

It was nearly dawn.

Oron was awake, and sitting crouched beside Uira, watching the mystic Saldum as the sorcerer came out of his trance. Far away upon the horizon the moon—the Isotis Moon, a full moon with demonic powers in its light—hung, dulled by the first breath of daylight, against the deep purple of the cool long night.

Saldum opened his eyes and exhaled a long, slow breath. A slight frosty cloud misted around his chin for a moment. Oron stared at him.

The acolyte spoke quietly. "I am ready. Do you wish to give me the Star?"

"Do you need it?" Oron asked him, through the silence of the camp.

Saldum replied, "Keep it. Give it to me later. It may protect you."

Oron asked him, "What have you done, Saldum? Gone inside yourself? Made your inner strength strong?"

He nodded. "I have called forth the great powers within me, light and heat and energy from the suns and stars and fires of my beingness. I do not think even Mosutha can stand against me, now. His force is fleet, mine is slow and strong. Warn your men, Wolf, to stay apart from me. My strength is that great."

Oron grunted. He turned in his crouch to look upon Uira and reached out a hand to her. Then, quickly, he brought his hand up in a throwing motion. A large stone, pointed and heavy, whizzed through the air, flying directly for Saldum's face.

A moment from the acolyte's forehead it shattered into a powder.

"You see," Saldum told him quietly.

Oron smiled reflectively. "Great strength," he commented, appreciation in his voice. "Great strength, indeed. Will Mosutha's men in the fortress have such power?"

"Some, Wolf. Guard yourself well. And remember this: if one of them does not fall at the first stroke, move on. Do not give him his opportunity, in that heartbeat, to gather himself for the return thrust. It would blast you to ashes."

Oron pondered it, then cast his eyes toward the sky. "It is nearing dawn," he spoke. "Time to move."

"When we approach the citadel," Saldum remarked, rising lithely and supplely to his feet, "I will unleash the first of my magic to aid you."

The acolyte turned, facing the soldier behind him. "Around this corner, down the sloping path, lies the room of gold."

"Lead us," said one of the men. A torch fizzled and fumed in his hand, its light revealing his stern, untrusting expression.

"We cannot. It is cursed for us if we do," proclaimed the robed man. "We have sworn ourselves to Mosutha and are signed with the Star. We will die, should we touch his gold. It is cursed for his minions."

The argument sounded plausible to the soldiers. Yet one of them voiced, "Cursed for you, and not for us?"

"Go forward and learn. When did he ever expect to turn it over to outsiders? There is more gold in the world, and for wizards it is easy enough to transform wine and bread into gold and silver. Barbarians must . . . work for theirs in other ways."

Hanmor's men traded eyes silently in the torchlight, agreeing silently amongst themselves.

"I go now," spoke the acolyte. "I will continue down this tunnel, for I know the way. Let no man of you try to follow—that is not part of the bargain. Return by the path you came by."

"Don't worry, bright one. We've no intention to go hunting in Mosutha's prison. We've come for gold, we'll take our gold and get away from here. A bargain is a bargain—even between true men and hell-traders."

No more needed to be said. The barbarians were convinced, and the trap was as sweetly baited as any could be. With a shuffling of his slippers and the whispering of his heavy robe, the acolyte moved off down the corridor, where sight of him was lost quickly and the noise of him faded almost as suddenly.

"Let's go and get it," said the mistrustful warrior. "Gold's heavy, and we'd better get started if we're going to haul out enough to take care of us all. . . ."

Mosutha was seated in his chamber, one arm propped upon the arm of his chair, chin resting upon the fist of that arm in a thoughtful pose. Around him swirled the remnant mists of blood-fumes and smoky incense.

To the soft knocking on his door he answered, "Enter."

One of his men stepped in, bowed, and made a sign. "They are led to the gold, O *isilla.*"

"And they suspect nothing?"

"Nothing, Master. I bantered with them to suspend their doubts, and they think we are greater fools than they."

"The others, in the feasting room?"

"Drunk and wasted, my *isilla.*"

"And our prisoners?"

"Secured, and fed last night. We will feed them again shortly."

Mosutha nodded, well pleased with these reports. "The barbarian woman?"

"I inquired after her before coming here. She attempted a rash act—threw a burning lamp at one of the brothers. His face was burned, but otherwise he will recover. Sadly, he was a young adept and could not move to protect himself. Two now look after him."

This disturbed Mosutha. "And what is become of her now?"

"They have chained her to a wall, but otherwise have not harmed her. She will be fed and tended to."

Mosutha shook his head impatiently. "Barbarians. . . ." he muttered. "But souls are souls, and Ernog is ancient and hungry. He will feast well when the ritual is done." Still, he was troubled, and his man noticed.

To the inquiry of concern, Mosutha replied, "We have another enemy afoot. He is a barbarian with a small army. I have heard this from one of my elementals. He approaches now."

Shocked, the acolyte exclaimed, "Will he attack us here?" The possibility seemed ludicrous. "Destroy him now, Master, with a sending!"

Mosutha made a face. "He is guarded by a renegade strength. My worry is not that he will harm us, but that he may distract our intention and interrupt the proceedings. I cannot have that. The woman in my chamber, she is dear to this animal." Mosutha stood up then, pensive, he fingered the star amulet that hung upon his breast. "I want you and six others to stand watch on the walls. Keep your senses alert, for with the first appearance of their coming we must destroy them. We will use the woman as bait, and that will throw them off. But they must be dispatched quickly. Is this understood?"

"Completely, my master."

"I will not have my ritual interfered with. I have journeyed half my life in preparation for it, and the Isfotis Moon comes but once in a generation. I have sold my shadow to Hell for this gain, and there is—" He ceased abruptly, aware that he was revealing far too much to an underling.

"We live to serve you, O Voice," his man assured the sorcerer. He sounded like a pupil eager to aid his master. "We will guard and protect you, for your interest is ours. We have given ourselves to you willingly. Order us and command us, that we may be enlightened, O *issila!*"

Mosutha's eyes glowed with pride. "That is well," he replied. "Go now and do as I have said. Keep your watch. The ritual must be set in motion."

His acolyte bowed, made the sign, and exited.

Mosutha absently walked the floor, hands behind him, deep in thought. "Chosen of the gods. . . ." he pondered, whispering to himself. "How can one barbarian with a sword defeat the might of eternal Hell?"

The first of the screams carried like the long, delayed howl of a dying beast, reverberating through the honeycombed stone corridors in stretches of agony and torment. More came. And more followed. A chorus of the damned: shrieks, screams, howls, the groans and outcries of strong men suddenly lost in some deployment of sheer horror.

The soldiers lined along the farther corridors froze with the fear that bit into them. They could see nothing in the darkness, but they could hear—could *hear*, palpably in the darkness—the drained, throaty howls of damned men lost to—

"*What is it?*" screamed a loud voice.

Footsteps answered him—and more screams.

"It comes!" came a cry. "It—*godsssss!*"

In the darkness.

Echoing in the darkness.

"The gold!" screamed someone. "What of the—?"

"It's *eating . . . us . . . ali-iiieee!*"

"Gods of the gods!"

"Turn back, damn you, *turn back, you bastards!*"

Shoving, in the darkness. Armor rattling, faces and arms scraping against stone, the raucous noises of men falling, and screaming—kicking their legs, sobbing like children.

"*It's . . . eating . . . uh-uh-sss. . . !*"

One with a torch advanced, down the tunnel. Those before him burst past, yelling, throwing their arms out to the walls of the corridor, stamping madly, crying, sobbing.

"Sorcery!" screamed someone, his voice caught by the tunnels and whirled through the underearth, echoing insanely, bouncing back, reverberating, "*Sorrr . . . cerrr . . . eeeee!*"

The one with the torch moved ahead . . .

"*. . . eee . . .*"

. . . shifted his flame to his left hand . . .

"*. . . eee-eee . . .*"

. . . and drew forth his sword with his right. A final survivor rushed toward him, and the soldier held out his sword to bar the coward's way.

"Get *back*, you damned—!"

"The *gold*, curse your mother!"

"*Forget* the gold, fool! *Fool!* It's eaten them alive!" Shrieking, he pushed his way past, cutting fingers on the sword edge, but escaping down the corridor.

Grunting in disgust, the man with the torch paused, looked back, looked ahead. A shadow lurched before him, a living shadow. He held out his light to see.

"Godsss. . . !"

His stomach recoiled. It was half a man—half a man, with one side of his face eaten away, one arm nothing but bone, and what was left of the face distended in a look of excruciating pain, the blood streaming down him, the tongue gone, the flesh dripping like rain down his—

"*Godsss!*"

He dropped his torch and turned to run as the half-eaten man fell behind him.

Something warm and sticky struck him on the back of the neck, he reached behind to fling it away—and shrieked.

Hanmor was nearly knocked to his back as his men pushed out in a furious crowd, hurling themselves as quickly as they could out from the corridor, into the main hallway. Two—five—six of them—a dozen—twenty of them.

"Close the door! It's sorcery! It's devoured the men!"

"Gods be damned, we're—!"

"Hanmor, close the door!"

"Close the—!"

He didn't understand. He grabbed one of his soldiers, a huge dog, yellow-bearded, and with the unfamiliar glow of terror in his eyes.

"What is it? What—?"

"Some . . . *demon!*" the man yelled at him. "Some . . . *thing*, Hanmor! Invisible! It eats flesh! Ate the men! Ate them! Ate their flesh!"

Hanmor pushed him aside and went to the door. He looked down the tunnel. All was dark, but a voice cried out hollowly from the depths, "Don't close the door! Let me out!"

Hanmor looked, saw nothing, but heard the footsteps.

"Close it!" hissed a voice behind him.

Hanmor looked back down the darkened tunnel. No one, but the voice carried to him, "Save me! Keep the door—!"

"Hanmor!" growled a voice. "Do you want to let it *out?*"

His hand, knotted and veined, shivered on the open iron door.

"Close it, damn you!" someone else shouted. "You don't want to die like that?" He threw himself against the door; the huge iron latch pulled from Hanmor's grip.

"Save m——!"

But the soldier pushed; someone else joined him . . .

"Ssssave m——!"

. . . and the iron door slammed closed with a dull sound.

Hanmor, stunned, did not reprimand his men.

"Mosutha!" breathed another beside him. "That foul bastard's crossed us! There was something in that room, something with the gold in that room that—!"

"Go-od-sss. . . !" came a hollow, shrieking voice from within the corridor, and then the heavy thudding of a body thrown against the inside of the closed door. "Open the door, open the door, *open the door!*" came the muffled scream.

Just on the other side. . . .

Hanmor looked at his men; none moved.

"Name of the gods, open the—!"

None moved. . . .

"*door-rrr!*" And the scream—muffled, distant behind the thick iron. The weak pounding of a fist. A groan. The slump of a body, the clattering of bones—

Then, a sick chewing sound, barely audible. . . .

"*Damn him!*" Hanmor howled. "Damn him, damn him, damn him to a thousand thousand hells!" He threw himself against the door, kicked it, hammered it with his meaty fists. "Damn that wizard, damn him to—!"

He stopped. Turned. Stared at his men. The war-chief's face was greasy with sweat, his eyes burned terribly red with the final ache of wrath in them.

"Find them," he breathed, whispering so lowly that he could barely be heard.

His men, shaking, quivering, stared at him.

"The prisoners," he told them. "Find them. Free them. Let them loose, find them weapons—*free them!* Let them kill the sorcerer with us! We'll murder every whore's son in this hole and sunder this mountain to rubble! Come with me! *Find them!*"

By midmorning they were approaching the fortress. On the other side of a sloping ridge, it was obscured partially by mountainous outcroppings. They could discern clearly the walls surrounding it, could see the lines of the rock that shone on the towers of the place.

Oron paused in his advance to stare upon it, to measure how best to take it. Uira was close by him, and Thos, but the Wolf turned to Saldum for his advice.

"What sorcery will you use to aid us?" he asked.

"Fire," Saldum answered. "I will build a fire, make the smoke grow huge and give it the shape of a phantom. They will think an evil monstrosity is upon them, and expend energy in defeating smoke. This should draw their attention adequately to let you and your men get in."

Oron agreed to the plan. "Now tell us how to enter. There must be a main entranceway."

"None as such; the wagons could have entered only by the way they originally left, and that is by the main gate in the southeast corner. You may be able to glimpse it from here. No, it is hidden. But the gate is well tended."

"Another passage, then. Some small hole, a way over the walls—"

"As I see it," the sorcerer confessed to him, "your best opportunity is to attack the main citadel. Do you see it there?" He pointed.

It stood out boldly—the tallest tower of the fortress, appearing to lean very close upon the breast of the mountain.

"How to get in?" Oron asked.

"It has but one entrance, and that leads into the courtyard. But there are windows, if you can scale the wall."

"Coming down from the mountain? Can we get on the roof of it? Or throw out a line to make a bridge?"

"You have rope," Saldum answered. "I have never seen it from the outside—there was never any reason to do so—so there may be a handier access, Wolf. But you'll have to discover that for youself. You must move quickly, though."

Oron grunted.

Saldum pointed again to the southeast. "See where that precipice juts out slightly from the mountainside? If we gather there, we will be hidden by the mountain. There, I can conjure my smoke. If you and your men can manage to climb and get into the main fortress—"

"We will do it."

"It will be difficult."

Oron grinned. "Difficult," he repeated, musing on the word. "We come in anger, to kill for revenge," he told Saldum. "What is difficult about that? There is no difficulty. I want Mosutha dead; he will die."

Saldum nodded appreciatively. "Then let us hurry. Even now Mosutha must be preparing his ritual to the Moon. His strength gathers. If he calls up his force before we can attack, he will be far too powerful for us to stand against him. Far more powerful than your sword, my friend—or your anger."

Hanmor led twenty men, with only two torches for all of them. They made their way down shadowed corridors that promised instant death at any misstep.

"Damn me," the war-chief swore, "but he must have the prisoners hidden somewhere in here! The dog! I know they were led into this—!"

He turned a corner, torch out, stopped in his boots.

Before him, in the very bowels of the fortress, was a huge stone cavern, cut out of the inner rock. A large area, and on both sides of the tunnel where Hanmor stood, cells had been broken into the rock. Cells—rooms—each fronted with long iron bars driven into roof and floor, with holes at the height of them to provide entrance. No swinging doors; only wide apertures through which the prisoners were dropped. . . .

"We have found them!" he whispered tautly to his men.

"Any of the robes around?"

"I don't see them, but they may be near. Advance! Get these people free! Arm them with any spare weapons you have!"

14

Mosutha, third son of a dispossessed farmer-hunter,
last of his blood, wanderer, intellect, student of life
and betrayer of life, sorcerer, seller of his soul and
seller of other souls to dark shadows, and possessor of
secrets that had lain hidden in swamps and mountains
and tombs for millenia. Mosutha, alone, stood in a
quietly arrogant pose in the upper chamber of a tower
in his fortress. He was staring out an open window.
Below him in the courtyard the preliminaries for his
momentous ritual to Ernog were being accomplished.
Torches were being lit, drums and gongs set in place,
red carpets laid out, boxes of accessories—swords, incenses, jugs of wine—placed within his protective circle of the seven-pointed Star. And overlooking it all
from the end of the courtyard, its back to the high-
arched peaks of the mountain and its legs folded to
hold the mighty flaming bowl of sacrifice, sat the
statue of the demon itself. Its visage of chiseled stone
seemed one moment angry, the next placid, as high-
moving clouds variously obscured the day's sunlight
and then swept on to brighten the sky, and the courtyard—and Ernog's ancient, moody brow.

There came a knock on Mosutha's door. He called
out, and a man entered.

"Master, shall we release the prisoners? Drag them

out into the courtyard?"

Mosutha, his thoughts elsewhere, considered it and replied, "Yes. Do so. It is better that they cower in the shadow of the demon. The fear will aid the ceremony."

"Yes, O, *isilla.*"

"Line them up on either side of the yard, so that we can lead them speedily to the flames and drop them in."

The man bowed and made a sign. "It is done, O *isilla.*" And he went out.

Mosutha watched the slow progress beneath him.

. . . .Mosutha hated the people of the Valley. Long ago he was a shaman—to what tribe, I know not. But he was banished for trying to work strange magicks. He traveled south—far, far south, into the swampy regions of Kostath-Khum, beyond even where the mighty Serir River divides the world in half. It took Mosutha many years to journey there, and for many years he lived with the devils of that land, and learned their magic. He discovered there the secret of the ancient demon-gods. . . .

". . . He is but a boy," hissed the elder serpent. *"Let us eat him."*

"He comes to us for knowledge. Shall we not give him knowledge? His heart is full of hate. Shall we not use his hate as a weapon?"

"What does he promise us?" inquired the elder serpent of his son.

"He comes to the swamps seekng old magicks. He wishes to harm the world, for it has harmed him."

"I hate men as much as he, but—see you!—men drove me away, long and long ago, and now I should give my weapons to a boy with a heart full of hate?"

"What shall we do with him, then? Feed him to the lamiae?"

The half demon-half serpent elder choked something like a laugh. "Bring him in. Feed him the Fire-Spirit. Make him die, and pull out his heart—blacken it at the furnace and let his spirit look upon it—and if he agrees, then place it again in his breast and let it blacken him forever. Let him trade his soul to Hell, and become an unman. Then we will teach him magicks. Let him brand himself with the Star, and then we will fill him up with knowledge, and he may harm the earth. . . ."

"It shall be done."

"Bring him in."

And he was brought in, and the shadows were bright with flames, a ring of serpent-things hissed dryly at him, their master sat upon its throne, and around them the walls of the cavern dripped with the seeping moisture of the swamp.

"You have entered Hell, mortal youth. An you be strong enough, yes, we will teach you things. But you will damn yourself. . . ."

"Give me power," he said, "to kill my people. For they have wounded me, cast me out and banished me. I am no more of them. I have no soul any longer, but let its shadow belong to Hell, for my heart is there already, and my mind and will."

"Let it be done, then. Place the human on the altar and feed him the flames."

He screamed. And screamed. And screamed.

Looked upon his charred heart..

Felt his broken ribs bent back from his severed chest, felt his heart pulled out, and, hot, flaming, replaced to torment him forever. . . .

He screamed, and screamed, and screamed. . . .

And was reborn, in a swamp-womb of serpents and ashes.

Mo'sou-tha'ah: "Hell-returned" in the language of

the serpent folk, his demonic masters.

Mosutha, his mind full of things—memories and promises, vengeances and aching things, monstrosities and small heavens, large hells—watched the slow progress beneath him, and felt within himself the pulse of his devouring heart. . . .

"Drag them out!" Hanmor growled, fearing to raise his voice lest it echo, and carry to warn some of Mosutha's men.

The prisoners were in a panic, all of them gibbering and yelling, coughing, raising arms and waving hands. Hanmor's men tore loose chains they found hanging from iron staples in the walls and fed them through the holes above the prisoner bars. One by one, they began hauling prisoners free.

"Hurry!" Hanmor grunted at them. "It'll take all day, you're too slow!"

Four of his men wrapped a chain around one iron bar of a cell and yanked at it. The chain broke; but they replaced it, pulled further and, with a loud grating sound, the bar tore free.

The opening was still too thin for anyone to pass through, but the iron bar proved to be a very efficient tool. By butting one end of it into the ground against the rough jamb of a cell and applying their weight against it near the top, two of Hanmor's men were able to lever free two more bars. The prisoners pushed through to freedom.

"Weapons!" they cried. "Give us weapons!"

There were not many. Hanmor's men retained their swords but gave over knives, hatchets, daggers—whatever spare blades they had hidden in belts, boots or under their jerkins. Chains and loosed bars served, as well.

And the freed prisoners, weak and exhausted from

their debilitating capture but roused to new strength by their escape, lent all the energy they could muster to help the others still in the cells.

The moments sped by. Hanmor ordered a number of the freed men to keep a watch at both ends of the tunnel for any sign of intruders, and the creaking, groaning, splintering and shoving went on.

On the wall, two acolytes stared out across the wide ridges and treetops far below them. They saw nothing. They were adepts, schooled by a man trained by the ancient serpent-folk: and yet they were men, young men, and more used to spending their time indoors, burning incenses and chanting chants and conjuring nightmare forms. Had either of them been more alert, he might have noticed a peculiarity on the ridge far down to the left of them. Only a hint, the merest suggestion—not of the wind or of a breeze, not of the passing of some pack of animals, but of the passage of men: slight movement behind a ring of trees, hurrying shadows, a glint of metal, tiny to the eyes.

But they did not see.

They did not notice the furtive Wolf close upon their door. . . .

"We must bind them well," one of the acolytes said. "We will lead them out one cell at a time. Otherwise, they may become unmanageable in the face of their deaths. Chain them together and line them—"

The other three looked up, surprised at their leader's sudden silence.

The tunnel was full, choked with men and women, crowded with angry faces, gaunt limbs, knives and axes and swords.

"*Kill them!*" Hanmor shrieked, hell-fire in his eyes. "*Kill them now!*"

The acolytes cried out, jumped away, tried to brandish their chains as weapons, moved to use the fire in their fists. . . .

Forty, fifty, sixty weapons slammed down upon them. Bones crunched, heads split ripely, arms and hands and pieces of arms and hands exploded in a welter of blood and screams, and the rocky walls of the tunnel were splashed suddenly with dripping rivers of bright crimson.

The ridge.

Oron and his men hurriedly gathered up dry scrub and small branches for Saldum.

"Move on now," the sorcerer told them. "I will follow shortly."

Oron eyed Thos, surveyed his gathered men. "That ledge," he pointed out to them, "that leads above the fortress. We take that route, and get in however we can."

Cool breezes blew down upon them, the dried leaves of the dead branches and scrub whipped and scraped, Saldum's robes whispered about his feet.

"Let's get on with it," Thos grunted.

Oron looked to Uira.

She reached out and touched his arm, and nodded toward the mountain.

They moved off as Saldum, leaning over his pile of scrub and tinder, spread his hands outward, muttered a few words, and created the first flames of his magic.

"Are all of them out?" Hanmor cried.

"All of them!" came his answer from many throats.

"Then listen to me, all of you! You prisoners; do you know your way out of this hole? No? Were you blind? The way through there leads up into the tower! You have your choice! Follow us out, or make your own way! But kill every robe you find! Kill the bastards! We're fighting our way free, and anyone who makes it outside into the courtyard rides free with us today! *Free!*"

On the wall, other acolytes had joined the initial two. All scanned the landscape that stretched before them: the high clouds, gray against the more deeply gray sky, the azure green of the forests, and the sepia and black of the mountainside, far distant, barely-discernible beyond the thick forestlands, hints of the purple Nevga.

"He believes more come," spoke one.

The others said nothing.

"Barbarians?" one asked.

"He has spoken with his elemental, and it is true. More come to war upon us."

"Fools," was a curt opinion.

"Fools, perhaps. But these people of the forest are a livelier breed than the dogs of the east, who forever — "

"Look you. There . . . do you see it?"

"That? It's but a cloud."

They watched, disturbed, as the foaming smoke rose quickly toward the sky, holding together as no fire-smoke ever did, building into long columns and fusing together, then, into a gigantic ball, a thrashing globe of gray and black mist that began to float toward them as though mindful of its watchers.

"Warn the Master," one of them ordered, his fingers tight upon the crenel stones. "This is no barbarian trick. There is a power here."

He saw six of them, straight ahead, in a small antechamber. Hanmor considered himself quite fortunate, and perceptive, for having taken that turn in the tunnel.

"At them," he whispered to the crowd behind him, and then, in a booming voice meant to startle the robes, *"At them! Kill the dogs, every one of them!"*

They burst through the opening, ripping down the arras that partly covered it. Seated around a small table, their hands busy carving wooden implements and devices, the six acolytes stared up, astonished, then threw themselves back, lifted their hands and screamed words of power.

But Hanmor and his men were upon them—warriors and freed prisoners, men and women. Swords rose and fell. Chairs were splintered into kindling. One of the robes screamed as his head, in a red torrent, jumped from his neck. A freed man cried out as a bolt of white fire slashed him up the arm. His hatchet found its mark, despite his agony, and a second acolyte went down with a cleft skull, brains flying.

"Kill them, kill them, kill!"

The air was filled with the spray of blood and the sweeping mist of busy steel. Howls of agony. Ripping cloth. One of Hanmor's soldiers, too slow, looked up into the powerful, tattooed hand of an acolyte; in the next moment his eyes were ripped from their sockets, blood shot out in streams from his ears, and his head twisted on his shoulders with the sound of ripping rotten wood.

Then Hanmor's sword found the acolyte's back and he was carved open to the spine.

"On, on!" screamed the war-chief. "Into the fortress! Kill them all!

Another acolyte went down.

And another, taking a freed man with him—his arm buried to the elbow in the prisoner's belly as a sword skewered him through the side.

And the sixth went down, seeping blood—"Onward, on!" screamed Hanmor—but not dead.

Panting, blood dripping from his nose, but not dead.

He lay quiet, listening to the hastening, squishy sounds of wet boots on stones. Then he rolled over and fingered his bloody lips. He was alive, and they had thought him dead. He looked to the open door; dozens of bootprints painted red on the flags, and his five brothers dead—stabbed, beheaded, cleaved open—and only four of the barbarians.

He pulled himself erect and went out, out through the opening the barbarians had entered by. Into the tunnel, and down it to the next corner. He hurried along, wiping at his bloody nose, until he came to a short stairs. At the top of it was a door.

He opened the door and went through, closed it behind him, and raced down the hallway.

Surely it was more than smoke. It was some elemental thing, and the acolytes suspected it.

"Get the rest," one of them said. "Warn the Master, but do not—!"

Already others had been roused by the man who had gone to alert Mosutha. They were hurrying across the courtyard and taking the steps to the wall.

"Fight it . . . fight it, my brothers. . . .!"

There were ten, eleven of them on the wall, arms outstretched, robes flapping, eyes burning white and yellow, as the black cloud sped toward them beneath the gray autumnal sky.

"It attacks us from the south!" the alarmed man exclaimed to his master.

"And what is it? What form does it take?"

"It is a cloud! It seems like smoke, but it alters its shape—"

"From the *barbarians?*" Mosutha nearly yelled, apo-

242

plectic. *"Sorcery?* From a pack of *barbarian animals?* Are you a——!" He stopped abruptly. "Saldum!" he swore. "The dog has sold himself to Oron!"

"Master, we must—!"

And a second door crashed open, the man with the bloodied nose burst in.

"What is this?" Mosutha growled to him. "What has happened?"

"The prisoners!" he gasped. "Freed!"

"Freed?"

"Hanmor—and his dogs, O *isilla!*"

"Hanmor is dead!" Mosutha shot back at him, purpling.

"He is not dead! He attacked . . . killed five of us . . . surprised us . . . came from the tunnels. . . !"

Mosutha threw back his head and let out an animalistic howl of profound rage. "I will not have this!" he screamed. "I will not have this! I . . . will . . . not!"

"Careful," Oron cautioned his men. "Careful. . . ." He had Uira by the hand and was leading her along the narrow ledge. Behind them filed Thos and the others, carefully placing their boots on the unstable rock and advancing with arms against the mountainside.

Far below them they saw the tops of the fortress towers, the roofs of buildings.

Oron peered ahead. "It slopes down," he announced. "Steep. We'll be able to—"

A scream. A man had stumbled. Oron glanced back. Arms reached for him, the man teetered uncertainly, boots scraped on the ledge. Pebbles, knocked loose, danced down the steepness and made pinging sounds.

The man grunted and tried to steady himself, but one foot was slipping over the edge. He threw himself to one side in an effort to gain balance.

"Hold him!" Thos growled. "Grab him and pull

yourselves against the—!"

But the warrior screamed again, slid, and was gone. A flash, a blur—eyes looked over the rim to see him falling . . . falling . . . shrinking from man-size to boy-size to the smallness of an insect. His tiny black body caromed against jutting rocks far, far below, and exploded.

"Erith!" someone swore.

Uira gasped with the sudden horror of it.

Oron's hand tightened on hers and he began to move ahead, boots scraping on the rock. "It slopes down. We'll be able to get close enough for ropes. . . ."

Hurrying down the stairs, Mosutha swore volubly. Behind him came three acolytes, the one with the bloodied nose and two others. Fearful—and angry.

"They will not—!" The wizard reached the bottom of the stairs and started across the floor, toward the wide doors that let upon the courtyard: and a pack of freed men erupted from a side door, saw him, and howled as they surged forward.

"Dogs!" Mosutha yelled, throwing up his arms.

His acolytes quickly stepped before him.

One of the freed men went down, ripped by invisible flames. Blasted, his open chest smoked and sent out charred bits of flesh and muscle. He was knocked down by the onrush of his companions. Mosutha dropped back; his acolytes shielded him and bought him access to the courtyard.

But the freed men jumped upon them. One robe went down, grunting, as his brains catapulted into the air on the edge of a sword. Screams lifted, blood jetted, bodies thrashed. . . .

Mosutha growled, turned, and ran on.

"We could jump it," Oron pronounced. He glanced

at Uira and Thos.

They were on the ledge, leaning forward dangerously. The thin precipice tilted even more perilously farther along, as it progressed along the mountainside; further advance was impossible. But below them—perhaps twelve spear-lengths beneath and eight spear-lengths out—was the roof of the building. It was a steep drop, and the ledge they stood on offered them no momentum whatsoever for a jump. Any of them, trying it, might easily miss the low wall that edged the roof and fall, crashing and spinning, to the base of it.

"No other way ahead?" Thos growled. He knew he couldn't make it; more, he disliked the thought of wasting lives just to get inside the sorcerer's walls.

"A rope," Oron told him. "I can jump across, Thos'll throw me the rope and we'll secure it—"

"And what will hold it here?" the giant asked. The mountainside was very nearly sheer, and what clefts and delves existed were very small. There were few protruding points, and those seemed too steeply angled to trust with a knotted lasso.

As Oron pondered it, cursing the mischance that had brought them so far only to mock them, one of the men near the end of the line called out, "The sorcerer comes!"

Oron craned his neck to see. Saldum, black robes flying, was hurrying along the dangerous ledge as unconcernedly as though it had been a wide forest path.

He grinned wolfishly to Thos. "Saldum," he said, "will secure it for us."

Thos shrugged his shoulders.

Bracing himself, Oron pressed himself against the mountainside. Uira looked at him, uncertainty in her eyes. He smiled at her, not forcing the smile; he was genuinely excited. Swallowing several deep breaths of air, he crouched low on buckled legs and stared, not at the edge of the roof, but beyond it. A handy trick he'd taught himself long ago; to look beyond his target and thus gain momentum.

Someone called out to him, but it was too late. Oron pushed, and a wild rush of air whipped him as, bent like a bow, he kicked out and dropped swiftly.

Even as it came close upon them they continued to discharge powerful sorcerous energies against it; and their power had no effect.

Yet they were unharmed.

"Smoke!" one of the acolytes yelled. "It is nothing but *smoke*, in the guise of a demon. *Smoke!* It is *harmless!*"

Wrathful with a rage he had never before experienced, fearful that his ritual would be undone, furious with Hanmor and the warriors for freeing the prisoners, Mosutha hastened from the scene of carnage behind him and hurried toward the doors that led to the yard. Ernog would yet have his ceremony, and it would be a bloody, terrible, wrathful ceremony, with corpses everywhere, flames everywhere, not only in—

"*Wizard!*"

Mosutha stopped short, at the top of the stairs that led outside, and turned, slowly.

Hanmor stood erect and tall, his bloody blade quivering in his fist, his bulk poised taut in an open archway just across the citadel's foyer.

"Now you die, wizard!" Hanmor bellowed.

Mosutha glared at him, and the yellow flames began to grow in his eyes. "Fool," he whispered, reaching his hands to the Star on his breast.

Hanmor let out a huge roar, a call to Death, and, sword up, threw himself across the stones.

"I could have helped you across!" Saldum called to Oron.

"I'm here, now! Saldum! Are you strong enough to hold a rope while our men pull themselves across?"

"Yes! Easily strong enough for that!"

Thos, who had the looped bundle of rope, passed it to the man next to him and ordered it continued down the line until it reached the sorcerer. Oron meanwhile tested the strength of various merlons along the edge of the roof and found one that satisfied him.

Saldum cast the rope to him; Oron caught the end and secured it. The sorcerer pulled it tight, looped his end about his waist and tied it. Bracing his feet on the ledge, he pressed his hands behind him, clinging to the mountainside.

The barbarian standing next to him watched, worried, as Saldum hummed a word and rolled his eyes up, took in several deep breaths, then ordered, "Go."

The man did not move.

"Jump, damn you!" Oron yelled to him. "The rope will hold!"

Still the man did not move. Another, behind him, growled, "Stand aside! If it doesn't hold, I'll swing across!" He shoved the procrastinator, but that forced the warrior off-balance. Grunting as the air flew from his throat, he lashed out with his arms and wildly caught hold of the rope as his feet slipped from the ledge. Sweating, cursing, he dangled there.

The rope held.

"Move across!" Oron ordered him. "You're holding up the others!"

Shaking, the man let go with one hand and began swinging, hand-over-hand, along the length of rope. He looked down once and saw the toes of his boots waving against a misty gray blur that dropped down forever. He fought the urge to pause—and fought back a sensation of vomit welling—and gained the wall. Oron helped him up, even as the next man threw himself out upon the line and started across.

Some of the warriors, too impatient to await their chance, leapt across the chasm to land, tumbling, on the rooftop. Thos was the first of these, daring himself even though fearful that he might fail. But once he'd done it he stood beside Oron and, swaggering, ordered others to do the same. The rooftop began to fill up.

"Wait," Oron told Thos, "before heading in. I want you to lead half the men into this building, but I'm going across to that one." He pointed to the tower next to them.

"Why that one, Wolf?"

"It is Mosutha's. Esa may be in there."

"Esa?"

"A woman . . . of my tribe."

Understanding kindled in the giant's eyes. "As you will, Oron."

The last few started across, and Saldum had yet to show any effect of the wear upon him. Uira was the last to pass over by the rope, and Oron strongly took hold of her when she reached the creneled roof, hauling her over the merlons with exaggerated strength.

Then Saldum jumped across, effortlessly. He undid the rope at his waist while Oron unfastened his end from that side of the roof and retied it to a block at the opposite side. The distance between this building and Mosutha's tower was not as great as that just crossed, but the tower rose another two stories above them.

"Can you jump," Oron asked Saldum, "into that window? Onto the ledge? Secure the rope inside?"

"Yes, Wolf."

"And—"

"And slay any who interfere? Yes, Oron. And if your Esa is in that room, I will alert you."

Behind them, Thos lifted a huge stone door in the center of the roof and dropped down into the topmost chamber of the building. Half the men began following him. . . .

Hanmor unleashed a howl of rage as his sword swept down at the sorcerer.

But Mosutha, his expression grim, lifted a hand and caught the sword. It stopped instantly in his grip.

Hanmor's face went white, and terror crept into his expression as he looked into the wizard's incredibly deep, virulent stare.

"Fool," Mosutha whispered again, in the pause of that shock. "Tread the paths of Hell forever, dog!"

Before Hanmor could move with his free hand to defend himself, or release his tight grip on his weapon, Mosutha lashed out. His right hand, fingers bent clawlike, flashed with the speed of a viper. Hanmor, astonished, screamed in pain as the sorcerer's hand buried itself to the wrist in his chest, breaking through bronze armor, leather padding, cloth tunic, flesh and bone.

"Tread Hell!" Mosutha shrieked, twisting his hand inside Hanmor's body.

The war-chief hurled back his head and let loose a barbaric, unending howl of utter agony. Mosutha, moving his fingers serpentlike inside the man's chest, grabbed the pulsing heart and, with no effort at all, ripped it free. Hanmor howled again in shock as his ribs broke and his armor shattered.

Eyes dreadful, hovering on dying legs but still alive, Hanmor stared at his own squirming, pumping heart in the sorcerer's hand. Blood was everywhere; coating

Mosutha's sleeve and hand and robe, gushering in a thick spray from Hanmor's demolished chest, pouring in thick rivers down the chief's front.

Mosutha sneered and flung the heart away, released Hanmor's sword arm and, turning, shoved the barbarian from him.

Hanmor, the war-chief, with life still flickering within him, crashed backward onto the floor and gasped, writhed, contorted, shot blood into the air, and died—died, looking still into the burning yellow eyes that reflected the flaming craters and burning pits of Hell. . . .

15

"It is empty!" Saldum called to Oron from the window ledge.

Waiting until the sorcerer had secured the rope inside the room, Oron threw himself out and quickly, hand-over-hand, made his way to the window. Uira followed, and the others.

The room was vacant—it was not even lit, although there were torches on the walls and, upon various small tables, oil lamps. Oron didn't waste time lighting them; by the light of the window he saw two doors at opposite ends of the room. As his men climbed through to join him, he crossed to his right and tested the latch of the first door.

The latch gave, the door opened creakily. Sword high, Oron cautiously reached his head through to see what lay outside. It was a corridor, a hallway—desolate, but with a torch burning far down where the way led around a corner.

Oron looked back into the room. "Check that door," he ordered a man.

One of his warriors did so, testing the latch, then pulled the door open, carefully, and stepping outside. "Empty," he called back. "Looks like it leads to a stairway, Oron."

"Follow it," were his orders. "Take half the men

with you. Whomever you find—whatever you find—kill it, if it wears a robe. But if you find the blond-haired woman—"

"She will be protected, Wolf."

Oron nodded sternly to him and looked to the sorcerer. "Saldum?"

"I will come with you. Lead the way, Wolf."

He stepped into the corridor; Uira, Saldum, and half the men in the room followed.

"Begin the drums!" Mosutha shrieked to his acolytes as he ran into the courtyard. He waved bloody hands at them and screamed at the top of his lungs, "Begin the drums! Begin the ritual! We raise Ernog to destroy our enemies!"

His acolytes were scattered in all directions—some still upon the walls, some engaged in battle with the few of Hanmor's warriors and freed men who had gained the outside.

"*Begin!*" Mosutha howled insanely, his voice ripping huskily as it reached a pitched intensity. He threw himself into his magic circle, took out handfuls of incense from the boxes at his altar and cast them about him, flicking Hanmor's blood onto the incense powder, and filling up the ditches of the carved circle.

Acolytes ran to aid him, lining up behind drums, taking up ritual swords, which hung along the walls, to defend themselves against their attackers.

Around Mosutha, a ring of tall flames leapt up and he cried out to the cloudy sky, "Rise, Ernog! Come you, Ernog! in answer to this slaughter! Reign, Ernog, with your sorcery! Ernog! *Keth-es-theta mo-u then-ra'da!*"

A bloody acolyte screamed and fell across the stones, an ax in his back.

"Rise, Ernog! *Keth-es-theta. . . !*"

"Where is Hanmor?" rose a chorus of angry voices.

"*. . . mo-u then-ra'da. . . !*"

"Hanmor is dead! *Hanmor is dead!*"

"*. . . Keth-es-theta esitu, Ernog, Ernog, Ernog!*"

"Kill the sorcerer! Kill the sorcerer! *Cut through the flames!*"

At the end of the corridor five acolytes came running down a stairs and met them head-on. Oron wasted no time in throwing himself against them. The foremost robe, utterly unprepared, let out a mad howl as the Wolf's blade ripped through his belly and left him staggering on a long stream of entrails and pouring blood.

"Kill them!" he screamed, continuing forward with his momentum.

Uira, right behind him and armed with her dagger, jumped into the air and kicked out with her long legs. She caught a second acolyte on the chin; his head snapped back as the concussion smashed him against a wall. His head knocked loudly on the rock and he slumped, unconscious, to the stones.

Then the pack of warriors, swords and axes, fell upon the remaining three. One barbarian shrieked madly as white flame slashed him across the face. But the robes were brought down in a welter of flying limbs, shooting blood, and echoing screams.

Saldum, who had stayed back during the melee, joined Oron as the attack ended. His expression was impassive as he looked upon the smiling rogues of the Wolf's command. They were happy as children, blood-smeared and gore-spattered, with the first kills to reward their difficult, tedious journey for vengeance.

But Oron noticed Saldum's intensity. "What is it?" he asked the sorcerer, panting strongly.

"You wish to find Esa?" Saldum asked him in a low voice.

Oron's eyes went wide. "Where is she?"

253

"She is near."

"How do you know, Saldum?"

"I . . . know," was his answer. "I can feel her . . . her pain, her agony."

Oron's nostrils flared, his mouth tightened into a grim line. "Tell me where she is, Saldum."

He lifted his hands and shook his head . . . feeling . . . sensing . . . then looked quickly down one avenue of the T-shaped corridor. "There."

Oron glanced down the hallway, then back to his men. "Half of you head down that way," he ordered them, nodding behind him. "The rest of you, come with—"

But before he could finish, four more men in robes appeared from a doorway. Uira screamed. Oron half turned, pushed her against a wall and crouched, then threw himself to the floor. As he dropped, he heard screams from his gathered warriors and the clash of steel on stone.

"They are in the square," said one of them, leaning at the window.

"The soldiers?"

"Mosutha has begun his ritual! They are attacking him!"

The other let out a sibilant hiss. "We must go to him, my brother!"

He at the window turned. "But the girl," he said. "Use her! Cut her open! Spill her blood within the circle! Raise a force to aid the Master!"

The second showed his teeth in a brilliant snarl as Esa, hanging beside him, whimpered and jangled in her chains.

In the feasting hall, two dozen drunken men roused to the sounds of screams from the courtyard outside.

They were alone in the chamber, and they noticed that the doors to the hall had been closed and bolted — from the outside.

When several of them took to the doors and tried to force them open, they quickly learned that their brute strength could not avail them against the heavy barricades.

Swearing, they pondered what to do. The muffled screams and the clattering din of rising and falling swords, just outside, maddened many of them and fired their blood.

"We must force—"

It was then that they smelled the smoke, and looked around to see that — somehow, impossibly — the walls of the chamber were glowing hot, tapestries were catching afire, and the very wood of the tables and chairs was beginning to smoulder with a rapidly increasing heat. . . .

"Rise! Rise, Ernog! Rise you from Hell! *Keth-es-theta esitu. . . !*"

Oron rolled forward, pushed himself aside and leapt up — directly beside one of the acolytes. His sword punched into the dog's belly; the acolyte, gasping as the first runnel of blood vomited from his lips, swiveled to grab Oron by the throat. But Oron ripped his blade free, shoved the robed dog away and turned to kill more.

But they had swarmed past him, were moving and fighting and falling within his pack of steel-busy warriors.

A heavy slap on his shoulder; "Down here!" Saldum urged him.

Oron's eyes lit up.

"To free your Esa!" Saldum yelled at him.

The Wolf glanced into the bloody mob beyond—

rising and falling swords, splintering bones, shrieks, screams, death.

"Uira?" he panted.

"She is safe! The Star! Run, Wolf!"

They were screaming, howling, burning alive. They pushed at the barred doorway until, ranting, they could no longer hold their hands to it. It was far too hot. Arras coiled up, high overhead, like brittle parchment caught in sudden flames. Drunken men yowled and picked themselves off the floor, where the very stones were glowing white-hot. They began stripping away their clothes; they screamed for wine and water to douse their thirsts and splash their bodies. Some tried it, with what little wine remained, and their flesh began to boil on their bones. Others tried to scale the walls to reach the windows, but the stones of the walls seared their hands and arms, and the stacked tables and chairs crumpled, the wood brittle and charred, eaten through with the incredible heat.

Some of them began to flash afire as the floor beneath them scraped, crunched, grinded, as gusts of smoke and lappings of true flame rose up from the skewed rock and the smashed flags.

"Ernog! Rise you from Hell!" *Keth-es-theta esitu. . . !"*

The knife slid easily into her belly, and the blood dripped down her thighs and legs in pouring sheets, sprinkled on the floor, collected in a pool. . . .

Esa, clattering in her chains, shrieked insanely.

"Raise the blood!" yelled the one at the window. "Call up the blood-spirit! Make of it—!"

Esa screamed and screamed, twisted her thighs, pulled with her arms, tried to kick, shook her hair, sobbed, screamed. . . .

"Silence, barbarian!" He stabbed her again, this time in the thigh, and intoned over the shining blood. *Mis thutu es le O-thustras. . . !*

"Hurry! *Hurry!* The tower is collapsing, Ernog—!"

A sudden howl of rage—the death-scream of a god. The sound of rasping steel.

And the roar of an animal-soul that nearly sundered the rock walls of the chamber.

They turned, astonished, frightened that some demon had been loosed.

But it was no demon—only a man. Only a wolf in man's flesh, dressed in man's bones. Only a barbarian with a sword.

Oron.

Esa's weak whimper of recognition fell from her lips in a sob.

He stood, his shadow thrown into the room, tall and huge, bloody sword thrust out before him like some victory tooth of combat, with the forest-mist of animal wrath burning in his shadow-black eyes. And beside him, another, dressed in black, and white-faced, yellow-eyed: a brother of the Star.

"Kill them!" howled the man at the window, lifting his hands to make doom.

They streamed into the courtyard, wave after wave of them—freed men and warriors, armed with weapons, armed with muscles and fists, and they threw themselves berserkly against anything dressed in a robe. They screamed as white fire cut them down, charred their faces, ripped open their bodies. But still they came on, climbing over the oiling corpses, splashing through the blood, working their weapons, throwing their bodies forward. . . .

Far above, thunder rumbled and lightning erupted across the sky, the arched webbing of it cracking the dense gray clouds—ancient, shattered porcelain.

Urged on by the lightning came the winds: tidal winds, winds that sent bodies tumbling across the bricks of the yard, winds that smashed the trees far below on the mountainside. Winds that whipped the circle of fire surrounding Mosutha into a tall wall of hellish flame.

The winds, and the lightning, and the deaths and the screams—

—and the earth, quaking, ripping, erupting. The earth, moving and sundering beneath them, heaving. The mountain roared as a thing, a giant, brought suddenly to artificial life. And through the gray sky and beyond the arching skeletal fingers of lightning came the silver rays of the early moon: a large moon, an eye—another living thing. . . .

The Isfotis Moon.

"Ernog! Keth-es-theta esitu. . . !"

"The wizard!" screamed some of Hanmor's men. "He releases the demon!"

"Ernog! Keth-es——!"

They could not see him behind his flaming wall. But the sky saw him, and the thunder heard him, and the earth answered. . . .

Across the courtyard gigantic ruptures appeared in the wall of the main citadel, steam gushered out, and the blackened dead bodies of the men that had been trapped there poured out in molten suits of armor. . . .

"Ernog! Rise you from Hell!"

"He brings it!" screamed the men. "He brings the thing from Hell!"

Then new howls of anger and outrage joined them—howls from Thos and the men of the forest, gathered at another entrance to the yard.

"The wizard!" Thos yelled.

"Where is Oron!"

"Where are the others?"

Thos immediately took charge. "At them!" he growled. "Brothers! Throw bodies onto the fire! Take the sorcerer! *Take Mosutha and feed him to Hell!*"

The one at the window dropped first, struck in the chest by a bolt from Saldum. It was invisible, but the concussion of it split his body open like an overripe husk, and as wet screams lifted from his mouth he was thrown back, entrails spilling from him and trailing bloodily across the stone.

Oron, with no sorcery, moved with his sword. The dog beside Esa threw out an arm and a searing blast of energy blackened the wall behind the Wolf. Oron had no time to cross the stones.

He threw his sword.

Point first, it sliced the air, a gray lightning-shade, and skewered the acolyte through the belly. He grunted; pushed back by the impact, he threw his hands out in a wild grab for support and clutched Esa's legs.

She screamed.

Oron jumped.

Bones cracked loudly as Esa's body was pulled, stretched, twisted by the dying acolyte. His bloody hands, fingers clenched, dug red furrows down her thighs and calves as he crumpled. He threw his head back and stared up at the woman. Her face, silent, glared down at him between her dripping breasts, her hips were pulled awkward by the weight of him, his blood mixed with her blood on the stone. . . .

"*Eff'a . . . noth-u . . . ri-suth . . . koy-asthon. . . .*" Dying words to drag her soul down to Hell with him. . . .

Then Oron's mighty hands gripped his head. Together, they fell to the ground. Oron twisted. The acolyte's head, trapped between powerful fingers as in a vise, offered no resistance. They bent around, around, the neck snapping loudly, bones bursting through his throat and shoulders.

Drool spilled from Oron's lips as, in his fog of wrath, he continued to push, push, push the acolyte's head. . . .

"Oron!" Saldum's voice was a warning.

The Wolf looked up, shaking; he threw the head from him, the acolyte's corpse slumped. Stepping from the body, Oron looked up at Saldum, a red mist in his eyes—then he looked to Esa, saw her hanging above him, red-stained, limp in the chains.

"Oron," Saldum whispered quietly, standing close. "Oron, she is dead. . . ."

He stared. His belly collapsed. His heart stopped. He rose shakily to his feet, unaware of his body, unhearing, unseeing because of the fog that wrapped his senses.

"Esa. . . ."

His fingers scraped her white flesh . . . touched the red blood of her. . . .

"Esa. . . ."

And suddenly, from the depths of him, erupted an incredible animal-howl of desperation and savagery and wrath and hatred and agony, agony, agony. . . .

"Pile them on!" Thos howled, dragging the smashed body of an acolyte across the courtyard and yelling for his men to do the same. *"Pile them onto the fire!"*

Hanmor's warriors looked up, startled, and the surprised freed men and women stared at the giant, dressed in bloody animal hides, stained with the gore of many killings, as he dragged a corpse with one hand and waved his red sword at them with the other.

"Pile them on! Kill the sorcerer!"

The earth shuddered beneath them, betraying their senses, nearly throwing them off their feet. The crumpled bodies—soldiers, warriors, acolytes—jumped into the air with each bursting pulse of the rocking mountain.

"Pile them on!" Thos shrieked madly as he hurried toward the center of the courtyard. "We are men of Oron's! Pile them on and *kill the sorcerer!*"

One of them moved. Then another. And another. Hanmor's men, barbarians. . . . All bloodied, some burnt, wounded, with fear and death in terror in their eyes—their enemies killed, and Hell erupting below them.

With a large grunt Thos lifted the corpse in his hand and sent it sliding across the rock. It crashed into the flames of the circle and rolled, and though flames licked at it and danced above it. . . .

"Ernog! Keth-es-theta. Rise from Hell!"

. . . the flames were partially jammed, and a hint of Mosutha's wavering form was glimpsed behind the fire.

They moved quickly, then frightenedly, under the giant's command, and began dragging the corpses of their enemies and comrades toward the circle, and piled them upon the ring of fire.

"Quickly!" Saldum encouraged Oron, his warning taut.

He stood alone, sword point resting on the stone, staring at the corpse that hung on the chains. The woman who, ages ago, had promised to become Oron's mate and wife and love. . . .

"She is dead, Wolf."

"I should—" His voice, a whisper, was barely audible. "I should . . . cut her . . . down. . . . Free her . . . lay out her body. . . ."

The floor rumbled, cracks appeared in the walls of

261

the chamber, the flagged stones of the floor groaned, the stone window creaked.

"She is dead, Wolf. And she was dead, even as you tried to save her.'

Everyone there in the room stood silent, staring at their leader—Uira, with tears rolling down her eyes—and sharing with him, even in this extreme moment, his anguished sorrow, his loss.

He looked at Saldum. "Her spirit?"

"Safe," was the honest reply. "It was safe at the moment of death. These dogs altered nothing; harmed only her form." He nodded to the butchered corpse sprawled at Oron's boots. "He tried—filth!—but all is finished with his death."

"*His* death!" Oron growled, and turned, glancing out the window.

As if in answer to his intention, thunder boomed low across the heavens and the floor quivered again threateningly.

"The mountain is collapsing," Saldum warned Oron. "Ernog is pushing up from Hell!"

Oron, not dazed but thoughtful, continued to stare out the window for a long moment. From the courtyard far below rose the screams of unending violence and the maniac slaughter, and dimly Oron could hear the chanting, throaty syllables of Mosutha's incantation.

"Now. . . ." he whispered, quietly, softly. He faced his warriors, faced Saldum and Uira. "Now!"

And with renewed determination—without the mad energy he had displayed so far—the Wolf of the Valley crossed the shaking floor of the tower and led the way out into the corridor.

The flames, crushed by the piled corpses, sputtered weakly and sent up stinking columns of thick black smoke.

"Fools!" Mosutha shrieked, revealed behind the flames.

"*At him!*" Thos cried. Lifting his sword, he clambered over the smoking bodies and jumped at the sorcerer.

There was no combat. The giant's first swing was stopped in midstroke by Mosutha's strong grip, and the stunned Thos, struggling within that heartbeat of panic to free his blade, felt the sorcerer's open left hand sweep across his belly. Thos shrieked as the top half of his body spun crazily into the air. Tumbling backward and spewing out a geyser of fanning gore, it blinded and confused the warriors behind him.

They pulled back, terrified, and Mosutha laughed at them and jumped from his circle.

"Take it!" Saldum ordered Oron, as they led the quick race of boots down the stairs of the tower.

"Let Uira keep it! She will need the protection more than—!"

"*You* will face him, Wolf! Take it! Take it, in the name of your father!" the sorcerer yelled at him, not realizing what he said.

Oron, astonished, did not pause in his hurry, but a look of pain and anger bore into Saldum's eyes.

Saldum did not understand, but he would not let Oron refuse the Star. "Remember what I told you! His power is crafted into this amulet! Use it against him!"

Reaching the bottom of the stairs, they hastened across the corpse-piled foyer of the citadel, even as more upheavals sent loosed bricks and cracked rocks crashing down around them. Outside, standing on the short patio that led into the courtyard, Oron paused and faced Uira.

"Give it to me."

"Wrap it around your blade, Wolf," said Saldum.

He did so, swiftly looping the chain over and around the crosspiece of his sword twisting it tight so that it could not slip to distract him while he fought. Then he stepped down into the yard, Saldum following.

Uira and the others, on Oron's unspoken orders, stayed where they were—in the open, but at the edge of the courtyard. If he were killed. . . . If he were killed, they would do what they could.

Mosutha was far away, across the landscape of rock and smoke, flames and crowds and stretched corpses. The wizard stood before the towering idol of the demon, and he seemed to be a moving black shadow, bald head bent back, robed arms waving frantically for the evocation of his power. From their distance, Oron and the others could hear Mosutha's yelling voice, though it was dimmed by the booming and the crashing of the storming sky and by the grinding and crunching of the stones and rocks around them. Lightning flashed high up, and behind the thick gray thunderclouds Oron glimpsed the Moon, for though it was afternoon the day had turned dark as night with the storm. With the storm—and something more. . . .

He turned and faced what remained of his force, looked every one of them in the eyes, stared long at Uira. Then he started across the stones of the yard, and Saldum hastened beside him.

The fierce winds of the storm whipped keenly at them, sweeping Oron's long hair back from his forehead and flattening his beard against his cheeks, whipping Saldum's robes with snapping slaps. The two did not slow their pace, however, as they advanced upon the wizard; they bent into the wind and walked quickly around the piled corpses, stepped through rippling puddles of gore, kicked aside severed arms and heads. Halfway across they passed the great circle of the Star and did not pause to look at it. Thos's corpse, halved, and the charred, still-smoking bodies ringed there, did not deter them. They marched on steadily, the sounds of their boots lost to the blowing roar of the wind.

Mosutha had yet to turn and face them, but Oron kept his eyes always on the wizard. As he and Saldum came nearer they parted so that, as though planned in advance, they approached Mosutha separately, circling around on both sides.

A sudden concussion beneath the ground stunned them. Saldum was pulled to his knees, and while Oron kept his balance he was hurled a short distance into the air as the rock of the courtyard abruptly shifted like a wave in the ocean. Fissures appeared along the edges of the yard and great gusts of steam and black smoke, red-tinged, shot up, pulled back.

Mosutha turned, looked at Saldum, faced Oron.

"It comes!" he screamed out, and thunder echoed his proclamation. "It comes! The shadow of Ernog rises from Hell! *Up from Hell!* Your people are destroyed, barbarian! Now sorcery reigns upon the earth, and I in the name of *Ernog* am king . . . *king of your soul!*"

Oron, silent, continued to approach, steadily, angrily, sword out, teeth clenched.

"You will feast on Death!" Mosutha howled at them, and laughed.

They came on.

Another concussion ripped beneath their feet and sent a geyser of steam and loosed rock high into the air at the other end of the courtyard. Now the atmosphere on the mountain was becoming thick with a blanket of steam and hot fog, and despite the drizzle of the storm the air was heating up quickly.

Mosutha turned from Oron to Saldum. The acolyte now was but a dozen steps from his erstwhile master—close enough to deal death.

"*Saldum!* You are *traitor* to me! You could have reigned beside me!"

"Reigned as a corpse? I own my own blood, monster! I am a *man!*" Saldum shot back, pausing and making a sign before him with a flurry of his hands.

"A man!" Mosutha returned mockingly. "A *man!* Then *die* like a man . . . *traitor!*" He lifted his arms before him and fisted his hands. Thunder boomed, lightning crackled, gas and fumes fired from the ruptured ground. "In the name of Ernog, who empowers me!" Mosutha lowered his arms, fists together, and a glowing stream erupted from them.

Oron cursed. It happened so quickly that he was barely able to see it. Saldum screamed as the blur in the air—Mosutha's energy—struck him. His own shield held but a moment: the white line in the air, rather than slicing through him, surrounded him, wrapped him up. He appeared wavering and uncertain, as if trapped in a murky crystal, a bubble of heat.

And then he was gone. Without a scream, torn apart. Across the courtyard, Uira shrieked. The clear bubble vanished and, where it and Saldum had been, there was now only a red mist that hung for a heartbeat in the air, then was blown away on the stong winds.

"*Dog!*" Oron howled, and ran forward.

Mosutha, within the shadow of the idol, laughed at him, lifted his arms, and screamed to his demon deity.

Clear energy shot from his fists. Oron threw himself to one side, as he would have from a thrust or a hurled knife. Still, the bolt of magic found him—struck him . . .

Mosutha screamed in maddened wrath.

. . . stunned him, but did not kill him.

266

Brought to his knees, Oron shook his head to clear his senses. His blade, tight in his right fist, glowed as though charged by a lightning bolt. The Star amulet, wrapped securely around the hilt of it, bloomed with a brilliant shining, and Oron realized that he owed his life to it.

Mosutha's own power. . . .

"Barbarian!" the wizard screamed. "The Star! Dog of the Valley, you—!"

Oron growled deeply and pushed himself up. The exertion awakened him. Mosutha, a scant three paces from him, shrieked another command and threw out an arm. Again Oron sought to escape it, this time by ducking his head, curling up and rolling forward on the ground. He felt a stream of heat pass along his back and seep into his boots.

Then he was up, and at Mosutha. The wizard, astonished, fell back, jumped as the Wolf's blade sliced at him. One edge of the sword ripped through Mosutha's robe, baring the flesh beneath.

"Esfeth k'nor——!"

But Oron was at him again—seeing nothing but a red mist, hearing nothing but the drumming thunder of blood and wrath that pounded in his temples. He saw Mosutha turn from him and dodge a second stroke, then a third. The sorcerer broke into a run, hurrying for the security of his idol. Thunder screamed high above and another eruption of black smoke and hell-fire poured up through the courtyard, sending bodies and brick and stone high into the air.

Mosutha leapt to the stairs that led up the right side of the idol. Oron followed him, chasing his steps with sword-stroke after sword-stroke, never giving the sorcerer a moment's freedom to turn and unleash his magical strength.

"Dog . . . dog. . . !" Mosutha panted, terror in his

eyes. "You cannot. . . . I am . . . *Ernog!*" he shrieked.

At the height of the stairs was a small plateau, the flattened top of one arm of the idol that, serving as a platform, led to the huge burning urn that Ernog held in his lap. Mosutha ran across the platform; Oron followed, and lunged at him.

Sword up.

Mosutha howled.

Oron struck the platform and skidded painfully on knees and elbows.

Before him, Mosutha lay stretched, sliced from his lower back down the length of one leg.

He tried to crawl.

Oron rose to his feet.

"I am . . . *Mosutha!*" His eyes glowed yellow, he stretched out a trembling arm to cast a furnace of power upon his enemy.

With an animal grunt gasping from his throat, Oron struck down with his sword; the blade smashed through the sorcerer's hand and split the length of Mosutha's arm in a spray of blood.

"Dog!" the wizard bellowed, waving his useless arm. "Dog! I am Mosutha! Ernog—!"

Oron sliced again with his blade—not with a killing stroke, but to catch the wizard across the belly. Spurts of blood jetted up from the torn cloth of the robe, and Mosutha screamed out agonizingly, trying to protect his ripped belly with one hand and a gushering, mutilated arm.

Oron stood above him, sword down, point aimed for the sorcerer's heart. His shadow, black, rippled upon Mosutha's writhing form.

"I am Oron," he whispered, staring the wizard in the eyes. "I am Oron, the Wolf, of the tribe of Ilgar the Moon-Hunter. You killed my people, you slew my chief, you murdered my mate and woman. I am no one. But I am Oron. Wizard . . . you die now, and you die knowing that it is Oron, the Wolf, who slays you, and sends you screaming to Hell!"

Mosutha clamped his red teeth, kicking his feet in a vain effort to escape.

Oron lifted his sword.

"Barbarian, in the name of Ernog—!"

"Die, in the name of Ernog, sorcerer!"

And he came down with his blade, fell to his knees atop Mosutha and drove the sword deep into the wizard's chest, pushed it so that the steel ripped up to the neck, yanked his sword through the throat so that the sorcerer's head, still screaming, dropped free. Carved open, the carcass spewed blood down the arm of the idol, into the sizzling coals of the flaming urn. Oron, howling his victory howl—the anguished, plaintive, tremulous cry of the forest wolf—skewered the sorcerer's head on the point of his sword, lifted it for the sky and his warriors and the gods to see, then flung it into the air, where it tumbled against the lowering gray clouds on a spinning trail of gray and scarlet gore.

EPILOGUE

The Man Without a Tribe

He tore the Star amulet from his sword and cast it into the steaming coals of the urn, and looked across the courtyard at the disjointed piles of corpses. Down from the patio of the main citadel ran his warriors, Uira at their lead, screaming his name. The wind whipped his hair, cooled the sweat on his aching body, stung the wounds on him.

No fires or geysers of smoke erupted from the plateau, no temblors from Hell rocked the bricks in the prelude to the emergence of the Hell-demon Ernog. With the death of Mosutha the cord was severed, the link between Hell and earth sundered.

Oron turned, where he stood upon the platformed arm of the idol, and stared into the sky. The thunder was distant, no lightning threatened, and through the thin drizzle the moon glowed in a darkened afternoon sky. Only the moon.

All dead, save for Oron and Uira and seven warriors. All dead.

As the afternoon darkened into dusk, they made their way back down the mountainside, away from the fortress that lay half in ruins, away from the piles of torn and mutilated bodies. As night fell they reached a flatland ringed by thin forest, close by the camp they had made last night, and here they built fires and roasted the small animals they flushed from the woods.

They spoke little. Fatigue . . . fear . . . awareness weighed heavily upon them. Oron was their leader, that much was known and did not need to be vocalized. Three men who had been of the tribe of Hutar, two of the tribe of Soth, two of the tribe of Kesh the Farmer: all that remained of the many many huts of men and women and families that had lived for generations along the Nevga and within the wide forests fed by it.

They ate, and one by one fell asleep, until only Oron remained awake, body still thrumming with excitement despite his wounds and his immense fatigue, mind still racing with a thousand pictures and sounds and memories, despite his sleepiness.

Wizard, you die now, and you die knowing it is Oron, the Wolf, who slays you. . . .

She is dead, Wolf. And she was dead, even as you tried to save her.

Save me! I am burning! I am being tortured! I feel the ache and the death in my bones! My shade is heated on coals!

My uncle was not a man to help others. If it will cause him pain. . . .

Yet there are things I will not do. I will not call up demons, because they can eat your naked soul. I am a man, not a demon. Men are new and swords are new, but magic is very old. . . .

Kiss me, my Oron. . . .

I wished to marry her. Her name is Esa. . . .

You will be given your weapons and you will go. Forget the path that leads you to the village of Ilgar the Moon-Hunter.

Banished?

Forget the path. . . .

Forget the path. . . .

Uira stirred in her sleep. Oron moved to her, knelt

271

down beside her, stroked her hair, and watched the quiet slumber of her worn features.

Are you afraid?

No, Oron, I am not afraid.

He lay down beside her, rested his arms about her, yawned, and began to doze. Uira, in her sleep, nestled closer to him, pushed her face against his beard, and stretched her legs along his.

No, Oron, I am not afraid. . . .

Oron, the Wolf, of the tribe of Ilgar the Moon-Hunter. . . .

And Oron, the Wolf, leader of men, banished from his tribe, slayer of the sorcerer, fell asleep beside his mate and slept in the deep night of the forest.